SOME RAIN MUST FALL

Some Rain Must Fall

MICHEL FABER

CANONGATE

699789
MORAY COUNCIL
Department of Technical
& Leisure Services

F

First published in Great Britain in 1998 by Canongate Books Ltd,
14 High Street, Edinburgh EH1 1TE

10 9 8 7 6 5 4 3 2 1

Copyright © Michel Faber 1998

The moral rights of the author have been asserted.

The author wishes to thank the Scottish Arts
Council for a writing bursary, which has kept
a variety of wolves from the door while he has
written these and many other stories.

The publishers gratefully acknowledge subsidy
from the Scottish Arts Council towards
the publication of this volume.

Earlier versions of these stories have appeared in various
publications: 'Fish' (*Scotland on Sunday*, 1996) 'The Red
Cement Truck' (*The Printer's Devil*, 1997), 'Half a Million
Pounds and a Miracle' (*Chapman*, 1998), 'Some Rain Must
Fall' (*Pulse Fiction: The Winners of the Ian St James Awards*,
1998). 'Fish' was broadcast on BBC Radio Scotland in
1996.

British Library Cataloguing-in-Publication Data
A catalogue record for this book is available on
request from the British Library

ISBN 0 86241 823 2

Phototypeset by Intype London Ltd
Printed and bound by WSOY, Porvoo, Finland

To Eva,
For help of every imaginable kind

Contents

Some Rain Must Fall   1

Fish   19

In Case of Vertigo   27

Toy Story   34

Miss Fatt and Miss Thinne   43

Half a Million Pounds and a Miracle   65

The Red Cement Truck   76

Somewhere Warm and Comfortable   83

Nina's Hand   93

The Crust of Hell   107

The Gossip Cell   136

Accountability   148

Pidgin American   161

The Tunnel of Love   184

Sheep   216

Some Rain Must Fall

FRANCES STRATHAIRN came home to find that her partner had cooked her a meal.

'First day at your new job,' he said. 'I thought you'd be exhausted.'

My relationship with this man is in crisis, Frances reminded herself, kissing him on the lips. *There is no doubt about it.*

But of course there was doubt. Exhausted, she collapsed on the sofa and ate her meal, which was excellent. Her own recipe, followed to perfection.

'So how are the kids?' he asked.

It wasn't a question about any children belonging to him or her: they weren't that kind of couple. He was asking her about the pupils at Rotherey Primary School.

'It's too soon to tell,' she said.

The first thing she'd got them to do was tidy up. Wellies in neat rows. Coats on pegs. Story books arranged from largest to smallest. Every pencil sharp.

Neatness was not her own personal bugbear: she merely knew, as a professional, that it was what the children craved. She was their new teacher and had been imposed on them at short notice; a contract must be made. They needed to demonstrate their goodness, their usefulness; they needed her to demonstrate her authority.

Most of all, they needed life to go on, with a maximum of fuss.

'Next: does every one of you have an eraser?' asked Frances.

The rustle and click of a dozen pencil cases being disembowelled.

'Anyone whose eraser is smaller than this, gets one of these,' she smiled, holding up one of the bagful of brand-new giant Faber-Castells she always brought along to new classes.

General wonderment as every child realised he or she qualified for one of these magnificent gifts.

Out of the corner of her eye, Frances observed one of the school's other teachers watching her from the doorway of the next room, no doubt wondering if Frances was really worth three times an ordinary teacher's salary.

'Now, I want every one of you to look through your project books and choose a page that you think has your very best handwriting on it. When you've chosen, I want you to lay your books open at that page, all together on the floor just here ... No, not on top of one another – all showing fully. Edge to edge, like bricks in a wall. But with a little space in between. That's right ... Give each other room. Good ... Good ...'

Frances squatted down, giving the children the hint that she could play with them at their level, while reminding them with her bigness and her spreading halo of skirt that she was something other. Though scarcely interested in their handwriting at this stage, she noted that nobody was conspicuously incompetent: Jenny MacShane, their teacher until last week, can't have been too bad.

On the morning of the second day, the two children who

hadn't turned up on the first day presented themselves. That was a good sign: word of mouth among the mothers, perhaps.

Frances read the absence notes: upset tummy for little Amy, doctor's appointment for little Sam. Fear, most likely, which might have grown unmanageable if they'd been allowed to stay away longer. She welcomed Amy and Sam back to their school, gave them their erasers. They were slower than the others to settle in, so Frances decided, among other things, to put off the essays until tomorrow.

Frances herself was slow to settle in to her new house on the hill above Rotherey village.

Her last lodgings had been in a ramshackle apartment – dog's-dinner decor, hastily convened furniture. She'd liked it there: it had once been the occupational therapy wing of a mental asylum, before Care in the Community had evicted the inmates. It still had some intriguing features: the odd mark on the wall, peculiar plastic things sealing some of the power outlets, a wicker clothes-basket woven by unsteady hand.

This house in Rotherey was a council house, cosy and generic; a policeman and his wife had lived there, and had respected all its prefab integrities. Not so much as a WANTED poster in the loo.

'The anonymity of this place gives me the shits,' she said to Nick, her partner.

'Well . . . Can I change anything for you?' he offered. 'I've got the time.'

Enjoying a sabbatical while he waited for his doctoral thesis to be assessed, he did indeed have the time, but there was nothing Frances could imagine him doing with this house. Rather, she wanted *him* to change.

'Let's go to bed,' she sighed.

The next night, though, she stayed up.

'How long, do you think?' he asked, just to sort out the sleeping arrangements.

'As long as it takes,' she replied.

As with everything, he was fine about having to sleep on his own; well-behaved, well-behaved, well-behaved. She wished he would haul her up to the bedroom and fuck her. It would be inconsiderate and inconvenient, God yes: she had no time for sex tonight because she had the children's essays to examine: eleven responses she must keep distinct in her mind, eleven plans of action she must conceive by the morning – as well as needing some sleep, of course. And yet she longed for him to knock her off course, or at least dare to try.

In her lap lay the children's essays: 'About Me, My School and My Teacher'. To each one she had clipped the best ID shot she'd been able to cull from the school's photographic montages of prize-giving nights, sports teams, Christmas concerts.

The first essay to hand was by Fiona Perry, the blonde one with the tiny ears and the oversized T-shirts.

Our school is called Rotherey Primary School. It has three big rooms, the oldest kids are Primary 6 and 7 and that is the room I am in. We do the hard stuff. Next year I am going to Moss Bank Accademey. Our teacher says thats where the fun really begins. Our teacher isnt at the school anymore. The last day I saw her she had to go home because she was crying. The next day was the day I was off sick with food poisning (the wrong kind of fish). But my best friend Rachel says our teacher just lost her head that day and now shes not coming back. We have a new teacher now who is you Mrs Strathiarn who is reading this essay!

Frances turned the page to see if there was any more, but that was all Fiona had to say, so she turned the sheet face-down on the couch next to her. 'The wrong kind of fish' – she smiled sadly. The wrong kind of fish could make a child an absentee on a day which might have changed its life for ever. Fiona Perry had missed a Wednesday presumably quite at random; yet by that evening her parents, along with the parents of all her classmates, had been phoned with the news that all the children could stay home until a replacement teacher for Mrs MacShane was found. In her essay, little Fiona was turning on the charm for the newcomer without missing a beat; Mrs MacShane had simply disappeared from her young life as if rubbed out by that lovely new eraser.

My school is called Rotherey Primary, wrote Martin Duffy. *I am in the big grade, Primary 6. I use to live in Bolton when I was young. My mum says that what happened with Mrs Macshane has got nothing to do with me and I should forget about it. Lots of people have asked me about 1,000 times and some times I tell them and some times I dont. But every time I do tell I forget it worse and worse, because really as soon as Mrs Macshane started crying I got embarsed and covered my eyes and I didnt see much. So thats my story.*

As if to punctuate, a toilet flushed. Nick, coming down for one last pee before sleep.

Don't you realise our relationship is in crisis! she felt like yelling to him, which was such an absurd impulse that she laughed out loud. He heard her laugh and came to her, his wrists still wet from hurried towelling.

'Something funny?' he wanted to know. His sense of humour was the best thing about him – one of the best things, anyway. He stood there, naked above the waist, a spray of glistening water-drops across his ribcage, a glow cast

Some Rain Must Fall 5

over his contours by her reading lamp. Her breath caught with the pain of soon not being with him anymore, because she would push him away, make sure he would never come back.

'Come here,' she murmured. He obeyed.

She would make love to him fast, here on the couch, then get on with her work. Undressing, she speculated on what Martin Duffy had really seen through his ten little fingers, which were tinged with the Marmite he had for breakfast. The covering of eyes was a social gesture, a message to one's peers asking for confirmation of the transgressive status of an event . . . She slid her rear over the edge of the couch to let Nick get inside her from where he was kneeling. So, did Martin Duffy really not see much? She doubted it. She might have to work on him, if there was evidence that his apparent robustness was a defence mechanism. Being new to the village made him vulnerable straight off, though on the other hand it would have prevented him getting too attached to Jenny MacShane . . . Right now Frances had to admit that her clitoris wasn't getting enough friction, especially with that damned condom, and her back was being repeatedly stabbed by a metal zip on one of the cushions.

'Let's go upstairs,' she said.

After orgasm, drunk with endomorphins, she drifted off to sleep, nestled against his back.

The school is fine and my old teacher is fine. This was the entire text of Greg Barre's essay. Which one was he again? She couldn't picture him, even with the aid of the photograph – admittedly an out-of-focus shot of a Nativity performance: a blur of cotton-wool beards and cardboard wings.

'What does this kid make you think of?'

She handed Nick the photograph across the breakfast

table. He checked his fingers for margarine and took hold of the tiny square of card by its edges.

'Shy,' he decided after a moment.

'Why?'

'In Christmas plays they always give the non-speaking shepherd parts to the shy ones. The girl in front is obviously the one who says, "We have followed a star," or whatever. This kid just has to tag along – maybe hand over a gift.'

She smiled at him as he handed back the photograph, a real eye-to-eye smile, the most genuinely intimate exchange they'd had for days. He was perceptive, all right. When it came to strangers.

'You'd make a good father,' she purred, still conscious of her flesh tingling with satisfaction and sleeplessness.

'Let's not start that again,' he advised her tersely.

Something flashed disconcertingly in her line of vision. It was the photo of little Greg. She hadn't accepted it back yet, and Nick was irritated all of a sudden, waving the image at her as if she'd already lumbered him with a child he didn't want.

The school was walking distance from the house, which was a pity in a way. A long drive in the passenger seat of someone's car would have given her a precious last chance to read the other essays. How could she have fallen asleep last night? She was like those useless men that women were always complaining about in advice columns.

'Good morning Mrs Strathairn!' chorused the children when she walked in.

She was 'Mrs' to them. She was always 'Mrs' to her classes, by professional decision. She felt that children trusted her more if they believed her to be a conventional spouse and mother, as if this made her an emissary from that story book world where family equations were not negotiable.

Unconventional and coolly feminist among her peers, she was able to compromise instantly and enthusiastically when she saw the need for it. Perhaps this quality more than any other got her chosen ahead of colleagues in her field, at least in fiendishly delicate situations like this.

She'd figured out almost immediately which of the children were the touchy-feely ones, and she drew them to her as bait for the others. Her talent was to radiate safety and the restoration of order. It was a gift she had possessed well before all her years of training.

Already children were pressing themselves to her, whispering things into her ear just for the thrill of leaning against her soft shoulder. The ones she was most worried about weren't these, but she worked hard to charm them anyway: they would help thaw the others out.

'Rachel? I'm told you know how to use the photocopier in the office. Could you make ten copies of this very important document, please?'

Rachel (*I don't play with many people at all I like doing work much more*) hurried away to the sacred machine, glowing with pride at the confidence shown in her as she prepared to step into an off-limits zone and tame the mysteries of technology.

Frances had a feel for the group as a whole, its tensions and safety valves, its flame-haired explosives, its doe-eyed emollients. The shock of the last day the children had spent with Mrs MacShane was working its way through their systems at different rates; Frances guessed that either Jacqui Cox or Tommy Munro would be the first to crack, in some spectacular incident that would appear to have no connection with their old teacher. Jacqui (classic hot-house flower, very particular that her fellow pupils spell her name 'the proper way') had written in her essay:

I like my teacher very much and I wouldn't want another one, at least not permantly. She has all my old work and it was her that wrote my reports and she knows why she wrote what she wrote. So when she comes back she will be able to keep me straight.

Tommy Munro, an ill-coordinated, excitable boy with startlingly long eyelashes and a prem head, wrote much the same essay to the best of his more limited abilities: *My old teacher is fine and everthing els is to.*

But his old teacher wasn't fine, at all, and Tommy was struggling with the impossibly unfair challenges of ruling straight margins and glueing sheets of cardboard together, his emotions corkscrewed deep into his pigeon chest.

Miraculously, nothing unusual happened on the fourth day, at least nothing any ordinary teacher wasn't paid to deal with. Just a heated argument about who was supposed to bring the sports chairs inside now that it had started raining – class beauty Cathy Cotterill, overwhelmed by responsibility. Red-faced, grimacing with a bee-stung mouth that would soon be grinning broadly again, she was one of life's intuitive survivors. Her essay had devoted two matter-of-fact lines to the circumstances of Mrs MacShane's departure, then went on to fill a page with *I don't play football much I rather play hop scoch. On Monday I get Jim I am not very good at Jim* and so on. Her anger had in-built transience and a limited scope: as an emotional firelighter she was a dud.

Exercising authority like a physical skill, Frances calmly took hold of the flailing ends of the dispute and wound them around her little finger. The yelling stopped, the threat of mayhem disappeared without a trace, and within ten minutes she had her entire class sitting at her feet, spellbound as she paraphrased text and showed photographs from a book about albinism. Frances had quite a number of these sorts of books:

odd enough to promise children a frisson of the bizarre, informative enough to fill their heads with the crunchy cereal of fact, irrelevant enough to be unthreatening. The sight of white Aborigines with pink eyes was enough to keep even Tommy dumbstruck while the cleverer ones frowned over the finer points of genetics.

As the rain dimmed the skies outside and the fluorescent strip-light took over, the children looked a bit albino them-selves, a phenomenon Frances pointed out to suppressed squeals of queasy delight.

'Maybe it's catching,' she teased.

At hometime it was raining so heavily that even those children who lived easy walking distance from the school were picked up by relatives or neighbours in cars. All except Harriet Fishlock and her tiny brother Spike from the tots' grade. (Frances found it hard to believe his name could really be Spike, but that was what everyone called him.)

'I don't know how I'm going to get Spike home,' sighed Harriet, fussing her pet-sized sibling into his greasy duffle-coat, 'without him getting totally soaked.'

Harriet lived in a shabby caravan park on the edge of the village with her alcoholic mother and a stepfather who could get spare parts for cars if necessary. There were rumours of sexual abuse, and a social services file running into dozens of pages.

'I have an umbrella,' said Frances. 'A super-duper giant umbrella. I can walk with you as far as the petrol station.' She watched the flicker of calculation cross the girl's face: yes, the petrol station was not in view of the wretched caravans: yes, the answer was yes.

Together they walked through the streets of Rotherey, the pelting rain screening the shops and houses as if through frosted glass. Everything was an indistinct and luminous grey, a vast sea with a mirage of a village shimmering on the waves, through which car headlights cruised slowly like distant ships. To get the best cover from the umbrella, Spike and Harriet walked on either side of Frances, and after ten minutes or so Frances was surprised and delighted to feel Harriet fumbling to hold hands with her.

Near the edge of the village, a red light pulsed luridly through the gloom: a police car parked outside the MacShane house. The police were there every day, apparently, though what they hoped to achieve at this late stage was hard to imagine. Perhaps they thought David MacShane would come back to pick up his mail or feed the dog.

The rain was thrashing down absurdly now, as if in fury, almost deafeningly noisy against the fabric of the umbrella. Luckily there was no wind, so Frances was able to hold their protecting canopy still as spouts of water clattered off the edges all around them.

'This is awful!' shouted Harriet.

'No it's not!' Frances called back. 'We're safe under here, and the rain won't last!'

They passed the petrol station; Frances said nothing. She understood she was crossing a Rubicon of trust and would soon glimpse the farther shore of caravan-land.

'This is where we live,' said Harriet when the park was in view. The rain, softening now, shimmered like television static all over the dismal junkyard of permanently stalled mobile homes. Frances knew that to accompany the children any farther would be to push her luck.

Yet, as Harriet and her brother were leaving the canopy of their new teacher's umbrella, Harriet made a little speech, spoken at a gabble as if escaping under pressure.

'Mrs MacShane used to come here sometimes after school. To see a man who's moved away now. They made loud noises together inside his caravan for hours, then she'd go home to the village. It was sex – everybody knows that. That's why Mr MacShane got so angry. He must of found out.'

The secret relayed at last, Harriet grabbed her brother by the hand and hopped gingerly into the marshy filth of her home territory.

In Frances's home – or rather, the house she would live in for the duration of this assignment – all was not well.

The wild weather (highest volume of rainfall in a single day since 1937, the radio would have told her if she'd known how to find the local station) had battered through the roof's defences, and there was water dripping in everywhere.

Frances walked through the upstairs rooms, squinting up at the clammy ceilings. They seemed to be perspiring in terror or exertion. In the bedroom especially, the carpet sighed under her feet and the bed was drenched: Nick had brought the buckets in too late. Returning downstairs. Frances almost broke her neck on the slick fur of the carpeted steps; perversely, this somehow knocked the edge off the contempt she felt for the house – as well as shaking her up badly.

'I did check all the windows were closed when the downpour started,' Nick told her a little defensively. 'I just didn't expect the place to leak, that's all.'

They looked up together at the droplets of rainwater gathering on the umbilicus of the light fitting. All the power in the house might blow any second.

'I want a child with you, Nick,' said Frances, hearing herself speak as if through the din of a rainstorm, though the brunt of it was actually over now, leaving the after-effects to carry on the harm.

Nick stared at her uncomprehendingly, as if her comment might decode itself into being about buckets or laundromats.

'We've talked about this before,' he said, warningly.

'I want it.'

She wanted him to take her upstairs, smack her down on the sodden bedsheets, and start a little life that would grow up to walk under an umbrella with her one day.

'I've told you,' he reminded her. 'You could maybe adopt one, as a single parent, and I could see how I feel. No guarantees.'

'It's not the shared responsibility I'm worried about, you bastard,' she said. 'I want your baby and mine. From the beginning. Nothing on the slate except *our* genetics. A clean start. Adopted children bring their damage with them from the womb, from the day they leave the womb. Already in the cradle they're soaking up their parents' fuck-ups.'

'Oh! Well!' he exclaimed, gesticulating aggressively. 'What a pity the fucked-up human race has to keep bringing children into the world, instead of leaving it to experts like you!'

Mesmerised by his violent display, she followed the sweep of his big hands, longing for him to hit her, batter her to the floor. But even in anger he was hopelessly, infuriatingly safe.

'Damn right!' she screamed in a misery of triumph.

'You know what you are?' he accused her, shoving his face right up to hers so she could see his lips forming the words with exaggerated clarity. 'A – con*trol* – freak.'

After they'd finished arguing, they stripped the bed, turned up the central heating and went out to Rotherey's only restaurant, a combination hotel and snooker hall which also did Indian.

Inevitably, the mother of one of the children from Jenny MacShane's class was there too, buying a carry-out, and she stumbled straight to Frances and Nick's table.

'I just want to thank you for what you're doing,' she told Frances blushingly. 'Last night, for the first time since . . .

you know ... this terrible MacShane business ... our Tommy slept right through without having nightmares or wetting the bed.'

'That's good to hear,' smiled Frances.

'I just want to say that I don't care how much you're getting paid, you're worth every penny.'

'Thank you,' smiled Frances. Warmth came harder to her when it was parents or other teachers wanting it.

'I just wanted to know ... Is there any chance of you staying on? As Tommy's permanent teacher?'

'No, I'm afraid not,' smiled Frances. Her lamb korma, none too hot when it was served, had stopped steaming altogether. And she could tell that this woman was going to go away and tell the other mothers that Frances Strathairn wouldn't stoop to work at a teacher's wage.

'Much as I'd love to,' she sighed, making the effort. 'The powers that be wouldn't let me.'

The mother went away then, walking with a peculiar shambling gait and a posture which suggested congenital inferiority. Frances stared at the door she had gone through, and picked at her food irritably. God, how she disliked herself for pleading impotence when that had nothing to do with why she must move on! This pretence of being the passive slave of higher authority – it was a deplorable lapse in dignity, an act of prostitution.

And to top it all off, she was going to break up with her man.

'I've seen you like this before,' observed Nick quietly from the other side of the candles. 'You always get like this just before the job's over. Those kids that survived the bus crash in Exeter, remember? A few days before you finished up there, we had almost the same argument' – he smirked – 'almost the same restaurant. And that time in Belfast—'

'Spare me the details,' she groaned, tossing her fork into

the mound of rice and taking a deep swig of wine. 'Ask the proprietor if there are any rooms free for tonight. If so, book one.'

He stood up, then hesitated.

'For how many people?'

'Two,' she chided. 'Bastard.'

Next day, the children started breaking down at last, more or less as Frances had been anticipating, with one or two exceptions. Tommy Munro seemed to have sidestepped the process, behaving with unusual maturity and poise for a brain-damaged kid; maybe, because he was so used to being confused and mistaken all the time, he'd come to believe that the incident with his old teacher must have happened in one of his nightmares.

Greg Barre, however, blew his crewcut top just after lunchtime, starting with a misunderstanding about which times table he was supposed to have learned, and climaxing with a shrieking fit. Mrs MacShane's name was thrown up in the ensuing hysteria and several children were soon weeping and accusing each other of causing what had happened or failing to stop it when they should have. Martin Duffy wailed his innocence with fists clenched against his day-glo sports shorts; Jacqui Cox wailed her guilt with arms wrapped tightly around her head. The teacher of the adjacent class rushed to the doorway, trembling with fear, her face twitching with a ghastly nervous smile like the ones sometimes seen on people about to be executed.

Frances gave her the hand-signal for 'I'll handle this', and a nod of permission to shut the door.

Then she moved forward and took control.

By the end of the day, she had them all quiet again, entranced by her own soothing murmur and the gentle patter of rain on the windows. She sat in the midst of them on a high stool, keeping the stories coming and the airwaves humming, hypnotising herself to ignore the fact that her rear end was numb under the weight of Jacqui's body in her lap. Jacqui was going to be a big girl, at least physically. Emotionally, she was too small for life outside the womb, and she clung to her teacher's waist with marsupial tenacity, pressing her face hard into Frances's bosom. She had been weeping for hours, an infinitely sustainable whimper: nothing that half a lifetime of reassurance couldn't fix.

Greg Barre was playing quoits with Harriet Fishlock and Katie Rusek, happy as a lamb, wearing the sackcloth trousers he'd worn as a shepherd in the Christmas play. His own were drying out on one of the radiators; he'd soiled them at the height of his frenzy. Frances had recognised she couldn't afford to leave the group to attend to him alone, and had chosen Katie to bear him off to the toilets and help him get changed; a risky choice, given the rigid gender divisions in this little world of Rotherey, but Frances judged it was the right one: Katie was mature and self-assured, Greg was afraid of her and secretly infatuated too. Most importantly, Katie was smart enough to perceive that the situation – half the class weeping and throwing hysterics, a boy with shit in his pants – was beyond the control of just one adult, and she caught the devolution of responsibility as if it were a basketball. In her essay she had written:

My name is Katie Rusek and I am in Grade 7 of Rotherey Village School. Something very bad happened here last week. Our teacher Mrs MacShane was giving us a Maths lesson when her husband came in to the class room with a shot gun. He swore at Mrs MacShane and hit her until she was on the floor. She kept saying please not in front of the children but it didn't make any difference. Then her husband told her to put the end

*of his gun in to her mouth and suck on it. She did that for a
few seconds and then he blew her head to bits. We were all so,
so scared but he went away and now the police are looking for
him. Every time I think about that day I feel sick. I ask myself,
will I ever get over it?*

From her perch, Frances watched Katie Rusek watching Greg
Barre prepare to throw another quoit. Desperation to
impress his guardian angel was making him suddenly
awkward, a faltering of confidence which both Katie and
Frances, from their different angles, noticed instantly.

'Let's play something else,' the girl whispered in his ear,
before he'd even thrown.

Frances murmured on. She was telling the class about her
squelchy house, her wet bed, how she'd spent the night in
the Rotherey Hotel. She made up a story about how she and
her husband had tried to sleep at home but the water had
come up through the mattress and soaked their pyjamas. She
described how she and her husband had balanced the mattress on its side near the heater and watched the steam begin
to rise. She kept returning to the theme that her house was
in chaos just now but that she could manage because she
had people to help her, and soon everything would return to
normal. All the while she pressed her cheek against Jacqui
Cox's wispy skull, stroking her gently at key phrases.

She talked on and on, effortlessly, the words coming from
a reassurance engine idling deep within her; her words and
the rain maintaining a susurrating spell over the children.
Most listened in silence, some played games, completed word
puzzles or drew pictures. No drawings of guns or exploding
heads yet: Jacqui might do one of those for her next week
sometime. In the days following that, she would smooth the
new teacher in and then move on to God knows where.

Jacqui convulsed in her arms, jerked awake the instant

after falling asleep, and repositioned her ear in the hollow of Frances's breast, reconnecting with the heartbeat.

'It'll be all right, angel,' Frances purred. 'Everything will be all right.'

Fish

THESE DAYS, Janet let her daughter sleep in bed with her. It wasn't what child psychologists would have said was best, but there weren't any child psychologists anymore, and her daughter needed help just the same.

Janet had tried forcing Kif Kif to sleep alone, but the little girl would scream with nightmares about God knows what – sharks, probably. Now she was sleeping dreamlessly, cradled in the curve of Janet's waist.

All around the bed, the flywire was stretched taut from floor to ceiling, the support struts and entrance zipper glowing in the candle-light. Janet shut her eyes against the tick-tick-ticking on the wire and tried to drift off, but it was no use; there was always the anxiety that something was eating through the wire, through the canvas of the zipper, and you would open your eyes to find . . .

She opened her eyes. Nothing had changed.

There were still the same thirty or forty little fish (newly spawned wrasse, perhaps? – it was hard to tell in the dark) hovering in the air, bumbling against the flywire, trying to get in. Individual fish bobbed off from the cluster, floating up to bump against the ceiling.

Janet drew another cigar from the box on her lap, wishing it were a cigarette, *craving* a cigarette. She struck a match: the fish scattered. The room was alive with shining little bodies, flitting against the furniture, knocking ornaments off shelves, disappearing into dark corners. Almost immediately, however, they began to swim back to the flywire, and the tick-tick-ticking began again. Kif Kif squirmed in her sleep, digging her hard little six-year-old's shoulderblades into Janet's side.

'It's all right darling,' murmured Janet, stroking her through the blankets. 'Nothing to be afraid of.'

Next morning Janet and Kif Kif dressed up in their camou-flage to leave the house. The fish, which now lay gaping and dead on the floors of every room, had got in through the narrow gap between front door and hall floor. The little plank of wood which Kif Kif put there nightly had been levered out of place from the outside while they slept.

An act of paltry sabotage like this might happen to them every week or so; the devotees of the Church of Armageddon (the 'Army' for short) didn't like to pass a house by without attempting to advance their cause. As far as major attacks went, Janet and Kif Kif had been lucky. Only once in the last year had they returned to their house to find it smashed open, all the windows and doors unhinged, and all the food and clothing taken. Dripping, blood-like, down the bedroom wall had been one of the painted graffiti slogans of the Army: THE FIRST SHALL BECOME LAST!

On that awful day, Kif Kif had kept guard with her machete while Janet restored the defences. By late afternoon the five-year-old was splattered with fish blood and muck, although she hadn't been attacked by anything too dangerous. Most of the fish she'd wounded had swum away, to die inside deserted buildings and gutted cars, but some had been hacked too severely to do anything but wobble slowly to the ground and die twitching on the crumbling asphalt. When Kif Kif had suggested that these fish should perhaps be taken to the Soup Kitchen for use as food, Janet had hugged her fear-shaken little girl and wept.

Today Janet and Kif Kif locked the door behind them, as quietly as possible, for sound was so much louder these days than it had sounded in the days when there were things like cars, factories and people running.

The million sea creatures moved noiselessly. Schools of barracuda swept without warning in and out of broken windows. Starfish wriggled on the bonnets of rusty cars. Octopi cartwheeled in slow motion through the air, their tentacles touching briefly on the tips of barbed-wire fences and the tops of awnings. Even the open-mouthed shriek of a shark attacking would be obscenely silent, so there was actually no point in keeping your ears cocked, though you always did.

At a cautious trot Janet and Kif Kif put a zig-zag of streets between them and their house, to confuse any Army members who might spot them. One day, of course, the Army might stop being nomadic, and concentrate on each occupied house they chanced to find, taking advantage of every occasion when it was left unoccupied, until at last its inhabitants had been killed by what they preferred to call the Holy Reclamation Of Nature.

Then again, it was also possible that one day the Army would amend its religion to permit its devotees to do the killing themselves, rather than waiting for the Holy Reclamation Of Nature to do it.

'Far enough now,' said Janet, her breath clouding the dry, grey air.

Kif Kif threw the plastic bag of dead wrasse into the gutter, where it burst open on the sharp edge of a broken wheelchair. A large eel floated out of a sewer-hole and slid through the air towards the spillage.

'Hungry?'

'Uh-huh.'

Coming back from the Soup Kitchen, feeling warm and sprightly with the city's only hot meal in their stomachs, Janet and Kif Kif leapt and skipped towards home. Small fish of all colours and shapes cluttered the air around them, frightened out of their foraging places by the commotion. Carp nibbled at the plankton nestled inside an exposed automobile engine. Barracuda circled a small dolphin which had become tangled in a shop awning and starved to death there. A manta ray of moderate size floated over their ducked heads and settled against the wall of a factory. Slowly it slid along a line of newly painted graffiti (ANY CRETURE THAT CAN READ THIS, YOU'RE DAYS ON EARTH ARE NUMBERD!), obscuring the words one by one. Janet repeated the slogan to her daughter on request.

'He's reading it,' smirked Kif Kif, making Janet laugh. They both knew the ray had mistaken the moist paint for something edible, and would be lying maw-up on the ground by tomorrow morning, after which the Army would probably find it and eat it. Since the Church of Armageddon had no equivalent of the underground Soup Kitchen which kept Janet, Kif Kif and the other unbelievers alive with salvaged tinned goods, it subsisted by fishing; Army nets could be seen occasionally, spanned between buildings in intricate layers.

It was rumoured that the Army didn't actually eat any of the tinned and packaged food they carried off from the houses they broke into. It seemed they merely confiscated it, to deprive Unbelievers of any unfair advantage. In the same way that they liked to crack the shell of an Unbeliever's house, to let the vengeance of Nature swim in, they liked to make food disappear, to signal that God was no longer prepared to provide. At least not to human beings; there was plenty to eat, of course, for everything that swam.

Accepting the divine wrath with bizarre enthusiasm, the Army were definitely on the side of the fish. There was hardly a public building in the city that was not marked with their commonest graffito: LET THE DRY LAND DISAPPEAR!

'A bit quieter now, Kif.'

Janet and Kif Kif were nearing their home streets. An acrid breeze started up, smelling of large, half-eaten fish. Janet's nose wrinkled with distaste. She reached out for Kif Kif and gathered her in as she walked.

'Sorry it's so nasty,' she said, but, looking down at the child's abstracted, placid face, Janet realised the apology was wasted: Kif Kif didn't seem to have noticed the smell.

Janet's mood soured as she considered that her daughter had grown up in a world which stank to high heaven. Kif Kif had never smelled air untainted by decay. She'd never seen a growing fruit or a flower, as every form of vegetation was immediately eaten by the fish before it even came to bud. She lived shut up in an unheated, poorly lit prison, trembling and twitching with nightmares every night. Even now, as they walked along the deserted street, any of a hundred broken windows might suddenly spew out a deadly streak of grey, and then what could you do? Janet had heard from other Survivors what it was like to just stand there while a huge shark, its jaws locked open, glided through the air towards the smallest prey. The Army certainly wasn't wrong in thinking the world was no longer intended for human beings. Kif Kif with her dinky little machete against the hatred of all creation—

'Mummy, look!'

Janet was jerked out of her brooding.

'What? What?'

Kif Kif pointed over the roofs of the houses, half-way across the city. Horrified, Janet watched a blue-black killer whale emerging from the low grey clouds, followed by another whale, and another, and another. They hung huge in the sky like black zeppelins, and the air seemed to grow claustrophobically dense with their displacement of it. Janet would have sunk to her knees but for the grip she had on Kif Kif's shoulders. At her back there was nowhere to hide, only more crumbling streets, more fragile, half-broken buildings; a mile of ground a whale could cover in less than a minute, and, beyond that, the empty sea. The killer whales began to move, towards Janet and Kif Kif's part of the city. Their tails swept the air lazily. They kept together. They were attacking.

Not far from the street where Janet and Kif Kif stood, there towered an old building which had survived intact, marble statues and all. The foremost whale wove through skeletal office blocks with a grace that belied its massive size, and passed very close to this old building, almost clipping it with its aeroplane wing of a tail. Then it loomed on, its shadow spilling straight towards Kif Kif and Janet. By the time it reached where they stood it was swimming about thirty metres above the ground, the motion of its tail blowing their hair all around their faces. Directly overhead, blotting out the sun with its monstrous bulk, it opened its mouth. A thousand needle-sharp teeth swung down like the hatch of an aeroplane. Water clattered on the asphalt: saliva in the wind. Janet screamed.

But the whale glided over them altogether, its great shadow smothering them as it passed.

'It's coming back! It's coming back!' shrieked Janet as she watched the whale describe a slow semi-circle and cruise towards them again.

Once more, however, it passed them over, and headed towards the old building, while the other whales floated in formation nearby.

Turning again, it swam back towards Janet and Kif Kif, but in a smaller arc this time, so that its shadow didn't even reach the street where they stood. It was heading for the old building once more, and this time it did not pass it by. Some decision seemed to have been made deep in the creature's brain, and it hurled itself straight at its target, ramming into the stonework with its massive head.

Amid the noise of a muffled thunderclap, the old building shuddered, stones falling out of their pattern in small clusters. A pale statue swayed on its perch and toppled to the street below, smashing unseen and unheard. The other whales, following the example of their leader, attacked the building with him, ramming and ramming it until crucifixes cart-wheeled down through the air and bells rang with chaotic lack of rhythm. At last the church fell in on itself with the tremendous racket that only collapsing buildings make.

For an attenuated minute the whales circled the ruin, then they swam off towards another part of the city, their tails beating up clouds of shimmering debris.

Janet let out her breath shudderingly, then gasped at the pain of frozen muscles thawing. She wasn't really very grateful to be alive; life had been conceded too far beyond the extremity of terror. To be unconscious in the long gullet of a whale: that would have been *real* mercy, not this ghastly approximation of survival.

Only, she must *pretend* to be alive, *pretend* to have hope, spirit, feeling, for the sake of her daughter, so that her daughter wouldn't give up. She must be strong for her daughter, comfort her, get her home to bed, carry her there if need be.

Janet looked down at Kif Kif for the first time, and was shocked to see that the child's face was radiant.

'Oh, Mummy!' marvelled the little girl. 'Wasn't it amazing?'

'Amazing?' echoed Janet incredulously. 'Amazing?'

Anger started up deep inside her like convulsions, getting more violent as she let go her hold on it, until she was shaking with fury.

'Amazing!?' she yelled at last, and began to hit Kif Kif, flailing at her with the flats of her hands. The child fought back, and in a few moments they were in a real tussle, pulling each other's clothes and hair, until a warning shout from Kif Kif ended it. Janet found herself being pulled along the street by the wrist.

'Come *on*!' shouted the panting child crossly. 'Stupid!'

Janet stumbled along, stumbling partly because she was too tall to be led properly by a six-year-old. She glanced over her shoulder to see what the child had already spotted: a school of moray eel gathering twenty yards away, attracted by the commotion of the fight and the smell of human flesh.

Janet gained her stride, scooped up her unprotesting daughter in her arms and ran and ran.

In bed that night, safe behind the flywire, Janet tried to explain why she had been so angry.

'I thought you were terrified of sharks and big fish like that,' she said lamely, hugging the slightly alien child tight to her side. 'You have nightmares every night . . .'

Kif Kif pawed sleepily at an itchy cheek and nose.

'I have nightmares about other stuff,' she said.

In Case of Vertigo

SISTER JENNIFER

swung open the boot of her car and lit the butane stove she kept set up in there. The open hatch of the boot shielded the flame from the wind; she was not concerned about the small risk of blowing herself and her car to high Heaven. She would get there by less spectacular means.

SISTER JENNIFER

opened a tin of spaghetti and shook the contents into a small saucepan to heat. It was the same breakfast she had every day, except for the days when she had none at all. As soon as the butane had done its work, she turned it off and sat inside the car again, balancing the hot pot of spaghetti on the gnarled steering wheel. She ate slowly and meditatively, with a fork, watching the sea-birds through the windscreen. Her car was parked well back from the edge, so she couldn't actually see the sea.

SISTER JENNIFER

murmured a prayer of thanks for what she had just received. It was one of her peculiarities, this: saying prayers of thanks *after* rather than *before*. So much could go wrong between being presented with an opportunity and actually being able to enjoy it; it therefore seemed pathetic to thank God for something that might yet be snatched away. Of course, the other sisters hadn't seen it that way, but she was on her own now.

SISTER JENNIFER

let the spaghetti settle in her stomach for a while and had a drink from her thermos, then took off her parka to see if doing without it was feasible. Unfortunately the food and drink hadn't warmed her enough yet, and she felt instantly cold, so she put it back on. This was rather a shame, because the parka covered much of her nun's habit and (more crucially) she couldn't wear it and her veil as well. If anyone came, she must of course go to them directly, and there might not be time to organise her clothing for maximum effect. She could throw off the parka in an instant, but might have to leave the veil. Still, the crucifix on her breast would surely give the right message.

SISTER JENNIFER

got out of her car to stretch her legs. They were long legs, after all. She walked back and forth along the deserted cliff-head, clasping her arms to her sides, her hands deep in her jacket pockets. Her fur-lined boots made no sound in the damp grass as she walked; her parka made a small rustling noise like a battery-operated toy. The sea and the sky made the sound peculiar to cliff edges, as if all the noise had first been sucked through a gap in the horizon and then regurgitated with something indefinable missing. The sea-gulls kept disappearing below her line of vision; she didn't want to get too close to the edge in case of vertigo.

SISTER JENNIFER

returned to her car, had another drink from her thermos and at last began to feel a little warmer. A layer or two of cloud had been blown away from the densely overcast sun, allowing more warmth to glow through its shroud. The parka could come off soon, quite soon. She wondered what time it was, noted that once again the dashboard clock had experienced a hiccup in its power supply and was flashing 00:00. The radio might tell her the time, if she was prepared to listen to its chatter and its pop music long enough. She tried it for a while, suffering, but was still none the wiser when a vehicle pulled up not far from hers at the cliff edge.

SISTER JENNIFER

switched off the radio and removed her parka, revealing the big dark crucifix on her white breast. The new arrivals stepped out of their camper-van and inhaled ostentatiously: a man and a woman. Festooned with sunglasses, cameras and binoculars, they had evidently not come to commit an act of desperation, despite the fact this spot was nicknamed Suicide Point.

SISTER JENNIFER

let the man and the woman walk to the edge and fiddle with their equipment. She tried to relax, but adrenalin had leaked into her system: her head was noisy with her own voice rehearsing the reasons why life was worth living. No pain was so great that God could not find room for it in his bottomless repository of sorrows. To have made the decision to die must mean that you have decided you can no longer carry the burden of life. And oh yes, there is no denying that the burden can grow too heavy. But, if you are ready to throw that burden off the edge of a cliff, to smash yourself to pulp on the rocks below, and be washed out to sea like garbage, what is there to stop you trying something different? No, no, *not* returning to the life you cannot bear, *not* shouldering the burden all over again, but handing the burden on to someone else – in fact, allowing it to be lifted off your shoulders, by God. Yes: by God, who stands at your side at this very moment, as near to you, and as real, as I, but a million times more powerful . . . !

SISTER JENNIFER

waved at the couple through her side window. They were going already. Perhaps they had seen everything they'd come to see; captured it inside their camera and binocular lenses, souvenired it on a strip of undeveloped film. Perhaps they were simply disappointed to find another human being here, at this spot which was so renowned for its desolation. Perhaps they were especially discomfited that this other human being should be a nun. They might think she was about to interrogate them on their marital status, or ask them to donate money to a leprosy mission in Indonesia. That was the sort of thing her fellow nuns might have had on their minds, she supposed. It was difficult to recall. It was so long since she'd been in the company of her sisters in Christ.

SISTER JENNIFER

watched the camper-van reverse, turn, and drive away. When it was quite out of sight, she swung open the door of her own car and lowered herself out. She squatted right next to the car's body, its padded door shielding her from the buffeting wind as if it were a wing trembling to enfold her. She kept her habit rucked well above her hips until she was finished, then shut herself back into the car, shivering. She considered putting her parka on again, had a drink from her thermos instead. Hours went by. The sun described its arc across the sky, aloof and beyond temptation. No one else came to the cliff edge.

SISTER JENNIFER

slumped back in her seat, the adrenalin long since ebbed away, the reasons for living no longer rehearsing themselves in her head. In time, she dozed. Waking, she prayed a little. Then she listened to the radio some more, this time finding out what time it was mercifully quickly. It occurred to her that she might be well advised to drive back into the town before the shops shut. She wasn't sure how her provisions were going.

SISTER JENNIFER

alighted again, walked around her vehicle, lifted the hatch of the boot. As she did so, a massive bird – some sort of giant heron or egret – flew over her car, its spear-like beak and dazzling white wingspan perfectly aligned with the vehicle. Involuntarily, Sister Jennifer's head snapped back as the great bird passed over, and she almost overbalanced, blinded by the sun. It was such an extraordinary moment that she was struck with fear, as if something would simply *have* to happen next, something which would surely rip her open like a paper bag. But nothing else happened. Dazed, she looked down into the boot of her car, seeing nothing there but the luminescing after-image of the sun.

SISTER JENNIFER

realised soon enough the true significance of the epiphany. God had given her yet another reason for living which she could pass on to others: the miracle of a bird in flight, the privilege of seeing a creature essentially different from oneself display its inhuman mastery, a display which one needed to be human and alive to witness and appreciate. It was necessary to keep living, if only to love the beauty of a bird, for birds themselves were incapable of loving it.

SISTER JENNIFER

waited until the flare on her retinas had faded and normal vision resumed. She rummaged through the supplies in the boot, verified that there was very little food left except more tins of spaghetti which, though she was hungry, she didn't feel like eating just now. She checked the drink situation. There was half a bottle of white wine left, which she carefully poured into the thermos despite the fact that it was no longer the least bit chilled. She tried to calculate whether it would last her until tomorrow, sipped it as if to force the issue one way or the other. She remained unsure, and wondered to what extent she was merely being cowardly about queueing in the off-licence again. To buy time, she cleared the empty bottles from the boot, gathered them to her breast and walked towards the cliff edge with them. From a safe distance she lobbed them over, listening as always for the sound of their fall, which never, ever came. Then she walked back to her car. Suicide Point was growing cold.

SISTER JENNIFER

closed herself in, drank a little more of the wine, and put on her parka for the night.

Toy Story

GOD PLAYED ALONE: there were no other children where he lived. It meant, at least, that he didn't have to share any of the cool stuff he found round the back of the abandoned universe. Everything was automatically his.

The abandoned universe was such a weird place, because even though it had been shut down for ever, there were still lights on inside, as if nothing had changed. And, round the back, there was always new garbage, more discarded fragments of the impossible dream, more cogs and gaskets from the innards of infinity.

One day, rummaging in the trash, God found something especially good: a planet. He lifted it out of the bin, grasping it enthusiastically at first, then more gingerly; for even though it had survived intact till now, it was oddly fragile. Underneath his small fingers, the planet's protective coating of atmosphere had given way and he'd felt the powdery surface of its earth directly against his skin. Now he held the globe by its white poles and surveyed the damage . . . Had it been a perfect sphere to begin with? If so, it was ever-so-slightly ovoid now. The dusting of earth on his fingertips was bleeding into the atmosphere like a sprinkling of cinnamon on the vanilla extremes of north and south. On the scuffed and dented continents, a few new lakes were forming. Apart from this, there was no harm done.

God sat down, his back against the fence, and examined

his prize. It was a blue and green world, with more sea on it than land, warm and aromatic. He put his nose close to the atmosphere and sniffed. There was a heady layer of something chillingly astringent, like pine or ozone, and, beneath that, the mingled scents of loamy soil, of baked crust, of equatorial compost, of salty soupy seas and sweet effervescent rivers. It was the most marvellous thing God had ever smelled.

He had to take his planet home with him immediately, despite the possibility that there was even better stuff to be found in the rest of the garbage today. After all, someone might come along and snatch his world away from him, or tell him to put it back where he'd found it, because it was too dangerous a thing for a child to play with.

Struggling to his feet, he almost dropped the planet from between his fingers, which had grown numb with cold. He experimented with holding the globe differently, using the palms of his hands, fingers slackened, to spread the pressure. This was a success: perhaps the planet was less fragile than it had first appeared. He stood holding it like this for a while, allowing the tropical seam to warm his hands until the sensitivity returned to his fingertips.

Walking slowly home, mindful of the road, God carried his extraordinary find, revolving it whenever its changing weather began to prickle the flesh of his palms. Eventually he was bold enough to try embracing the planet. Again, success. By the time God was almost home, he was running, the planet cradled securely in the crook of one arm.

He hung it up in his bedroom, suspended from the ceiling. It was the only place for it, really. Resting it on a surface, like a table or a dresser, was too risky: some part of it might get gradually squashed, or come to grief for lack of light, or perhaps the whole globe might even roll off and be smashed on the floor. He'd considered keeping it on the floor to begin with, but this was out of the question too: he might kick it in a moment of carelessness or fury, and besides, it was too beautiful a thing to look down on.

So, he dangled it from the light in the centre of his room, attached by a few threads of cotton to the lightbulb just above. He'd removed the lampshade from the bulb, to give his planet maximum light, and to eliminate distractions: there ought to be only one focus of attention up there. God's planet looked beguiling and perfect, revolving almost imperceptibly but constantly in the breeze from the window, elevated to a level where no other toys were visible. For, though God still played with his other toys, he knew they were objects of a different order: sturdier, more useful; less complex, less special. There were toys which could, on the right day, amuse him so intensely that he forgot his planet existed, but as soon as he remembered, he was well aware that his planet was, unlike his other toys, unique.

Apart from playing at home, God continued to go out to the abandoned universe and rummage around the garbage. As usual, his eyes would goggle at the strange new things he found there. Incandescent rods, impossibly dense metals, bottled gases which plumed out in the shape of a star when smashed free, huge fluffs of silver fibre spilling out of the bins like foam, bright yellow protective clothing with holes in it, enigmatically specific crystal implements still snug in their black rubber cases, handwritten code-books whose densely inscribed pages were washed to a pastel blur, whole binfuls of computer disks smashed to shrapnel, and – too big for the bins to contain – broken engines of paradox. All the materials of universe-making were being thrown out here.

None of this mattered to God. He was concerned not with the universe's past or future but only with its present. He would play while there were things to play with, even if they came from the garbage. What else was there to do?

Inevitably, because God's planet was suspended from the ceiling, he paid most attention to it when he was lying in bed, looking up from his pillow. Tired out from playing all day, he would notice the little blue-green world through eyes already half closed. Usually he fell asleep then, and dreamed of travelling there, shrunk down to the appropriate size. These were funny dreams, highly romantic, with the almost holy air of myth and nonsense. Typically he would be, at one and the same time, his normal self, looking up at the planet from his bed, and a tiny, grown-up version of himself, wandering around on the planet, looking up through the impenetrable heavens as if for a glimpse of his own face. In these dreams, his tiny, grown-up self was constantly sur-rounded by other people, beset by responsibilities, driven by a mission; and yet, perversely, he craved aloneness and the freedom to play in silence.

Always by the end of the dream there would be some sort of crisis in which the citizens of his blue-green planet imprisoned him, determined to keep him there for ever; in nightmares, they even tried to bury him alive, so that he might, in time, enter the anonymity of the earth's crust as a sprinkling of irreclaimable atoms. Gasping for breath, he would wake in a shroud-like tangle of bedsheets.

Despite these occasional nightmares, he never lost his sense of the little planet's beauty and charm. A miraculous egg of confluences, it was innocent and clever, making moun-tains out of molten sludge, rainforests out of water and dirt, fresh water out of salt. It was alchemy achieved by instinct, the instinct of a world which was not aware of itself, but which had none the less found a use even for the spent breaths of plants.

Often, having intended to go to sleep, he would be capti-vated by the planet's gentle glow of ingenuity, and leap out of bed to discover it all over again. Standing on a chair, he would peer at the globe with a magnifying glass, almost touching the spongy skin of its atmosphere.

The magnifying glass was a pretty good one, also found in the bins at the back of the universe, but there were limits to what he could see through it. Extremes of weather, so thrilling in theory, were a disappointment from where he stood. Seen from the outside, even the fine distinctions he hoped to make between one kind of cloud and another – cirrus, altostratus, cumulonimbus and so on – were often impossible, as one kind shrouded another, layer upon layer. It was all fog, really, like a haze of tiredness over God's eyes. As for hurricanes, tornadoes, lightning, hail, falling snow, even rain: these were phenomena he would never see, no matter how intently he squinted. For, when there were clouds in the sky, they hid these spectacular sights from him; when there were no clouds, these sights did not exist to be seen.

The first time God realised this, perched on his wobbly chair in the middle of the room, he was sickened by how perfectly he was excluded, and hung his head.

His planet was so small, and he so big. Whole oceans were scarcely bigger than his hand, few countries as large as the eyes with which he strained to see them. Of course he delighted in being able to see the whole picture, in the round, but at the same time he longed for the details. Through a clear patch of sky, he could just about see the wood, providing the wood went on forever, but he saw no trees. Sometimes the frustration provoked him to fantasise unreasonably: to see not just a single tree but an infant sapling – no, better still: a tiny, tight-furled bud edging out, like a frog paw from charred forest cinders.

Yet, what he *could* see was so good that his dissatisfaction never lasted, and often he would stand staring at his planet for so long that his neck ached and his eyes stung and his bare feet went numb. He would watch clouds go ripple-shaped when they passed over mountain ridges, or turn into white banners around the tip of a peak. He would watch glaciers edging away from the poles like bubbles of fat around the white of a frying egg; he would note that the colour of an entire subcontinent had changed from parched brown to lush green, as if it had just decided it was bored with infertility.

He became familiar with the unique shape of each land-mass, even small islands which were lost in the blue of the oceans if he so much as blinked. The largest continent, some of which merged with the globe's icy top, was the most various in smell. Every millimetre of it produced a different aroma, subtly mingled like an exotic ratatouille. The earthy scent of agriculture would murmur under a pall of inciner-ated carbons; a sweet whiff of monsoon would swirl around the stink of fleshly decay; an intriguing hint of fresh straw-berries could be traced travelling across vast landscapes pungent with diesel and sodium. At its southern extremes, the largest continent hung down in two points like the collar of a shirt; its bulge of mountains poked up over the collar like an ugly face. Two of the other land-masses reminded him of faces, too: they were of almost the same massive size, very similar in shape, separated by an ocean, but both old men in profile – disappointed, long-faced old men, enduring sto-ically. The larger of the two smelled of blood, fresh blood, as if it were perspiring it constantly.

Of course God knew about all the people on his planet. Millions of them, too many millions for a child to count. Their cities studded every solid part of the globe except the ice-floes, and even these he examined from time to time, just in case. Though there was no way of being sure, God guessed that it was from the largest continent, with its collar full of humankind, that he first began to hear the voices.

For ages he took these voices to be from his own dreams, for they came to him as he was hesitating in the doorway of sleep, already wrapped in his blankets and the dark. In time, he realised they had nothing to do with his dreaming, but were spiralling down to his bed through the black space between him and his little planet, like motes of sonic pollen.

The voices were at first so faint that they meant no more to God than the rustling of his own pillowcase. However, after a while, either because he learned to listen more keenly or because the voices were louder, he was sometimes able to catch their drift. Not that it was necessarily the loudest voices which reached his ears; there was some odd scientific principle at work, causing almost all the millions of human exclamations to dissipate in the troposphere, while just a few were snatched up into outer space, gathering volume in exact proportion to the distance they travelled.

Occasionally God did hear a great cry which must have been uttered by a large number of people in unison: affirmations of praise and encouragement to Allah, Elvis, Victory, Freedom, Hitler – entertainers, perhaps, or sports teams. They meant little to God, these repetitions of a single, meaningless word, floating down to him out of context. Other, quieter fragments of speech, the little cries and conversations of individuals, had more chance of making sense to him.

It was the timbre of a voice which appealed to him more than anything, the music of it, which carried with it an echoing picture of the speaker and the speaker's circumstance. From fragments of a few words each, he could visualise enough to make him feel he'd been part of a life other than his own. Sometimes he was the one who had spoken, sometimes the one spoken to. He was child, man, woman, at any random moment from humidicrib to hospice. He felt himself lifted into a sled by strong gloved hands and a voice describing what the journey was going to feel like.

He felt the texture of someone's naked shoulder as they wept about something he didn't understand. Anxious friends patted him on the back as he coughed and spluttered over an expensive meal. He hoped his son would do well at school, that his daughter would be all right with such an idiot for a husband, that Santa Claus would give him a Galaxy Mobile.

No voice, as far as God was aware, ever came to him twice, or if it did, he certainly didn't recognise it. He did, however, learn to recognise particular calibrations of feeling – specific flavours or harmonics of emotion. Some exclamations, though stridently passionate, did not move him, and he would fall asleep even as they harangued. Others, meek and barely audible, had the power to shock him awake. For them, he would get up out of bed. Not because his name had been mentioned – his name was used so often he figured there must be no end of Gods on the planet – but because of a certain tone of voice, full of love and longing for the impossible. However sleepy he was, he would climb up on his chair and give the globe an extra nudge, to make time go faster, so that whatever was to happen would happen sooner, and whatever had happened would be longer ago.

Then he would sleep, and dream his dream of visiting his planet and dying there.

Or, if the last voice he'd heard was laughing, he would dream he was playing at the back of the universe, and finding stuff so indescribably cool that he couldn't even picture it once he woke up.

The strangest dream he ever had, though, was just after he'd heard a child's voice, almost certainly a young boy's, whispering down to him on an unusually quiet night.

'God?' The voice was shaky, close to tears. 'Are you there? Can I talk to you?'

There was a pause while God and the other child both held their breath, then nothing. God had lost him.

God jumped up and stood on his chair, putting his face close to the planet as it hung there. Even in the darkness he could see the white of the poles, some jet-streams, clouds. He could not, of course, see the boy who had whispered to him.

'Hello,' he whispered back, his lips touching the exosphere. 'It's me. I'm right here.' Clouds formed instantly under his mouth, as if he had fogged a window, but that was all. No doubt there would soon be weather too extreme to measure, in exchange for this attempt at conversation, but he was too sleepy to wait for it. His eyeballs felt swollen and he was shivering.

In bed, he fell into sleep as if from a height, as if he were a single, soft-spoken word falling through space. Then he dreamed of going to the back of the universe, his favourite place for finding new toys. This time, however, he heard, as he approached, the sound of someone rummaging there ahead of him. It was another child, the same size as himself, emerging bum-first from the charred shell of an ancient generator. God dashed forward in an ecstasy of loneliness, desperate to be as close as possible before the child turned to show him if it was a boy or a girl.

He ran and ran, all night, for ever and ever, until, in the morning, he woke, remembering nothing, except that it had been good, and he was happy.

Miss Fatt and Miss Thinne

TWO FAIRLY YOUNG ladies, having been friends since convent days, still lived together in a small cosy house. They were terribly used to one another, and took turns to do the scrambled eggs in the mornings.

Miss Fatt, who was not fat, regularly performed such tasks as extracting the different-coloured hairs from the bath plughole, scrubbing the dried toothpaste froth off the bathroom sink, and other jobs which Miss Thinne, who was not thin, detested. Miss Thinne took care of such tasks as washing and ironing, and her friend considered this a fair exchange.

Physicalities are important in this story: Miss Fatt was a slender woman with long legs, big breasts and a face like Marilyn Monroe's. Miss Thinne was likewise a slender woman with long legs, big breasts and, in her case, a face like Greta Garbo's, but fuller in the cheeks. Had they been in the habit of wearing each other's clothes they might have been mistaken for each other, at least in bad light.

But they weren't in the habit of wearing each other's clothes (however perfectly these might have fitted), because they considered themselves to be as different as chalk and cheese. This conviction (a totally mistaken one) was based on things like the division of the housework. How could they be even similar, they thought, if one of them retched while the other hummed contentedly over a toilet bowl? How could strangers have trouble telling them apart, when one of them spent three hours a week ironing, and the other had ironed for perhaps three hours in her whole lifetime?

However, there are deeper truths than division of labour, and in reality Miss Fatt and Miss Thinne were so much alike that they were almost a single organism, growing in two pale branches from an invisible root in the heart of the house.

On a typical day, the alarm went off at seven in the morning, and one of the women would reach out of bed and turn it off, this responsibility being accepted in turns, as the alarm clock was shifted nightly from one bedside table to the other. Miss Fatt might get out of bed, put on her slippers, and shuffle into the kitchen to make breakfast.

At the breakfast table, she and Miss Thinne would talk in the drab private language developed by people who share too many minutes of the day.

After breakfast, the women got dressed, Miss Fatt in her Wonderbra and fashionable clothes, Miss Thinne in her white uniform and regulation cardigan. Then they left for work in the car they shared, Miss Thinne getting off at the Community Health Centre, and Miss Fatt driving on to wherever she was wanted that day.

Occasionally she wasn't wanted anywhere and would drive back home, but usually she had plenty of work, what with her Marilyn Monroe looks.

A Typical Miss Thinne Day

Miss Thinne's duties as a community nurse were many, and she enjoyed every single one of them. She was one of those health-care professionals who had the knack of generating a sort of breezy warmth impossible to distinguish from genuine affection. This allowed her to get along with anyone, especially the sick and elderly.

'How are you today, Mrs Carbioni?' she might ask, while changing the dressing on that woman's perennial ulcer, or:

'There you go, love,' as she set a plate of food in front of a shuddering old crone, or:

'Have you given some thought to what I told you last week about smoking, Mr Sangster?'

She could be motherly when required, or sisterly, or like a devoted daughter. She never failed to get what she wanted, which was the best for her patients.

Her colleagues pronounced her a marvel.

'Eleanor's a marvel,' they said.

At morning tea back at the Community Health Centre there was congenial chat among the nurses. Each nurse discussed her patients' worsening problems around a large laminex table.

'Mr Simek is forgetting to go to the toilet and he can't seem to manage the phone anymore. Becoming very uncooperative too – a real pain! I think he'll have to be moved out of home pretty soon.'

'Poor old soul. He was a lovely dignified man only a few years ago.' This was Miss Thinne talking, of course.

'Yes, I suppose he was . . . It seems so long ago now, I'd sort of forgotten. You remember them all so well!'

'Eleanor's a marvel where that's concerned.'

Miss Thinne blushed, not out of modesty but almost out of shame for being so ideally suited to her chosen profession, as well as so ideally suited to her chosen home life and the companion who went with it: so ideally suited, in other words, to Life altogether.

Late in the afternoon she would leave the Health Centre and, if she didn't see the car waiting by the side of the road with Miss Fatt reading a magazine against the steering wheel, she would stroll to the bus stop.

A Typical Miss Fatt Day

Miss Fatt worked for a glamour agency, which meant she was a model most days, and more occasionally an actress. Being busty, she didn't get much fashion work, but there were plenty of other assignments.

On television, she'd played a criminal's girlfriend (or possibly wife) in an episode of a popular detective series, a good meaty part which had required her to convey Anxiety, Love, Bitterness, and finally Grief and Horror when her boyfriend (or possibly husband) went down in a hail of police bullets.

Her one movie role so far had required rather less acting than that, but at least she hadn't bared her breasts, unless you were going to split hairs over where exactly breasts began.

Mostly, however, she did commercials, through the agency of Carp & Bravitt. Starring and supporting roles came in mixed succession: one day she might be almost lost in a crowd of women gaping at a man because he was wearing a particular brand of shirt; the next day she might be the star, holding a can of floor polish with a smile. Next time after that, however, she might again be running in a crowd, following a seven-foot rabbit to a supermarket.

Obviously there wasn't much of a future in commercials, but Miss Fatt had high hopes for her acting career: in a few weeks, she would be playing another, different girlfriend (or possibly wife) of a criminal in another, different television drama, and in about two months she was actually contracted to play a sinister, sexy villainess in *Lethal Weapon VI*, a big-budget international movie. This was certainly a big deal, in any sense of the word.

'Heard about your film job coming up, Suzie,' said Mr Carp.

'Yeah,' said Mr Bravitt. 'A real stroke of luck. But you deserve it, Suzie.'

Both men thought she had excellent legs and breasts.

The makers of TV commercials were always very nice to her, too, because it was against their interests to have anyone miserable associated with the product. For Miss Fatt, a commercial meant nothing less than an afternoon of fun. Directors would ask her how she was going, did she want a cup of tea, would she mind awfully doing just *one* more retake?

'All right girls: big leap in the air now . . . Come on! I know it's daft, but let's all think happy thoughts about getting paid for this!'

In all her years in TV commercials, even as the lowliest extra, Miss Fatt hadn't had one unkind word said to her. She might not have impressed anyone as a marvel, *yet*, but she was, it was generally agreed, a really nice girl. And, when the shooting was over, Miss Fatt would swing into her little car and drive home.

First Month

It was on the 25th of April that Miss Fatt and Miss Thinne first began to suffer from their unusual problem.

Miss Thinne turned off the alarm at seven and slid out of bed into her slippers. It was her turn to make the breakfast, and with dutiful contentment she gathered together the makings, such as bread, margarine, eggs, tea and so on. But when she'd finished gathering them together, the hoard suddenly struck her as a monstrously large one. In fact, it seemed *so* excessive that she was a bit revolted: did she really have such a gluttonous appetite as this pile of food would suggest?

As if to answer her own question, she looked deep into herself and tried to examine her appetite, but glimpsed only the last trickles of it disappearing into a black hole. It seemed to have been lost as helplessly, as inevitably, as water out of a colander. Within a few moments she was entirely taken over by the realisation that *eating was not for her*: she'd been doing it for too long. What on earth was the point, after all, of putting things in your mouth, pulping them up with your teeth, and swallowing them?

'What's wrong?'

It was Miss Fatt, come into the kitchen in her slippers and nightgown. She looked at Miss Thinne as if to say, What are you doing just standing there? And Miss Thinne looked back at Miss Fatt as if to say, What are you in such a hurry for?

'I couldn't *wait*,' said Miss Fatt. 'I'm so *hungry*.' She ogled the eggs in the egg-basket, but they were hard-shelled and raw, intolerable minutes away from being ready to eat, so she went for the bread instead, snatching up slices of it straight from the packet.

'Oh my God, what a hunger,' she mumbled, stuffing herself.

'Go ahead,' conceded Miss Thinne. 'Eat it all. I'm not a bit hungry this morning. Couldn't eat a bite.' And she stood there, shivering in her nightgown, marvelling at the ability of a human to do what Miss Fatt was doing.

Miss Fatt frowned in mid-chew and pointed out with some concern,

'You should eat something.'

Miss Thinne opened the refrigerator and scooped a handful of grated carrot out of a plastic bowl. With uncommon delicacy she took her seat at the kitchen table and, while Miss Fatt continued eating slices of undecorated bread, she stared at the handful of carrot and reflected,

'You know, this is really quite a lot, when you think about it. It must be . . . four or five cubic centimetres, at least.

The whole human stomach wouldn't even be five cubic centimetres, would it?'

'Oh, much more than that,' demurred Miss Fatt, gasping in between swallows. 'Anyway, it stretches.'

'Ugh,' said Miss Thinne. 'I don't like the sound of that.' Carefully she transferred some of the carrot to her other hand and nibbled, like a suspicious animal, at the reduced amount.

Miss Fatt swallowed hard on her sixth slice of bread and was comforted by the realisation that if she put some eggs on to boil now, she could continue eating bread until they were cooked.

In due course, Miss Thinne and Miss Fatt went to work.

'And what do you do of a weekend, Eleanor?' a co-worker asked Miss Thinne over morning tea.

'I play the oboe in the Catholic Women's Sinfonia,' she replied.

'You're joking!'

'No, I learned it at convent school, and sort of never gave it up. It's a lot of fun.'

'Ha! Ha! Good for you!'

Miss Thinne blushed, sipped her tea, but did not touch her biscuit.

Miss Fatt went off to the countryside to be driven around. She was playing the wife of a man who had just bought the right brand of car. A camera mounted variously on the bonnet, the side windows and the back seat filmed the two of them smiling at each other, so pleased with the car's wonderful performance. Miss Fatt's seat belt kept her breasts separate, for easy viewer identification; the rear-view mirror was angled towards her, so that she could judge whether the wind was blowing her hair in an unphotogenic direction. If that happened, she had the authority to order the car stopped so that she could get a touch-up from the hairdresser – now if that wasn't star treatment, what was? 'How about a drink after?' proposed the actor at the wheel to Miss Fatt. There was no sound being recorded by the cameras, of course, so only expert lip-readers would have known he wasn't expressing his delight at the steering or suspension.

'Why not invite me out to lunch?' said Miss Fatt. She had never asked a man anything like this before.

The actor laughed. 'All right, love.'

Over the roar of the engine, which in the finished commercial would be replaced by exhilarating music, Miss Fatt's stomach rumbled and whined.

Second Month

By the 25th of May, Miss Fatt and Miss Thinne were developing rather different shapes from those they'd had for years. The cause was, respectively, eating and not eating.

In the mornings, Miss Thinne ate almost nothing, and Miss Fatt almost everything. Because the grocery expenses remained much the same, neither of the women made any fuss about this new routine; in any case, it had established itself so abruptly and so invincibly that they were forced to accept that it was meant to be.

Only once did they share any apprehension about what might lie in store for them, and on that occasion they merely caught each other's eye across the kitchen table and, pushing aside for a moment a bowl of porridge and a stick of celery respectively, they joined hands and squeezed until their grip trembled and tears welled up in their eyes.

'You're looking awfully smart, Eleanor,' Miss Thinne's coworkers said at first, for her weight loss made her look, well, *willowy*, at least in clothes.

'How do you do it?' was also much asked. 'Whenever *I* go on a diet, nothing happens.'

And then again: 'Being skinny's all the rage these days. When I was a girl, you were supposed to be plump and rosy!'

Miss Thinne was *thin* and rosy. The rosy part was from a make-up kit.

Miss Fatt did a lot of exercise each day, to keep her weight gain within reasonable limits. Her belly was still trim, but she was putting on quite a bit on her breasts, thighs and bottom.

'Shaping up for *Lethal Weapon VI*, eh?' guessed Mr Carp. 'You'll stun 'em, Suzie.'

'What a body,' sighed Mr Bravitt, out of earshot.

Miss Fatt's actor friend took her out to lunch and dinner regularly. A couple of times she'd even accompanied him back to his flat, which had very little in it except a bed and a refrigerator. She'd used his refrigerator, but not his bed, though she knew it was only a matter of time before he demanded some sort of sexual reward for his generosity. The problem was, sometimes his flat was just so much closer, as far as the next meal was concerned, than her own home.

Third Month

By the 25th of June the two women were becoming remarkable.

Miss Thinne was as thin as she had been at the beginning of puberty. Her thighs and calves had lost all superfluous fat; her clavicles and shoulderblades were becoming prominent, her fingers taper-like. Her bra became wrinkled with unoccupied space; her clothes hung loose and slid about on her as she moved. Her neck seemed to have grown; cheekbones appeared where none, even with the aid of cosmetics, had ever been before.

'You know, Eleanor,' suggested her colleagues. 'You may be taking this diet too far.'

'Think of your health, dear. We wouldn't want you to disappear into thin air.'

'You look great just as you are now, honestly.'

'But it's not that I'm dieting,' protested Miss Thinne mildly. 'I just don't want to eat anything.'

In that case, it was agreed, she should see a doctor.

But Miss Thinne knew that her metamorphosis was meant to be.

Miss Fatt knew it too, and took no action, apart from exercise and (lately) a girdle.

'D'you think Mel Gibson likes 'em *that* big?' joked Mr Carp, only trying to be nice. He thought that she was perhaps overeating out of nerves at the prospect of the imminent movie role. As for her television assignment playing the girl-friend (or possibly wife) of the criminal, that had come and gone, and Miss Fatt had received high praise for her performance. The director had been delighted, actually, that she was so much more curvaceous than she'd been at the audition. 'Good slattern potential,' he'd pronounced, and ordered a teddy for her, presumably from that shelf in the wardrobe department marked VOLUPTUOUS SLATTERN. But he'd said it in the nicest possible way, as a professional director to a professional actress.

Of course, this was a couple of weeks ago now, and she had gained more weight since then. A punishing regime of jogging and press-ups waged a losing battle against the six square meals a day with which she was covering her former shape with soft new flesh.

'My God you eat a lot,' said her actor friend one day. His perfect failure to understand excited a small flame of contempt in her, and she looked at him condescendingly, as if to say, But of *course* I do – what else would you expect?

Fourth Month

On the 25th of July Miss Thinne began her day by bringing a tray of food in to Miss Fatt. She herself took small bites of a Chinese lettuce as Miss Fatt devoured pancakes with jam, fried eggs and bacon, Welsh rarebit and a bowl of custard. Miss Fatt was eating perhaps even more now that she was miserable, for she had lost her chance to play the sexy, sinister villainess in *Lethal Weapon VI*. A week away from shooting, the casting director had caught sight of her new shape and immediately cancelled her contract, employing in her place another slender young woman with long legs, big breasts and a face like Marilyn Monroe's.

Friends advised her to sue, but in their heart of hearts they thought she had only a dubious moral right to win.

'Are you all right?' they asked her, meaningfully.

Since then, Miss Fatt had been playing sexy overweight women in commercials. The directors were just as pleasant as ever, but Carp and Bravitt tried to point out to her, in a subtle way, that she couldn't reasonably expect their firm to secure as many assignments for her as before.

'The use for big women in advertisements is limited, Suzie. You've either got to lose some weight, or do some serious thinking.'

'Serious thinking?'

'You could give up being sexy altogether. I could put you down in the books as a "housewife and mother" type. You know the kind of thing: sensible perm, cheap floral dress, spreading margarine on the kids' sandwiches with a golden sunny halo all around you . . . Chucking dirty clothes into a washing machine to a choreographed dance routine . . . Can you still dance, love?'

'No,' sighed Miss Fatt. 'Not really.'

'Well,' said Carp, a shadow of distaste crossing his face. 'Think it over anyway. But, you know, the best thing to do would be to lose weight.'

'I'll do my best,' promised Miss Fatt, but she knew that eating less was out of the question, and it was getting more difficult to exercise, what with the bulging belly and the expanding bosom. Her actor friend had broken off with her just at the point where she was seriously considering going to bed with him; the reason he gave was that he couldn't afford to refill his refrigerator several times a week. This was the first unkind word uttered to Miss Fatt since the change in her condition had begun.

The first unkind word uttered to Miss Thinne came soon after, when one of the elderly ladies whose malnutrition she was trying to correct pushed a plate of food away and jeered, 'Who are *you* to say I don't eat enough?'

'I . . . I'm sorry,' grimaced Miss Thinne.

Fifth Month

The 25th of August Miss Fatt and Miss Thinne spent at home, for it was a Sunday.

Ordinarily, Miss Thinne would have gone out to play the oboe with the Catholic Women's Sinfonia, but she'd had to resign from the group because she no longer had the lung-power to inspirate the instrument.

Miss Fatt would probably still have been working on *Lethal Weapon VI*, if she hadn't been disqualified. Mind you, by now she was no longer even what her actor ex-friend had described as 'a bit gross'. She was *rather* gross. Her cheeks were filling out and merging with the new fullness of her neck and chin; on the rest of her body a number of bones had disappeared, in the sense that they could be found only by determined palpation. A long crease trapped sweat and talcum powder under her belly, and her breasts sagged under their own weight. Her usual attire was no longer a Wonderbra and fashionable gear; it was floral dresses and a sarong which Miss Thinne had given her for her birthday some weeks before. All the clothes that no longer fitted her they'd already given away to charity shops, thus revealing their unspoken shared assumption that she would never be a size 12 – or even 16, for that matter – again. Giving away the twenty-one pairs of unwearable shoes was, well, almost unbearable, but what hurt most was having to put away all her rings (no, she would *not* sell them – not yet) for fear that they would strangle her fingers.

As far as her work went, she played only fat women now, usually in humorous contexts. She had sworn off drama since she had landed the role, in a TV movie, of the fat older sister of a beautiful young girl. The part had required of her a Poisonous Jealousy which took advantage of the younger sister's low self-esteem to make the girl feel unattractive, unloved and ungrateful. It had seemed a good enough role, but the director's method in coaching Miss Fatt had consisted of exhortations like:

'Come on, Suzie. Remember you're fat and revolting. You want *her* to feel as repulsive as *you* are – it makes you feel better. See the psychology?'

Miss Fatt was determined to stick to roles in commercials in which she could smile in floral dresses and be invited afterwards to have a cup of tea with the other extras.

She might have considered giving up work altogether, as the amount of exercise she had to do in order to maintain her fitness for it was torture, but, more than ever, the two women needed the income from their jobs. Not only did their grocery bill continue to increase almost daily, but they'd had to buy a whole set of larger furniture for Miss Fatt to sit in, and a number of giant soft cushions for Miss Thinne, to protect her protruding bones from bruising.

One day Miss Fatt came home to find Miss Thinne still lying in bed, too weak to get up.

Shrouded by the sheet, her body looked like a skeleton, but once uncovered by Miss Fatt it didn't look too bad: no thinner, surely, than that of a healthy seventy-year-old. As for Miss Thinne's weakness, she'd merely left the bowl of celery slivers too far out of reach. A nibble or two and she was on her corrugated feet again, ready and able to prepare Miss Fatt's mid-afternoon roast.

Sixth Month

On the 25th of September Miss Fatt visited Miss Thinne in hospital.

She came by public transport, having some time ago sold the car, partly to raise money for food, and partly because she'd been having trouble squeezing herself into the driver's seat.

'Hello, Eleanor,' she said at the foot of the hospital bed where Miss Thinne lay naked, her bedclothes thrown aside because of their weight on the starved white limbs. 'How's the leg?'

Miss Thinne had fractured her tibia in a fall, easily. The plaster cast resembled one of those white thigh-length boots Miss Fatt had once sported in an ice-cream commercial.

'Home in a week or two.'

Looking up at her visitor, Miss Thinne didn't by any means feel herself to be the more unfortunate of the two. Tears came to her eyes as she observed how ugly Miss Fatt was becoming. Her eyes were piggy, her mouth a puffy rosebud marooned in an expanse of mottled pink. The dowdy lace and wire of a huge bra from a charity shop peeped out above the folds of her birthday sarong which, unbelievably, was now too small. She seemed condemned to exude a morbid sexual grossness while Miss Thinne, naked as she was, seemed utterly sexless. Even so, the nursing staff found it in their hearts to say about her:

'Isn't she creepy?'

And about Miss Fatt:

'What a slug.'

Seventh Month

By October 25th Miss Fatt was no longer playing fat ladies in commercials.

She had, in fact, been removed from the books of Carp & Bravitt. Striving for a tact so impossible to achieve that he soon abandoned the struggle, Bravitt told her, at first, that it wasn't worth her while to be kept on the books, given how rarely the firm would be able to find work for her. Then, when Miss Fatt made the mistake of pleading with him, he told her she was not the sort of person, physically speaking, that Carp & Bravitt wanted themselves associated with.

Thus ushered into the ranks of the jobless, Miss Fatt waddled to the employment office, which was located (luckily) only a few doors along from Carp & Bravitt's office building, so that she didn't have far to travel in order to get the news that she was no good to anyone.

Riding home on the bus, the stamp UNEMPLOYABLE burning on her forehead, she was far too hungry to feel as awful as she should.

Limping with a stick and still in plaster, Miss Thinne was allowed to go home on the understanding that she would rest up, subsisting on sick pay.

Unfortunately, this was out of the question. She just couldn't do without her overtime and penalty rates – if anything, she needed a raise to fund Miss Fatt's ever-growing appetite. So, impressively sprightly in her slimline plaster cast, she returned to work, shocking her old colleagues.

'Lovely to have you back, Eleanor,' they winced.

The Eleanor they had back was a startling bird of prey, with teeth advancing as the flesh of the face retreated, ears like curls of pink wire, and pop-eyes.

Soon enough reports were brought back of Eleanor's inability to nurse owing to her frailty and, more damningly, to her appearance frightening the people she was supposed to be caring for. With the utmost sensitivity and goodwill she was therefore relieved of her duties.

Eighth Month

By November, Miss Fatt and Miss Thinne were practically fugitives (if such a word can be applied to people who rarely move) from the ant-eater snout of hospitalisation. They lived in fear of some officious social worker calling on them and 'assessing' them as unfit to stay at home.

Their metamorphosis having advanced swiftly, they were now utterly dependent on one another for simple survival. Miss Thinne had to be fed when she was asleep, or she would retch convulsively at the prospect of eating. Lukewarm vegetable soup poured carefully into her mouth in the middle of the night smuggled enough nutrients into her body to keep her alive, though she would wake up coughing and spluttering, glaring at her ministering companion in fear and outrage before coming to her senses.

Lately, she had the bewildering sensation that there were only a few thousand proteins, vitamins, minerals and whatever else floating about in her body, and that she could actually feel these being consumed and extinguished one by one.

In the daytime she would go out to the corner grocer to buy food. Unemployment benefits were hardly enough to cover this expense, but extra money had been raised through selling off everything except the bed, the cushions and the cooking equipment. Even so, they had to be disciplined in their budget: only powdered soup, potatoes, rice and oats were worth buying these days, as anything else was eaten too quickly, and with too little effect, to justify the increasingly frail Miss Thinne carrying it home.

Finally, on the 25th, Miss Thinne collapsed at the shop, fracturing two of her ribs on the grocer's burly arms as he leapt forward to catch her. Desperately though she tried to leave for home, she lost consciousness in the attempt and was, instead, promptly removed to a hospital.

Mere hours later, Miss Fatt's helpless bellowing for food provoked neighbours to call the police, so that she, too, ended up being taken to a hospital, albeit a different one.

In Miss Thinne's hospital, staff of various ranks said:
'Don't you worry, dear: you'll be right as rain in no time.'
Or:
'Well then, Eleanor, you haven't been taking very good care of yourself, have you?'
After a day or two, no longer *to* her but in her earshot, they said other things too, like:
'Progressive lipodystrophy.'
'Hypophyseal cachexia.'
'I think the little bitch must be *taking* something to flush

the IV fluids through her system without absorbing them. Search her bedside locker.'

In Miss Fatt's hospital, Miss Fatt was not addressed directly even in the beginning, because her problem was diagnosed as being mental in origin rather than physical. The fact that no one tried to communicate with her didn't matter much anyway, since she might not have been able to listen: her ears were swelling up into little puddings. She certainly couldn't hear the farrago of diagnoses and recommendations her doctors were thinking up for her in faraway parts of the building.

'Prader-Willi Syndrome.'

'Glandular dystrophy.'

'Staple her stomach.'

'Shorten her intestine.'

'Step up the reducing diet.'

'Suprarenal tumour.'

'I'd go for Cushing's Disease myself.'

Miss Fatt, for her part, had only one thing to say, only one suggestion to make.

'Feed me!' she cried. 'I'm hungry!' Her voice was squashed into a hoarse bleat by the fat in her throat pressing in on her vocal cords.

'You've *had* your thousand calories,' snapped a nurse. 'At breakfast.'

'Then kill me!' sobbed Miss Fatt. 'I want to die!'

'Don't be stupid, Mrs Fatt' was the nurse's retort. Like all the nurses, she found the fat woman in Room 13 monstrous and loathsome, but felt professionally obliged to pretend that she found her merely annoying and difficult, in case the patient might be shamed into making a recovery.

Ninth Month

On December the 25th, Miss Fatt lay on a cot, or rather two cots pushed together, in the psycho-geriatric wing of a large hospital far from the residential part of town. She was naked, not because of her almost constant feeling of suffocation, but because no institution nightgowns were big enough to fit her and, as no one was paying for her stay, it wasn't worth getting one specially made.

Miss Fatt was under treatment for suicidal tendencies arising from her delusion that she would continue to gain weight no matter how little she was given to eat or how many experimental drugs she was injected with. The room in which she was locked was free of edible substances and sharp implements; free of everything, in fact, except for the cots and a naked lightbulb overhead.

Trapped inside a quivering mass of fat, the tortured spirit of Miss Fatt was capable of nothing but stubborn outrage.

'I – need – *food*!' was all she said to her keepers, her voice almost strangled to a squeak.

'You're just an animal,' a nurse accused her one day, as she warily cleaned up the enormous droppings smeared all over Miss Fatt's cot-sides. Her slim, well-proportioned body was trembling with disgust and awe.

Others said: 'Slut.'

Others said: 'Cow.'

Miss Fatt just lay there, waiting for her meals. Her only distractions from the unbearable hours of longing were her agonies of breathlessness, headache, angina, sinusitis and thrombosis. The doctors were making bets among themselves as to what would be her eventual cause of death, and thrombosis was the favourite. Miss Fatt had heard one of them prophesy as much, while he was kneeling at her feet, examining her blubberous legs. He smelled strongly of an aftershave which Miss Fatt had once nuzzled in a TV commercial. Perhaps the seductive eyes, the bee-stung lips, the subtle cleavage of her former body had persuaded him to try that aftershave, once upon a time. Now here he was, dwarfed by her mass, telling her she would die soon of thrombosis. She ignored him, secure in the knowledge that she would not die of thrombosis or anything else he could understand: she would die of her unique condition. Only at mealtimes did she glimpse death, knowing that the food she wished for so desperately would kill her by and by.

Miss Thinne was supposed to be dying in an inner-city cancer hospital, but on this Christmas night, taking advantage of the relaxed security procedures on Jesus's birthday, she was instead able to be elsewhere.

She was in a taxi speeding towards Miss Fatt's hospital.

Her ischia, jutting out through her fleshless buttocks, made shallow dents in the cab's back seat as she excreted the last of the intravenous fluids from which she had disconnected herself hours before. A stolen overcoat hid from the driver's notice both her nakedness and the fact that she was too wasted to live much longer.

Having reached the hospital gates, Miss Thinne swung open the cab door and limped without paying into the dense, unlit greenery. There she waited, not breathing, listening for the sound of the taxi driving away.

As soon as the air was silent she walked up to the long cast-iron fence and slipped through the bars, needing only to shed her coat to achieve this feat of insubstantiality.

She didn't need to be told where Miss Fatt lay imprisoned: this final meeting was as inevitable as the metamorphoses themselves.

'Suzie'

Miss Fatt's slit eyes looked up at the high but unbarred window and saw, poking through there, the face and arms of her companion. Only the hair and skin lent some recognisable individuality to what was otherwise the common human skeleton.

'You've come,' squeaked Miss Fatt.

Miss Thinne heaved herself on to the window-ledge like a nightmarish white praying mantis, and lowered her spindly legs carefully down into the dark and humid room. Her forklike feet dangled more than a metre from Miss Fatt's helplessly supine body.

'Can't reach,' panted Miss Thinne.

'Just let yourself fall.'

Surrendering her balance on the window-ledge, Miss Thinne allowed herself to drop, landing safely on the soft mound of flesh below.

Sprawled on top of Miss Fatt, who had so very much flesh and no discernible bones, while *she* had such very obvious bones and hardly any discernible flesh, she understood for the first time that the way they had become alienated from each other was strangely natural, like the separation of liquid from solid in curdling milk.

Both exhausted, they lay together, silent, while in the corridors outside, Christmas carols were sung to those patients for whom there was deemed to be some hope of remission. A faraway firework lit up the outside world and cast a rectangle of bright light on Miss Fatt and Miss Thinne. For the last time they tried to use their estranged bodies to show their love for one another, but for the first time this proved impossible.

'I'm so hungry,' lamented Miss Fatt, the tears trapped in swollen creases at the corners of her eyes. 'But I know that if I eat anymore, even *one* more thing, I'll die. I mean it.'

'I know.'

'My heart will just stop.'

'Yes.'

'And you?'

'Me? I've . . . had enough.' This statement alone drained Miss Thinne perfectly white, her pitiful reserve of moisture and pigment apparently exhaled along with the words. Then finally:

'There it goes . . .'

She meant the last of the contents that had nourished her, and indeed her body started shuddering, as if the bones were claiming their right to break free from their flimsy prison of skin.

'Feel free . . .' were her last words.

'Yes . . . yes . . .' said Miss Fatt, inside herself only. Outside, the Christmas carols were sounding fainter as Miss Thinne's body grew still, and they had faded away altogether by the time Miss Fatt lifted the dead hand gently to her lips.

Half a Million Pounds and
a Miracle

ROBBIE AND MCNAIR knew the job was going to be trouble when the Virgin Mary fell off her pedestal and smashed to smithereens right in front of them.

'What do you think?' said Robbie, when they squatted down to examine the rubble. He could see very well the statue was beyond repair, but he felt he ought to defer to his boss's experience and authority.

'It's grit for roads now,' frowned McNair, turning little fragments of the Virgin over and over in his massive hands. 'Dr Prosser won't be pleased.'

Dr Prosser was the ancient official who'd contracted McNair to oversee the renovations to St Hilda's, a fine Victorian church which had lain derelict for most of this century. Funding had finally been found to rescue it from total collapse – half a million pounds' worth.

McNair had had reservations about the job from the start. His company's trade was restoring neglected old buildings, true, but he'd only done a few churches, none of them Catholic, and none of them in such a rotten state of repair that roof slates fell through the ceiling and you walked ankle-deep in pigeon shit and the statues were liable to brain you.

'Have you not got any Catholic fellows for the job?' he'd queried Dr Prosser.

'None here in Ross-shire,' sighed the bureaucrat.

'To do this place up,' McNair had warned, 'you'll need more than half a million pound, you'll need a miracle.'

'We've applied for more funding next year,' said Dr Prosser. 'That's how it's done. A year at a time. Just do the best you can to begin with.'

So McNair had taken on the job.

And regretted it almost immediately. At this stage, weeks in, he'd only just finished clearing the place of debris; he'd had to sub-contract a lot of extra labourers, and many over-loaded garbage skips had been carted away. St Hilda's was still a disaster area. The inner walls were full of holes, spilling out the disintegrating straw its builders had used for insulation. Half the floorboards were rotten, including (probably) the ones underpinning the splendid old stone font. Every structure, surface and fixture in St Hilda's seemed to be in a sort of renovator's Limbo: too frail or damaged to keep as it was, yet too solid and expensive to rip out and replace. The stained glass in the windows, for example, was a showpiece of Victorian craftsmanship – a pity only a few jagged bits of it had survived.

McNair and his apprentice, Robbie, stood in the nave of the church now, dead centre, deciding where to go from here. They'd spent thousands already and the place only looked sadder and emptier. McNair asked Robbie if he had any ideas.

The lad kicked pensively at the thick layer of pigeon cack on the floor.

'I reckon the only way to get this off is to plane it,' he ventured.

McNair sighed. He'd been hoping for something a bit more inspired than that.

'Why couldn't they have ploughed the money into Scottish industry, eh?' he exclaimed suddenly. 'Think of how many jobs half a million pound would create, eh?'

Robbie frowned, trying to imagine how half a million pounds might create jobs. It was as difficult as imagining how water could be turned into wine.

'They could have built a . . . a shopping centre, mebbe.'

'Eh?'

'In a place that hasn't got one. Uist, mebbe.'

'Eh? What are you talking about?'

'I was in Stromness once. The shop was always shut by the time I could get myself out of bed. I could've starved.'

Feeling the weight of McNair's incredulity, Robbie didn't say anymore. The effort of thinking of a way to turn money into jobs had exhausted him. Personally, he didn't see why, if there was a half a million pounds going spare for some Highland town, it couldn't just be distributed equally among the sparse population. Who'd need jobs then?

Another idea Robbie had for what could be done with half a million pounds was maybe building a giant cinema complex in some place like Invergordon. All right, so it just happened to be where he lived himself, but it would get loads of customers from the ships and the rigs, surely. Everybody was desperate for something to do.

Only the other day, Robbie had gone to a terrible disco in Alness, hoping it would transform his life in some way. It was the sort of disco where no alcohol was allowed so everybody made sure to be thoroughly drunk before arriving. Robbie had searched the entire hall, from wall to wall, to find a girl who didn't look as if she was about to fall asleep, or vomit, or bite him in the neck. He'd found just *one*. She was very short, seemed very nice, was very bored. She asked him what he did for a living. He said he was a stonemason, that he was doing up a church.

'Oh, that sounds interesting,' she'd said.

'Em . . . it's pretty boring, actually,' he'd replied.

'Oh,' she'd said, looking away slightly and tapping her foot to the mechanised beat from London.

Looking back on it now, Robbie couldn't understand why he'd said his work was boring. Shyness, he supposed, because it wasn't true. The challenge of making St Hilda's look like a proper church again – and not just that, but a different kind of church from the ones he'd grown up with – was pretty exciting, really. Re-attaching an intricately carved corbel, disguising the join with a cunning glue made of dust from the original stone mixed with cement: now *that* was satisfaction.

As for the problem of the smashed Virgin, Robbie got on to that promptly. Aware of McNair watching him in what he hoped was admiration, he consulted a telephone book and, using his mobile phone, called a church on the island of Barra, seeing as how it was such a Catholic place, and old-fashioned enough to have a Virgin of the right vintage.

'Hello there,' said Robbie, when he'd got through. 'We've had a little accident here at St Hilda's Church in Ross-shire. Yeah. And what I was wondering is, have you got any Virgin Marys you don't need?'

McNair covered his eyes and sighed deeply as a harsh *cwuk!* sounded through the phone.

'He hung up,' said Robbie superfluously.

'Let me handle this,' said McNair, motioning for the mobile.

McNair rang Barra back, explained who he was, translated the situation into officialese, mentioned the half-million pounds. Dressed up in this way, McNair's conversation with the Catholic priest managed to last many seconds longer than Robbie's. It might even have lasted a whole minute.

'No Virgin Marys, eh?' Robbie enquired when it was over and McNair was tapping his fingers dolefully on the table.

'He says they may be *Catholics*,' McNair said, 'but they're *Scottish* Catholics.'

'Which means what? They do without?'

'No, it means they make do with the one Virgin Mary they've got. No spares.'

The men sat in silence for a minute, gloomy. Outside, a vehicle pulled up, the rusty church gate creaked, the worm-eaten church door groaned, and a fragment of ceiling fell into the aisle. McNair suggested that Robbie go and see to the visitor and leave the Virgin to him. As a contractor of many years' experience, he had lots of contacts when it came to specialised bits and pieces. There was a place in Cornwall which was brilliant for supplying crenellated moulding, for instance, and another one in Morpeth which was pretty much cinquefoil city.

Robbie went out to talk to a joiner who had just arrived with two dozen lathe-turned balusters for the gap-toothed balustrades upstairs. McNair took the opportunity to ring his old friend Alistair at Glasgow Cemetery Supplies and asked him what he had knocking around in the religious statues line.

'I've got quite a few graveyard angels, all sizes,' offered Alistair.

'Any that could do for a Virgin Mary?'

'I dunno. The Virgin Mary hasnae got wings, has she?'

'Wings could be knocked off. The important thing is the dimensions and . . . em . . . the expression.'

'What sort of expression?'

McNair thought hard.

'Like . . . like those women in advertisements for instant coffee, just when they get to sit down and have their first sip. Except more serious.'

'I'm with you, I'm with you,' Alistair assured him.

Months went by. Painfully slowly but impressively surely, St Hilda's began to come good. Sealing and retiling the roof made a big difference, of course, especially to what was left of the half-million pounds.

Meanwhile, in the outside world, Robbie met the girl from the disco again in the Invergordon supermarket. She worked there as a checkout assistant.

'How's the church coming along?' she asked him as she scanned his paltry basketful of bachelor groceries.

This time he didn't downrate himself or St Hilda's, but told her a little about the challenges and how he was solving them. The girl had a lovely smile and looked quite pretty even in a supermarket uniform. Her name was Catriona. Unfortunately, she finished scanning Robbie's groceries in hardly any time at all, and had to ask him if he was saving coupons for the tartan teddy bears. He said no and before he knew it he was outside on the street. A good problem-solver when it came to stonemasonry, Robbie was at a loss here: he couldn't very well buy his groceries twice, could he? He supposed that meant it was all over between him and Catriona.

Back at the church, a stone angel had arrived which Robbie was turning into a Virgin Mary. He'd knocked the wings off no bother, sanded and polished her back, fixed her firmly to the pedestal. The angel had come without a few of Mary's trademark features, but Robbie was adding these himself.

The missing cord around her waist was easy: Robbie merely cut a length of thin rope, soaked it in cement fondue, tied it on and let it dry. Adding a veil to the angel's bare head was more difficult. Despite several attempts involving underwiring and gauze to give the cement-soaked fabric a full and flowing shape, it still looked as if the Virgin Mary had been flipping a freshly rolled pizza base in the air and it had landed on her head. Every few weeks Robbie had to admit his veil was rubbish, knock it off the statue's head and try again. All around the Virgin, the church of St Hilda was emerging from the rubble, but the veil refused to come good. Evaluating his latest attempt with a frown, Robbie wondered: how would a real Italian like Michelangelo have done it?

It turned out that Catriona was a bit of an expert on Michelangelo. Robbie knew this because . . . well, he'd seen her a few times lately. At the supermarket, and also at her mum's house. Catriona's dad was actually an artist but, due to lack of work opportunities in the Highlands, he'd moved to Edinburgh, and seemed to have forgotten to take his wife and daughter with him. He'd left his art books behind, though, and Catriona knew these intimately. With eyes closed, she could picture the Sistine Chapel ceiling better than her own bedroom, she said, then blushed.

In time, Catriona asked if she could come and see him working at St Hilda's some time. He said he'd discuss it with his boss, though in truth it was his own shyness which prevented him taking her along right away. There was a particular expression workmates had told him he wore when he was concentrating, a sort of dumb intensity, which he wasn't sure he wanted her to see. Also, he'd be covered in dust and glue and God knows what else, whereas when he visited her he always spruced himself up.

And so, putting off Catriona's visit a little while yet, he returned to St Hilda's and worked like a slave. McNair was impressed with the wonders his apprentice managed as the year wore on. Only the veil remained, frankly, crap.

One day, about eight months into the project, Dr Prosser

came to visit the church and, in due course, he stopped to appraise the renovated Virgin.

'Her eyes are supposed to be closed,' said the good doctor.

'Closed?'

'Closed!'

'Well . . . she's got to open them some time, has she not?'

'Also, she looks as if a pancake has fallen on her head.'

'No bother, easily fixed,' grimaced Robbie, pulling his mallet from a loop in his belt. 'It was a . . . an interim measure, like.'

He tapped the statue's headgear gently but firmly with the mallet, and it fell away in shards.

By winter St Hilda's was sound structurally; the weather proved it by raining and hailing down on it night and day without getting in. The floors were smooth and solid, if uncarpeted, and the aisles were symmetrical with repaired pews. The windows were sealed with wire mesh and ordinary glass: an interim measure. As a whole the place looked impressive but cold and rather bare. Resting at the end of a working day, Robbie and McNair drank coffee and discussed St Hilda's finer potentials.

'You know,' mused Robbie, 'I've been looking at them old Italian churches. Fellows like Michelangelo did some cracking stuff there, you know. Huge great paintings on the ceilings and all.'

'Yes, well,' said McNair, 'Michelangelo's passed on a few years ago now.'

'I thought mebbe there might be some painters living around here who might like to have a go at these ceilings,' persisted Robbie. 'You know: job creation.'

'I'll raise it with Dr Prosser next time he comes round.'

Robbie thought McNair was being sarcastic, but a few weeks later it turned out that McNair *had* raised it with the bureaucrat. Word came back that when the basic renovation of the church was finished, in 1999, the board might then consider the possibility of commissions 'of an artistic nature'.

'It'll be the next century by then,' objected Robbie.

'A millennium project,' grinned McNair. 'They might get Lottery funding.'

It was late November before Robbie found the courage to invite Catriona to the church. McNair was away for the day, of course.

Catriona stood in the transept, enchantingly back-lit by one of the big portable tungsten lamps. She had walked all around the aisles, shyly explored the chancel, but she kept returning to this spot, standing perfectly still, looking up at the ceiling.

'What are those?' she asked Robbie softly, not pointing with her hands, which hung at her sides as if she'd forgotten she had any. Robbie followed the line of her pale throat up through the air until he, too, was staring straight up.

'You mean those ornamental panels sunk into the ceiling? They're called coffers.'

'They're beautiful,' Catriona murmured.

'They're about the only decorative part of this place that's still in good order,' sighed Robbie. 'Everything else needs work or replacing.'

'Oh, but you'll do it, won't you Robbie?' she asked him.

'Sure,' he laughed, a little unnerved, because she sounded as if she was asking him to make some sort of solemn vow.

Noticing his discomfiture perhaps, she pointed at some vaulted arches converging above the transept and asked what the curvy bits underneath were called.

'Oh, them? They're called the . . . ah . . . groins,' Robbie said, then blushed.

Desperate to salvage the moment, Catriona asked another question, the first one that came to her.

'Don't you think the Virgin Mary looks as if a big pancake's fallen on her head?'

It was coming up to Christmas when the bad news came through from Dr Prosser. Regrettably, funding had not been approved for a further year's work. There had been changes 'at the top' and the whole project had been put 'on hold'.

When Robbie found out, he had to sit down; he felt as if someone had spiked his coffee with something fast-acting and maybe fatal. McNair, embarrassed, shrugged his shoulders as if to say it was just one of those things, but Robbie had come to love St Hilda's. He didn't care what denomination it was, didn't even care if he or anyone else ever attended it. He just felt he owed something to St Hilda's as a building.

On the last day of the contract, McNair and Robbie cleared out the last of their equipment, packed up the last of their tools. The church would be locked up until next year, waiting for another half a million. In the meantime, they could only pray it was weatherproof and vandal-resistant. McNair left, and Catriona arrived an hour later. Dolefully she and her man wandered around the premises one last time. Robbie tossed a protective sheet over the Virgin Mary's still veil-less head. Shrouded entirely, she looked like a Halloween ghost.

To finish with, Robbie went upstairs and locked the doors to the balconies. When he returned to escort Catriona out, he was annoyed to find that the sheet he'd thrown over the statue seemed to have half fallen off. He stopped, had a good look and gasped in shock. The sheet had in fact been elaborately rearranged with deft folds and tucks, and now framed the Virgin's face in an elegant drape: a veil worthy of Michelangelo.

'Did *you* do this?' Robbie demanded of Catriona.

She looked up at him in disbelief, then covered her mouth with her hands and suppressed a little splutter of laughter. Robbie, calling upon his highly developed skills of estimation, confirmed she couldn't be taller than four foot eleven. The Virgin's head was almost seven feet off the ground.

'You've got a lot to learn about women,' Catriona smirked as she led him to the church door.

Resisting her for one last second, Robbie faced the statue squarely and pointed an authoritative finger.

'Don't move,' he spake unto her, 'until I get back.'

The Red Cement Truck

UPSTAIRS, A STRANGE man was going through her things.

She could hear the drawers of her dresser being slid open and shut, the awkward little groans of wood against wood.

'At least he didn't rape me,' she thought.

Upstairs, there was a clatter: the contents of her jewellery box. Her senses were so heightened she could distinguish the sound of her engagement ring from that of her mother's brooch, and so on.

And on and on: the clattering went on and on: he must be trying to sort through the jewellery, to find the valuable pieces. What an odd thing for him to be doing! Why not just take everything and pick through it later? She almost wanted to go up and help him, to tell him that her ex-husband had had all the jewellery valued for insurance purposes, and that the estimates were listed in a little notebook under the stationery in the dining-room cupboard. Always the rational one, she found it difficult to be tolerant of how irrational this man was being, wasting time trying to guess the relative value of rings and pendants in her bedroom when the police might come bashing at the front door any minute.

After all, there had been a gunshot.

His footsteps thudded down the carpeted stairs; she heard the rustle of his soft leather jacket as he rounded the corner on his way to the kitchen. Evidently he was thinking straighter now. Many people kept a stash of money in their kitchen, in a jar or a drawer. *She* didn't, but many people did. She could hear him beginning to look, and was surprised to be able to perceive the difference between the scrape of her stainless steel saucepan across the shelf and the smoother shove of the cast-iron one next to it, or between the tangled clatter of forks and the meshing of spoons. Was she imagining it when she felt she could even hear the infinitely muted click of his fingernails on the plastic of the cutlery tray? Surely she must be! And yet – wasn't that the sound of the serrated Swiss knife she used for onions and tomatoes, being removed from among the others? In *his* hands, that knife was a deadly weapon. Was he going to come back in here and stab her?

Unlikely. After all, he had already shot her.

He was rummaging through the spice racks now, the coffee things, packets of spaghetti. Getting irrational again. Would he be on his knees, pulling long-unused baking dishes from the shelves below the oven, when the police arrived? It was pathetic, but she couldn't help him. Her body, so overdue for a change of position, perversely refused to move. Her pelvis, knocked 90 degrees askew from her ribcage by the impact, seemed to have settled in to its new orientation. Worse, one of her eyeballs was almost, *almost* touching the fibrous tips of the carpet pile. The carpet was actually swelling up with blood, raising its pile by fractions of a millimetre.

To be honest, she didn't think she could stand the sensation of nylon fibres tickling her eyeball, and she was right. The instant it happened, she was out of there.

Naked, she padded to the door of the living room and listened through the crack. He had left the kitchen now and gone into the bathroom. Of course he wasn't looking for money in there; he was using the toilet. She could smell the sudden stench of his anxious diarrhoea, and understood, with a sort of poignant fascination, that he hadn't meant to kill her.

The queer thing was, she felt more alive now than she'd ever felt before: even the stink in her nostrils seemed to be vibrating hundreds of tiny cilia on its way up through an intricate maze of sinuses. Experimentally, she pinched her nostrils shut with her fingers: the pressure of flesh against flesh, the awareness of untrimmed nail and porous skin, was startlingly immediate. Next, she reached out to the door handle, but before she could grasp it, the door swung open, as if blown by a draught. At the same time, just outside the house, the sound of a large vehicle pulling up at the kerb made her wonder if police or ambulance had finally arrived. If so, who would they take away?

The curtains of the living room, which had preserved the privacy, the *intimacy*, of her encounter with the man now suffering upstairs, rolled aside at a gesture of her hands, flooding her living room with light. It was eleven o'clock in the morning, and the world out there was brilliant with sunshine after a rainy start earlier on. The vehicle which had parked in front of her house, little more than arm's length from her window, was a cement truck so massive that only a section of it could be viewed, as if it were an absurdly enlarged detail from a painting, or a huge close-up filling a cinema screen. The enormous metal barrel was painted deep red, textured by corrosion, aged and weirdly organic. It revolved slowly, glistening with raindrops.

It was easily the most beautiful thing she had ever seen.

Next, a workman in red overalls stepped between the truck and the window, his back to her, almost brushing against the window-pane. With a ballet dancer's grace he slow-motioned his arms in arcs through the air, to guide the great red cement truck through her narrow street, on its way to somewhere else. She was alarmed, for the first time since hearing the gun go off. He must not walk away, this red-cement-truck man, without seeing her! Urgently she knocked at the window, or thought she did – at any rate, there was a sound of knocking on the glass, causing the workman to turn around. He squinted into her living room, staring straight through her nakedness at vacant furniture, looking down through her legs in case an animal might be trying to get his attention. He saw nothing. Her dead body was out of sight, below window level; her living one was invisible to him. Turning again, he continued his balletic motions, ambling sideways as the truck rolled on past, its barrel slowly twirling. Wherever its secret load of cement was going to be poured out, it wasn't here.

Achingly, unbearably lonely all of a sudden, she turned to her old self and considered being dead. But slipping back into that body was such a distasteful challenge: it would be like trying to put on a dress that was ill-fitting, torn, soaking wet and slimy. She put a finger in, nevertheless, wondering if she could cope with the cold.

A key screwed in a lock: it was *him*, leaving. On impulse she ran through the house, silent as a torch beam, and joined him at the back door.

He seemed to have changed since she'd seen him last, through other eyes. The hulking psycho who had fired a bullet into her unexpected presence as if by instinct, had shrunk to a round-shouldered fumbler with a lost expression, like a visitor left responsible for a crying baby with a dirty nappy. The gun which had seemed such a natural part of him as he pulled its trigger was in his jacket pocket now, a misshapen lump clacking against her jewellery – Christ! hadn't he even brought a *bag*? And she could smell, too, that he hadn't flushed the toilet – Who *was* this man, to have killed her like this? How had he won the right to be the last man to touch her?

His clumsiness in solving the idiosyncrasy of the back-door lock was excruciating; she could sense he would love to batter it open but was afraid of failure or alerting the neighbours, or both. Instead he fumbled on, twisting the key, now gently, now roughly, grunting with frustration.

Again on impulse, she ran over to him and laid her hand over his, slipping her fingers through his, feeling for the key. He shuddered convulsively and the door sprang open.

'Yes, yes,' she whispered in his ear. 'You bastard.'

He heard nothing, and yet he turned, his anxious bewildered face inches away from hers, scrutinising the unfamiliar furniture.

'Go on, go on,' she urged him. 'Get out.'

As if pulling himself together by a strenuous effort of will, he turned away from her and stepped out into the back yard, moving so fast that she had to run to catch up. Once again the supernatural keenness of her senses startled her: walking close behind him, she could hear not only his nervous breathing and the rustle of his clothing, but his heartbeat – distinctly in his chest, faintly in his temples. She could smell the rain-soaked grass under his shoes as he trampled it close to the soil; she could smell the unopened buds on the bushes, the scattered dandelions, the ivy on the back gate, the traces of detergent in her T-shirts and underwear fluttering on the washing line.

The thought that she would never wear those clothes again, that they would hang there until someone got permission to put them into a labelled plastic bag, made her want to weep. She glanced, one last time as she followed him, at the knickers with the faded strawberry pattern, washed so many times, yet still perfect for her, snug, warm, forgiving of the weight she was at . . . the weight she no longer had.

She could tell from the way her killer was dressed and from the appearance of the sky that it was chilly in the world today, but she felt nothing, not even the breeze that was fluttering her clothing on the washing line. She *smelled* the breeze, but didn't feel it. Under her naked feet, as she followed her killer through the gate into the back lane, the grit and cobblestones and shards of broken glass felt no different from the carpet in her house. She wept then, for the irrelevance of clothes.

He had a small blue van waiting in the lane; he opened the door on the driver's side and she got in immediately, sliding across to the passenger seat. She thought he would get in next to her, but he opened the hatch at the back instead, and retraced his steps to her house. Thank God for that! She hoped he would return with something valuable, to take away the sting of being killed for a pocketful of rings and brooches which the pawnshop might reject.

In the meantime, she examined the interior of the van to get to know her man a little better, and discovered to her bemused distaste that he was the sort who played scuffed and faded cassettes with titles like *Heavy Metal Gold* and *1993: The Big Ones*. But one thing was interesting: even with the van wide open, draughty with fresh air and uncollected garbage, she could easily detect the subtler odours of a woman's facial cleanser, toner, deodorant, blood. Not the blood of death, either, but the blood of routine fertility.

That was good, good, good: it suited her that he had a wife.

He returned, a minute later, with her television, then went back for her cassette player and her juice extractor. Evidently, that was as much as his nerves were up to. Slamming the van's hatch shut, he swung himself into the driver's seat with an anxious grunt and set the engine revving.

By the time they were lying in bed together late that night, she had learned a lot about him, including his name. She was whispering it now, over and over, into his ear, and every repetition added another furrow on his sweating forehead and deepened the crease between his brows. She could see in the dark, which was something his wife couldn't do, of course. But then his wife didn't need to see him, knowing him so well, knowing him so much better than anyone.

'You've been with another woman,' his wife said, dangerously sleepless next to him in the bed. She had her back to him, her cool hard shoulderblades only a few inches from his corpse-like, clammy body. Inside those few inches between them, *she* lay, fitting easily, yet exerting pressure.

'What are you talking about?' he coughed.

'I can smell it on you,' came the reply.

'You're off your head,' he retorted. An invisible hand stroked his prick, teasing the blood into it.

'I told you before,' stated his wife frigidly. 'One more time and it's the end.'

'I haven't done nothing,' he pleaded angrily. In his ear, a woman seemed to be whispering his name, urging him to let go and let it happen. In an agony of undischarged guilt and fear and desire, he reached out for his wife.

'Take your filthy hands off me,' his wife hissed. 'Save it for *her*.'

And in between them, as his vital fluid pumped out silently into nowhere, *she* curled up in the impossible space and went to sleep.

Somewhere Warm and Comfortable

SCOTT HAD TO stand on tiptoe to reach the magazines at the top of the rack; he was a late developer, at least as far as height went. A moment before he made his move, he checked that the newsagent lady was still bending down below the counter, searching for a customer's order: by the time she surfaced, Scott had fingertipped a magazine into free-fall, caught it, folded it in half, and shoved it down the front of his trousers. The glossy paper slid easily between the cotton of his underpants and the denim of his jeans; it was cold against his thighs. He wondered which one he'd got: it was either *Busty Babes* or *Men Only*: on tiptoe he hadn't been able to look and grab at the same time. But he knew it was *one* of them, by the space that was left up there.

It wasn't the first time he'd shoplifted, but it was the first time he'd shoplifted something other than Mars bars and football cards. This was a different league: these things were expensive. Funnily enough, he did actually have the money to pay for the magazine he was stealing, because his sister always gave him £2 out of the movie money to keep quiet about the fact that she hadn't taken him to the movies at all. She would go off with her boyfriend to his house, and Scott would hang around the shops until late afternoon, when Christine met up with him again behind the cinema and took him home. Christine had been going to her boy-friend's house every week for months now, so Scott had a bit of money saved up which he fantasised about spending on Lego. He couldn't, of course: Christine's boyfriend was a secret from Mum, so the money they saved on movies, swim-ming and the zoo was a secret too. He had no choice but to spend it on ice creams, Mars bars, sherbet – well, no, he didn't buy that anymore. That was for kids.

He wished he could simply have bought the sex magazine, because that would have proved he looked eighteen, whereas he knew he looked about eleven, a couple of years younger than he really was. Everyone treated him as if he was still in primary school, as if they could keep him sweet with a ticket to *The Flintstones*. He resented his sister for having become a sexual being so effortlessly: it was so easy for girls – sex just fell into their lap, didn't it? *She* didn't have to steal magazines of naked girls, that's for sure: she could be a naked girl herself, just by taking her clothes off. *And* she could have sex, which was more than he'd probably ever do, what with his big stick-out ears and puny body.

'*There* you are!'

He froze, rigid with panic, but it wasn't the newsagent lady collaring him, it was Christine.

'What are *you* doing here?' he said, his voice husky with nerves (or was it breaking at last?).

'Come outside,' she hissed at him, not angrily, but with urgency.

He obeyed, the magazine's hard spine and sharp feathery pages chafing his thighs as he walked. There was a public toilet behind the library with a big green door that shut with a latch. Whatever Christine wanted, she had better not delay him getting there.

'You've got to come with me,' she said.

'Come with you? What for?' He couldn't imagine being allowed into the house where the sex was had. Maybe she'd ask him to sit quietly in another room. No way!

'I thought I could go through it alone,' she said. 'But I'm scared.' Scott noticed suddenly that she was pale and had bags under her eyes.

He fell into step beside her; they were walking in the opposite direction from where her boyfriend lived. The magazine inside his trousers was starting to warm up and the way it pressed against the bulb-like genitals in his tight Thunderbirds briefs felt very good. He hoped the girls in the magazine wouldn't have anything obscuring the view between their legs, the way the naked girls in the *Sunday Sport* always did.

He looked up at his sister again as they walked, and this time he noticed that she didn't have as much make-up on as usual and that she wasn't wearing one of her 'cleavage' tops but a loose white jumper.

'Where are we going?'

'We're there.'

They had arrived at an ugly single-storey house with a large car-park and a plaque on the door. Inside, there was a sort of a waiting room and a sort of a secretary who told Christine to take a seat. There was no one else waiting.

'What are we doing here?' whispered Scott to his sister, who had gone the same colour as the telephones.

'I'm going to have an operation,' she told him. 'Just a little one.'

'An operation?' Scott leaned forward in disbelief, the magazine digging into his flesh. 'Why isn't Mum here?'

'Mum mustn't know about this. She'd worry herself to death. *You* know – because of Aunt Marian and Aunt Annie and Uncle Frank and Grandma and Grandpa.'

Scott swallowed hard. These were all people who had died

of cancer, some of them at a young age. Mum was always anxious about her own health, countering Christine's pleas for greater freedom with her own plea that she needed a bit of looking after, that she might have a time bomb inside of her, waiting to go off.

'Is it cancer?' whispered Scott.

'Not exactly,' said Christine, looking down at the hands clasped in her lap. 'It's a kind of . . . growth. The doctor says he can take it out and it'll never come back. But you know Mum would never believe that.'

They both sat back, a skin of anxiety forming over their conversation, holding the words under. The waiting room wasn't like any doctor's waiting room Scott had ever been in before; it had a patterned carpet and the receptionist had dark-red nails. She made a telephone call to someone who seemed to be a friend of hers; she talked in a sort of code and said 'Jesus' and worse things, albeit under her breath. Christine kept looking at him strangely, as if she wanted him to do something, but then every few seconds she would hug herself and sniff the way she always did when she was irritated by him. Scott picked up one of the magazines lying on an empty seat. It was one of those women's magazines about face lotions and lipsticks and bonking. He flipped through it, looking for pubic hair, but it was all hidden behind beach towels and bath sponges and big fancy lettering. There were some nipples, even a couple that were sticking out like crazy, but he couldn't get too excited about them. He was too old for that maybe: he was ready now for what he had inside his trousers. Besides, if the receptionist caught him trying to tear a page out of one of her magazines he would die of embarrassment.

After a few more minutes, Christine was called by a deep male voice behind a door. The look on her face as she was standing up to go was just horrible, like in horror movies when people smile and say they're fine but really they've got an alien creature hiding inside of them.

'You'll wait for me, won't you,' she said.

Of course he waited.

She was gone for about half an hour. The waiting room was deathly still, the receptionist having run out of friends to call. Scott read all the women's magazines; well, bits. Kim Basinger, no bimbo anymore, faces her thirties with newfound maturity and still turns heads. Aramis ignites the flame of passion. Rod Stewart says he has dipped his banana in the fruit bowl for the last time. Camille Paglia scoffs that most men don't even know what the word 'cunnilingus' means. Scott made a mental note: he would have to look that one up when he got home.

Finally Christine came out of the doctor's room. She looked the same as before, fully dressed, no white surgical gown or anything, no bandages that Scott could see. The only thing was, she was taking very careful little steps, as if walking on eggs.

'Let's go,' she said hoarsely.

Out on the street, she walked beside him for a few minutes and then had to stop and lean against a brick wall.

'I can't go home yet,' she gasped. 'We have to go somewhere else first. Somewhere I can lie down.'

'Why don't you go to your boyfriend's place?' suggested Scott.

'We can't go there.'

'Why not?'

'We just can't, that's all.' And she started to cry.

Scott was moved and frightened by his sister's distress, which was different from the tantrums he was used to at home when Mum and Christine fought about what she was and wasn't allowed to do. He was struck, too, by the way she kept saying 'we' – she *never* said that to him usually. He was always the accessory, the excuse, the tool with which she could propel herself far away, into someone else's company. He hadn't submitted without a fight; he had refused to get dumped at the zoo or a movie theatre, he'd refused to tell her which shops he'd be in while she was off doing 'whatever you do'; he'd demanded two pounds instead of one. But she looked fragile and small now, lost in her big white jumper as she slumped against the wall. He cleared his throat, trying to meet her half-way with the suggestion:

'How about we go to the movies?'

She laughed and a spray of clear, innocent snot came out of her pale nose. She wiped it on her sleeve and shook her head.

'I can't sit down on a hard seat,' she said wearily. 'I need to lie down.'

'How about the picnic area in the zoo?'

'Somewhere warm and comfortable, you idiot.'

She took him to the Art Gallery, where neither of them had ever been before. Richie Fuller's mum worked there as a cloakroom attendant.

'Put your parka in the cloakroom,' Christine instructed him, but he refused. The magazine in his trousers was rather bent by now, suppled up by the warmth and movement, and he was afraid that if he took his parka off people would see it poking through his football shirt. Christine looked at him imploringly, but he couldn't help her on this one, and she could see it in his face. Instead, she went up to Mrs Fuller and said hello to her, making forty-five seconds of cheery conversation. But when Christine rejoined Scott, she was as white as the marble statues guarding the entrance to The Nineteenth Century.

'Take me by the hand,' she whispered anxiously. 'Everything's going black . . .'

Scott hesitated, terrified. He wasn't big or strong enough

to catch his sister if she fell, didn't want to have an unconscious girl sprawled at his feet with people swarming around asking questions.

'*Take* me somewhere, Scott, for fuck's sake!'

He grabbed her hand, which was cool and damp, and led her into The Nineteenth Century, where there was an upholstered bench in the middle of the room. He sat down on one edge, guiding Christine as she collapsed onto the rest of it; she grabbed him round the waist with a groan. Once horizontal she immediately seemed to relax, adjusting her position with infantile abandon, treating his thighs as a pillow. Within moments she was asleep.

Scott sat as still as he could, so as not to disturb her. Her head in his lap felt strange: he couldn't see her face, though he felt her damp breath permeating his jeans through to his thighs, couldn't feel her head except as an indistinct pressure on the magazine, whose buckled spine and sweaty pages were cutting into his groin. He wondered if Christine was in a coma, or if she would vomit, like Auntie Marian always used to after an operation, except into his lap.

'Chris?' he ventured, shaking her gently.

'Leave me alone,' she slurred. 'Stay with me.'

For almost three hours Scott sat there, trying to shift his weight subtly from one buttock to the other so that only half of his bum went to sleep at a time. At one point, even his genitals went to sleep, torturing him when the feeling came back. Christine slept through his muffled complaints and his changes of position, but when he tried to lift her off him altogether, she whimpered and clutched. And so, he stayed. Impossibly bored at first, he soon passed into a state beyond boredom, in which he stared in a meditative trance at the four paintings he could see from his seat.

The one straight in front of him was of a naked woman

combing her hair at the side of a pool, with three old men peeking at her over the top of some shrubs. They had long beards and robes, and their faces looked as if they'd just seen a laser bomb go off nearby. The woman had a ghost-like, silvery veil between her legs, and glistening hair obscuring one breast. She was beautiful. Her eyes were as green and luminous as *Ghostbusters* ectoplasm. Her one naked breast was as real as his own desire. He would remember this picture until he died.

Closing time came, and a gallery guide asked Scott and Christine to leave. Fortunately, Christine woke up at the sound of the stranger's voice, seemingly in better shape after her rest, and together they left the building, Scott limping more than his sister by this time. It was six o'clock, already two hours later than Mum expected them home, and they still had to get there, of course.

'Are you all right?' asked Scott as they stood at the bus stop.

'I'll survive,' said his sister. The sun was setting and the wind turning chilly. She hugged herself, rubbed her palms against the white fluff of her jumper. Scott simply zipped up his parka. Lower down, the cold breeze was heavenly against his chafed and overheated groin. He longed to go home and get undressed, into pyjamas, into bed. Unknown to him, so did his sister.

'Hey, Scott?' She was crying again, reaching for his hand again. 'Thanks, kid.'

'No problem . . . old woman,' he retorted, stung and senti-mental.

Night fell and, running much behind or much ahead of schedule, a bus came to take them home. Even from far down the street they could see that all the lights in the house were on, as if to make up for the people who weren't in it.

Minutes later, across the threshold, Mum was beside

herself with rage; the house ricocheted with female shrieks as Scott stood listening half-way up the stairs.

Don't hit her, he kept thinking. *She's got the family curse – the same thing you're so scared* you'll *get.*

In the end, the daughter's voice began to prevail over the mother's.

'*Ring* her!' Christine shouted over and over. 'Why don't you just *ring* her?'

Eventually Mum calmed down enough to telephone Mrs Fuller, the dialled numbers beeping softly upstairs in Christine's empty room, too, on the endlessly quarrel-provoking extension. Scott tiptoed up to it, lifted the handset, listened to one mother reassuring another that Christine and her brother had indeed visited the Art Gallery. For how long? Oh, for hours. Wonderful to see in such young people. So nice to know that not all of them are hanging around the streets, going to crass American movies and getting into trouble with the Wrong Sort.

Scott heard Christine's receiver click off as their mother hung up downstairs. The house remained silent. Everything would be all right now. Scott walked across to his own room and there, at last, behind his own closed door, he extracted the crumpled, damp and torn magazine from his trousers. It was *Busty Babes*. He opened it, flicked through. It was full of pubic hair, pale-orange vaginas, women holding their breasts in their hands: everything he had always wanted. But he was so tired tonight, so full of emotions he couldn't digest, and not all of them his. Tomorrow; tomorrow he would examine these women properly; he would choose which of their bodies was for him, and he would show them what he was made of. Tonight, he just wasn't ready.

He ran a bath and washed himself with loving care, playing submarines time after time so that the thick, creamy lather sealed up the surface above his body. Afterwards he dried his tender, wrinkled flesh with the softest towel he could find, and dusted himself with talcum powder. Then he got into bed and watched Thunderbirds 1 and 3 circling his lampshade in the moonlight. The magazine was hidden under his bed: a little bomb waiting to go off.

'Goodnight, Scotty,' whispered Christine in his doorway a few minutes later, but he had already left her, gone to the land of wet dreams.

Nina's Hand

THE LAST NIGHT they slept together, Nina's right hand nestled under her pillow, as if seeking to stroke her face. A heavy sleeper nowadays, Nina barely moved from lights-off to alarm, and her hand had learned to live with this, smothered under a claustrophobic wad of warm polyester. In the morning, Nina lifted her head from the pillow and her hand slid into the light, a small, perfect clutch of pale roseate fingers.

Nina's hand was put to work immediately, gliding through the air like a trained bird, switching off the bedside alarm clock, rubbing the sleep out of Nina's eyes. Every morning these same first impressions: the minutely corrugated plastic of the alarm clock's button, the damp acquiescence of Nina's closed eyes and the textured thrill of sleep crystals skidding along the forefinger. Nina's hand was glad to be used, to answer the call. A long, idle night had been meekly endured: active subservience now was a leap into freedom.

Sometimes the nights were just *too* long, and Nina's hand would slip out from under the pillow while Nina slept, and wander around inside the bedclothes. There was the pleasure of settling on a part of the bedsheet which was cool and distant, the intrigue of finding vagrant breadcrumbs, the frisson of tasting the dark empty air outside the covers. Once in a while Nina's hand would visit other parts of Nina's sleeping body, parts that seemed, in one way or another, neglected during the daytime, and Nina's hand would ask them, with a hesitant touch of fingers, if there was anything it could do.

Nina's hand didn't wander so much lately, not since Nina had been working at the factory and sleeping more heavily than usual. The tedium of eight hours under the pillow was preferable to a repeat of what had happened recently when, loitering below the waist, Nina's hand had been squashed without warning beneath a collapse of thigh. The slow extinguishing of sensation that followed – an ambiguous hint to begin with, a terrifying fact by morning – must be what death was like.

The rewards for lying motionless all night were not glamorous, but they were plentiful. Routine challenges, to be sure: the throwing aside of the bedclothes, the grasping of the water glass, conveying it through space at a gently increasing tilt towards Nina's lips, a minor miracle of articulation beyond the scope of Nina's poor arithmetic to express. Then there was the launch from the bed, when a deceptively gentle flex of Nina's hand on the edge of the mattress tossed her entire body forward to land, erect and swaying like a lifebuoy, on the bedroom surface.

Nina spoke, or made some sort of sulky murmur of complaint, not directed at her hand, or at any other living thing, for she lived alone now. The protest used the language of sexual activity, but had nothing to do with all that, really. It had something to do with Nina's feelings about going to the factory.

Nina's hand led Nina into the bathroom, guided her on to the toilet, wiped her afterwards. Once upon a time a bath would have been run, and Nina's hand would have performed elaborate tricks with taps, shampoo bottles and soap. Slick with white lather, Nina's hand would slide and slalom at great speed over the entire surface of Nina's body. But since Nina had been working at the factory, there was no time for baths anymore.

Nina's feelings were often a mystery to her hand. The hand meant well, but got stuck on questions like why tears could be wiped anywhere, but urine only in a tiny mirrored room. Moreover, the causes of Nina's emotions often had no tangible connection with anything her hand had grasped; there was a world of things beyond the physical which seemed able to enter Nina freely, before her hand could throw itself up to greet or repel them.

Confronted by these supernatural enigmas, the hand's function was clear: maintain Nina's hold on the real world.

The act of dressing Nina was the first time each morning when Nina's hand was reminded that there was, in fact, another hand. Nina called it her left hand, and it lived on the dark side of her body: an identical twin of the right one, except for its eerie reversal of fingers. Nina's hand had a policy of working efficiently and cheerfully with this other hand whenever the task demanded it, and indeed some of their collaborations had the precision and panache of chor-eography, but in truth their mutual resemblance was an unsettling rather than a reassuring thing, as if each was flexing itself to supplant the other. Yet Nina's right hand sensed it had the edge on its sinister offsider, and whenever possible it performed tasks alone. In short, there was no love lost between them, and on the rare occasions when one hand was told to clasp the other without a practical reason, they sat limp and awkward in Nina's lap.

When there was something that needed doing, however, they could toil in perfect complement, like estranged twin sisters reunited in the workplace, who never spoke but remembered the intimacy of the womb. Just now, the two hands were pulling on Nina's clothing together, diving down and hauling up like simultaneously launched acrobats. Nina was not difficult to dress; she was thin, she lacked curves, and she always chose the simplest attire. Clasping Nina's bra, the hands' fingers touched, an awkward clash of blunted nails, but a few moments later their collaboration was over and they were independent again, the right hand reverting to a peripheral awareness of its sibling's existence.

The hand's affinity with Nina herself was more complex still. There was no simple answer to crude questions like Who made the decisions? Who gave the orders, and who followed? The relationship between Nina and her hand was like the fur on a cat's back: prickly and undignified when disturbed, but smoothing instantly and automatically, because it was genetically programmed to be unruffled. There were times when Nina commanded her hand to lift the lid of a scalding pot or grasp a rose by its thorny stem, and the hand's protests flailed unheard in the vacuum between thought and action. However, there were other times when Nina would stumble in a lurching bus and find that her hand had already clasped a metal stanchion, or when Nina would become aware of an itch and find her hand already on the spot, digging for it. They had an understanding too nearly infallible to be undermined by the odd cut or scalded finger; they were, in fact, almost a single, indivisible organism.

Taking charge now, Nina's hand led Nina to a mirror, combed her hair there, drew black lines around the edges of Nina's eyes. There were vague dark rings under Nina's eyes already, but these were evidently not decisive enough, and the extra ones Nina's hand drew were precise. Once upon a time, there had been a great many more cosmetic rituals than this to perform in front of the mirror, involving cotton buds, pigmy pots, wee phalluses of crimson wax, and minuscule brushes. Now, however, it was the black lines only. And why not? Nina's dwindling concern about her appearance made sense to the hand, which considered its own outward form almost never.

Nina's hand had started life as a tiny, pudgy thing, helpless as a beached starfish.

In time, it had grown into an impetuous little paw which smeared chocolate over Nina's cheeks, stacked coloured blocks, lifted floes of soapsuds from the bathwater it was swimming in, and, on the occasion of Nina's first visit to the seaside, even got to hold a real beached starfish between sandy fingers.

Adolescence had brought self-consciousness and sexual experiment: the squeamish thrill, for example, of having one's fingernails lovingly painted by the sinister sister hand, knowing that one must do exactly the same in return once the cold, translucent liquid had ceased to be wet.

Adolescence outgrown, Nina's hand had evolved into an unpretentious creature, smooth and slender still, but toughened by thirty-six years of use, unobtrusively callused, delicately wrinkled. In rare moments when Nina's hand made contact with a hand of a young person (Nina had no children and, now that her husband was gone, no prospect of having any) Nina's hand was shocked to find itself gross and hard by comparison. Alone against Nina's cheek or under her pillow, however, its faith in its own compactness was restored.

There were many things that Nina's hand had disliked intensely when younger: particular tasks, temperatures, textures. Nowadays, it could handle them all. In the preparation of breakfast, for example, Nina's hand was required to touch raw beef and other clammy meats, and to hover in a miasma of frying oil as these squalid substances cooked. Nina's natural appetite was slow to rouse in the mornings and she had always inclined towards a vegetarian diet, but these leanings were not accommodated by her new job, which demanded she be fully fuelled for action from the moment of arriving and not weaken or hunger for at least three hours. The impossibility of achieving this feat of endurance on a cup of tea and a few spoonfuls of avocado had revolutionised Nina's breakfast regime: instead of the gentle spreading of cottage cheese over fragile crackers, the deft excision of grapefruit segments, Nina's hand must hold a grease-spattered eggslice and turn some sizzling slab of protein over and over – a beefburger, perhaps, or sausages, or a ham omelette. Egg by itself had proved unequal to the challenge: only meat lasted the distance, as if the factory refused to be fobbed off with a mere ovum when it could demand flesh.

Feeding Nina was a little like factory work in itself, a repetitive conveyance of food to the mouth until time ran out, with just this one reward at the end: the wiping of Nina's lips, a complex motion for the hand to perform, a graceful corkscrewing-while-sliding manoeuvre which might have to be repeated in reverse, like a seal writhing contentedly on a lubricated shore.

Nina's hand thrived on little opportunities like this, which, admittedly, were growing fewer the longer Nina worked at the factory. There was no toothbrush to be deployed lately, no floss to fiddle with; when the eating was finished with, Nina would immediately leave for work.

Though taken outside each day in all weathers, Nina's hand understood little of the wider world beyond Nina's body. Confronted with the universe, it preferred to nuzzle into Nina's pocket or wrap itself around her throat protectively. It half knew that the street along which Nina hurried now was connected to other streets, a whole grid of streets which added up to something vast called a city. The bus which Nina ran to catch was similarly somehow a part of the other vehicles, collectively a body called traffic. The buildings flashing by, if one drove past them long enough, were supposed to coalesce into so-called suburbs, each with its own name and character. But awareness of such things was almost impossible for Nina's hand to hold on to for very long; the world naturally receded and was far away, a visual hum of scenery. Was it shameful to take more interest in the studded ceiling of the bus than in the sky above? More shameful still to lose interest in the ceiling when there was the more immediate thrill of coins nestling restlessly in one's palm? The feel of these cool, silvery slices of metal, exciting a prickle of sweat from the skin as they turned their faces over in preparation for being accepted as offerings, was far more compelling than any expanse of untouchable vacuity. Perhaps that's what Nina meant when she said (to worried friends suggesting she give up her job) that everything comes down to money.

It was money that Nina went to the factory to get, though there was never any money to be seen there, only gherkins and occasionally sauerkraut. Still Nina returned daily, and here she was again, laying her hand on the cast-iron gate, pushing it open with a groan of effort and begrudging.

Narrowly inside the long, squat building's entrance stood a machine whose knack was to bite numbers into big cardboard tickets. The first task of Nina's hand, upon entering, was to fetch Nina's ticket out of a slit, insert it into a slot, and wait for the sensation of the machine's bite to buzz the fingers. The potential for playfulness was there, but not the permission: insertion must be once only, and quick. Then there was an apron to be put on over Nina's clothes, a green rectangle of damp cloth with Nina's name written on it by some other hand.

The factory's insides were harshly lit and humid, like a giant concrete fishtank newly emptied of water, still wet, heated by a monstrous thermostat. The air had given up much of its oxygen to make room for steam and vinegar vapour. The work began without prelude or preparation: Nina took her place among a line of other bodies at a waist-high trough, inside which a flat rubbery spine moved empty glass jars vibrating along its surface. Behind and above the trough were wooden crates of gherkins, fixed at an angle so that the glistening green cargo was constantly spilling forwards. From these crates, Nina's hand and the hands of the other women must select appropriately sized gherkins to fill the jars: a snug fit only was allowed. A few big fat ones were best to begin with, tossed into the jars almost carelessly, some smaller thin ones to wedge in the spaces, then a couple of stubby or runty ones to finish. The left hand might do some of the selecting, make some of the clumsier insertions, but the right hand must do the real filling; this was precision work.

The speed at which the belt moved, however, was such that no single hand, nor even single pair of hands, could fill all the jars, nor even all of any one of the jars: that was why there were dozens of pairs of hands lined up against the trough. Nina's hand would engage with whatever jar was going past at any given moment, and add what appeared to be needed. Depending on Nina's shifting position in the line, sometimes the jar was almost full and her hand would top it up, sometimes half full and Nina's hand would find the correct cucumbers for the puzzle and squeak them into place, sometimes empty, ready for the fat ones.

When the jars were all full, borne along beyond the reach of the women, a different clutch of hands, male hands, ushered the jars into a steam-hazed machine from which they eventually emerged with lids clamped on, cooked in a fluid of dill, vinegar and water. The factory's layout was in fact a kind of pinched loop, like an electric element or an intra-uterine coil, with the jars describing a slow arc from the start of the conveyor belt, past the women, turning quite sharply into the main processor, and emerging to trundle along another slowly arcing trough, complementary to the first in the opposite direction, towards the exit. If the female hands filling the jars should overreach the crates, they would come into view of a whole line of other female hands, like mirror images, fetching the hot jars off the trough, checking them for peculiarities, stacking them in cardboard boxes. In the loop's centre, between the two arcs of conveyor, was nothing; nothing but three pylons holding the factory up.

The noise was louder than ignorable, legally below deafening, its clanks and thuds and hisses disguised by an aural fog of synthetic music from an industrial-strength radio. Occasionally a woman sang along to one of the tunes if it struck her as sufficiently symbolic of some event in her life. Nina never sang. Singing, fortunately, was not compulsory. Nor was speaking, and Nina never spoke, except when spoken to. Alone in the toilet, she sometimes wept, beating her fists against her bared knees. The weeping seldom lasted very long, and each time the same farcical thing happened with Nina's hand: it would be rashly sent up to wipe Nina's eyes, then hastily rinsed under the icy water of the toilet sink to wash off the vinegar; then Nina's hand, heavy with pity and condescension, would wipe Nina's eyes again.

Nina's hand didn't hate the factory the way Nina did, though it would have probably preferred to be employed almost anywhere else. The work was wearying – and yet it had, over time, made Nina's hand stronger, and strength was an attribute Nina's hand was secretly pleased to have. Brawny male hands had always seemed awesome in comparison to itself, but until recently it had assumed that the power to wrench wheels off cars or lift a woman off the floor must issue from that intriguingly ugly, arborous musculature. Now, however, Nina's hand possessed something of that strength itself, with no significant change to its trim appearance.

Crushing empty food tins or punching a dent in the kitchen wall gave it the satisfaction of an interior potential greater than the exterior might suggest.

Most of this extra strength was not, in fact, caused by the routine selecting and pushing into jars of the gherkins, though this was the least unpleasant work. The task that had really made the difference was one that each of the women was given in turn, for limited periods only, because of its brutal physical demand. This task had the technical appellation 'banging the jar'. About three-quarters of the way to the end of the line, the monotony of female bodies was broken by a different fixture: a squat wooden post, its top coated in thick grey rubber as if it had been dipped in a vat of the stuff. This post, with its shock-absorbing tip, was where each jar must be slammed down hard to ensure maximum settling of contents before the final few gherkins were added. Failure to do this resulted in underweight jars, which resulted in angry lectures from the factory foreman, which resulted in Nina ramming her right hand into her sodden apron pocket and ordering it to clench until the fingernails broke the skin of the palm. It was therefore very important to bang the jars hard enough.

Today, when Nina's turn to bang the jar came, she nodded agreement but excused herself for just a minute and walked off. It was only in the toilet that Nina's hand became aware Nina was feeling ill, as she knelt on the floor in front of the vinegar-dewy bowl and retched. The fluctuations of digestion were a foreign country to Nina's hand, but it understood that there were times when food, however solid and distinctively textured it might have been when going into the body, was changed somehow into a vile glutinous soup potent enough to halt all activity until it was ejected. Nina's hand, fastidious when indulged but stoical in a crisis, rose to the deed Nina herself was hesitating to command: it entered the retching O of her mouth and slid two fingers into her dilated gullet. When the vomiting was finished, Nina washed her hand and face and went out to bang the jar.

For a while, the work was much as Nina's hand had experienced it before. It grasped the jar, bashed its base on the rubber-tipped post, replaced it on the belt, and so on and on. Within minutes, though, an unfamiliar feeling began to make its way down to the hand, indicating that all was not as normal in Nina's body. Microscopic insects seemed to be buzzing in the nerves, alarming at first, ultimately soothing, like a self-generated massage. The hand felt itself swelling, increasing in mass, the way it had felt when first released from under the crush of Nina's thigh, but paradoxically it felt lighter too, as if the atmosphere of the factory had changed the laws of gravity and was inviting all things of great density to float up into the air. All the while, the banging of the jars went on, regular as a pulsebeat, forceful as falling cars in a wrecking yard. If anything, the rhythm was more powerful than before, settling into the groove of automatic command. Nina had become a machine whose actions her hand could no longer influence, but whose efficiency it need no longer oversee. Soon a state of strange equilibrium was reached, with Nina's massive and languorous hand riding on the impact of the banging, accompanying the jars on and off the belt as they leapt up and down, rather than having to seize them. Eventually, the activity became a moving fixture, like the sea, and above it hovered the soul of the hand, watching.

Of course there were seconds going by, bright flashes of time, winking in rhythm with eternity, but they never amounted to minutes. Each was joined to the last and the next, or disappeared suddenly, according to its wish. Within these seconds, folded inside them like hors d'oeuvres, were sensations: the sensation of bouncing up and down through the balmy, vinegary air, the sensation of banging the jar, the sensation of losing hold of the reason for banging the jar, the sensation of losing hold of the jar itself, the sensation of the jar shattering, of the sharp glass intruding into the space that Nina's hand had always shared with Nina alone.

Nina's hand levitated into space, a leap subdivided radially over time, so that it had seemingly endless leisure to consider its position. It perceived that it was far from Nina's centre of gravity, farther than it had ever been. Still languorous, it indulged a barely registered spasm of curiosity and opened itself to Nina's wishes and commands, but found itself disconnected from them utterly.

In the vast frictionless sky of moments that Nina's hand was suspended in, all the years of interdependence it had lived through with Nina glowed into perspective. The hand had never doubted it should exist only at Nina's side, but it doubted now. The hand and the woman had held each other back, undeniably. They had been, perhaps, a mismatch.

Now, no longer hidebound by Nina's fears and limitations, Nina's hand glimpsed all the million uses it could have been put to by other people, in other times and places ... Its nerves, still open to stimulus, received distant, second-hand instructions and experiences from the greater world of manipulations.

Insubstantially attached to a host of strangers' bodies, it flexed hitherto unimagined muscles in exquisite ways, adding tiny diamonds to a heart-shaped cluster of jewels, carving tiny wooden figures for souvenirs of Switzerland, assembling a compass from glittering debris laid out on a velvet cloth. By contrast, skin prickling in the dry heat of Africa, it began to pluck an exotic orange zither, gathered courage and speed, and played it until the strings shimmered with perspiration. Elsewhere, elsewhen, it restored a vandalised Pietà, fitting fragments of marble scarcely bigger than crushed eggshell back into the curve of a wrist. Next, sheathed in pellucid gloves, it reconnected severed nerves with microscopic surgical thread. Then again, it wielded a slender paintbrush whose tip was as soft as the hair at the nape of the neck, slicked to a red point as if with a droplet of blood, descending towards an almost-finished masterpiece. Tiring, perhaps, of the impossibly meticulous, it pushed a detonator that changed the world's topography in an instant, flicked a switch that restored power to a bombed Balkan village, waved a banner on a mountaintop. In the pursuit of more intimate textures, it planted a single yew tree in loamy earth, winkled a petrified sword from the bottom of a coral bay, stroked the snow-powdered mane of a husky.

These and innumerable other sensations, prowesses and dexterities passed fleetingly through the nerves of Nina's hand, but there was no end to them, and yet there was an end to the hand's capacity to receive. It had reached satiety at last, and so it abandoned, one by one, those of its vessels which were still permitting more to enter.

What it wished to experience most of all now was stillness, anaesthesia, darkness such as could be found under a pillow.

Thankfully, merely wishing for this darkness seemed to propel the hand towards it, as if volition was the means of flight in this universe of disembodied possibilities.

The air thinned, was less rich in sensation, and such sensations as passed through the hand now were soothingly familiar: the memory of breadcrumbs in the bed, the fine stubble on the jaw of a beautiful man in the morning, the brilliant floes of soapsuds in the bath, the discovery of damp viridescent moss in the world just outside the doorstep.

Finally, before Nina's hand curled up to rest, it relived just one more experience: the moment when Nina, newly sighted as a days-old baby, discovered something floating in front of her face, a rosy, quinquefoliate flower that was somehow, magically, attached to her.

The Crust of Hell

AFTER FOUR HOURS and seventeen minutes there was a raindrop, and Ivan sprang to life.

There were other raindrops, of course (though not many), but this was the only one to fall in the neatly demarcated rectangle chosen for Ivan's experiment, and he set to work with the equipment. He wanted to know exactly what happened to that raindrop after it hit the sandy soil: how long did it quiver there like a liquid pearl, how slowly did it sink in, how wide was the stain, how deep was the penetration?

With information like this, Ivan might just be the man to change the world.

The rain stopped after three minutes and fifty-two seconds, for good. Ivan did every test he could, then packed up. The temperature had dropped slightly, to 107 degrees Fahrenheit.

Back in the jeep, the guide was cleaning his teeth with that most prized of foreign tools, the *samanaf* – Swiss army knife, in other words. Out here, all familiar language was swamped by harsh incomprehension and transformed beyond recognition, just as the arable land was swamped and transformed by salt and sand. Ivan squinted at the guide and realised only now that this was a different man from the one who'd accompanied him here yesterday.

'Where's Yaphet?' he said, wondering if he'd get an answer in English.

'Yaphet go with Yaphet family, go with Yaphet house.'

So: Yaphet had folded up his hut of sticks, packed it on the back of a camel, and moved on with his wife and children. Why these people did this, pulling up what little vegetation there was in order to erect temporary dwellings, when if they only stayed put and tilled life into the soil they could have a self-regenerating homeland, was a mystery to Ivan.

'Will you be here tomorrow?'

The man shrugged, smiling broadly. His teeth were stained with lat leaf.

'Too much lat,' said Ivan, grinning in return.

The guide shrugged again, making a weary hand gesture that denoted sexual erection. He meant by this that the stimulant was the only thing that made it possible for him to work, to drive around the desert with foreigners, to fight members of other tribes, to fuck his wife – to do anything other than surrender to the heat and the aridity, curl up on the sand, lose the last of his water content and be baked, like clay.

'OK, let's go,' said Ivan.

He was the boss. Consultant to governments and multi-national corporations, modest-selling author of *Applied Agrodynamics of Meteorology*, he might as well have been an army general with a hundred deaths under his belt: he was white, he had money, plentiful food, a vehicle, a house with water in it. He was the 'OK, let's go' man.

It was exactly two months now since the Silbermacher family had been waved through the Ethiopian border on their way to Bharatan, this aggressively arid territory four hundred feet below sea level and half-way between what could be called Africa and what could be called the Arab States.

One of the first things the Silbermachers had learned when they got there was that a map, unless you already know exactly where you are, is nothing but a pretty picture. If you have been in the habit of picturing yourself somewhere in particular on a round and colourful globe, your sense of where you are on the planet is probably dependent on how much you understand of what's being said behind your back and what lies north, south, east and west of you. You know you are in Hungary because people are speaking Hungarian and *that* way is Austria and *that* way is Romania. You know you are in Seattle because people are speaking American and *that* way is Canada and *that* way is Oregon. In Bharatan, the Silbermachers understood nothing and nobody: so, they were nowhere.

Africans kept metamorphosing into Arabs, as far as Ivan's family could see. An apparently African man would disappear into the army barracks dressed in a goat-herder's loincloth and shawl; he would emerge in military khaki, looking suddenly like a member of the PLO. Understanding the language would have helped, of course, but unlike the previous rash of visitors to Bharatan, the Silbermachers were not linguists: to them, when the Bharatani spoke, it sounded like African-chief talk from old Tarzan movies, or sometimes it evoked memories of CNN footage from the Arab Gulf war of 1991.

Then again, all a Bharatani had to do to confuse the Silbermachers even more was get hold of a torn and faded Jim Beam T-shirt from the army rubbish dump, and suddenly he was in their eyes a black American, sauntering around in search of buildings to spray graffiti on.

The Silbermachers had no religion themselves and were ideologically opposed to tampering with the religion of native peoples, but as a result they hadn't the foggiest notion of what the Bharatani believed in, so this too remained a mystery. Ivan's teenage daughter discovered that the Bharatani considered the display of female hair, breasts and thighs wicked: that was about it.

'They're real, like, *inhibited*, y'know' was her assessment. 'Like those holy rollers down south.'

By 'down south' she meant somewhere in southern USA like Texas, of course, not somewhere in southern Africa like Malawi, though the slur would have been equally true of either place.

Not that the Silbermachers had that much to do with the common Bharatani, since most of those lived in the desert beyond the army enclosures. Clusters of huts housed the men, women and children who were no use to the foreigners, and in these portable shelters like birds' nests fallen from the sky, the Bharatani lived briefly and died. A narrow stream of water trickled through the settlement, polluted by sand, salt, shit and the occasional child's corpse. To drive through the settlement was a deeply affecting experience for the Silbermachers, though precisely what part of them it was affecting was hard to say. Everywhere dark-skinned, emaciated people were praying, jabbering to their God to deliver them – Allah, Jehovah, Set, Haile Selassie, who could tell?

The Silbermachers lived in a house in the military sector, because for all their liberal guilt they could not live in a bird's nest fallen from the sky.

They came from Seattle, from the US of A, by invitation, because a few years ago the Bharatani had evolved to the point where they at last developed a script for their spoken language, and some foreign linguists had eagerly received it for study, and the Bharatani's mass starvation had come to the notice of the Western world. The local government's brief was to cure the Bharatani of nomadism and get them to settle down and plant food, so that the shifting soil would settle down too, binding together to support life. Ivan Silbermacher's brief was to find out if there was anything that could be done about the soil's relationship with the weather.

Ivanka Silbermacher's brief was to maintain her relationship with Ivan. She was his wife of twenty-three years, an attractive and resilient woman who could generate a certain amount of energy in 120-degree heat, despite having been born in a cold country. Her skin was dark tan against the white blouses and skirts she always wore: she joked that she looked more like a gypsy than ever. She could make delicious refrigerated casseroles that didn't taste as if their ingredients had come from cans. She could charm obstructive bureaucrats. She could stare down hostile Bharatani. She was a wonderful lover.

The most obvious thing Ivan and Ivanka had in common was their given names, but these were near-identical by coincidence only. Ivan was fourth-generation American Jew, with Ukrainian forebears in some distant past that meant less to him than (say) the fact that Kellogg's Frosties were less sweet now than in the pre-healthconscious days of his childhood. Ivanka was Hungarian, and hadn't come to the US until 1968. At twenty, alone in a strange country and speaking almost no English, she found the odd coincidence that her next-door neighbour's name was the masculine equivalent of her own just about as complex a talking-point as she could manage with one of the natives.

'Ivan – Ivanka – it's the same!' she had smiled, relieved to be able to get through a sentence without committing some fundamental error.

Ivan had been interested, sincerely interested, in Hungary's political situation, and that had made her feel warmly towards him, because all the other men she'd met so far only wanted to talk about TV, food, the weather and sex. The irony was, of course, that she hadn't the vocabulary to talk about Hungary's politics with Ivan, however much his interest in it made her displaced little body come alive for him, and instead she mouthed broken clichés about TV, food, the weather and, later, sex. She'd tried to say what it was like for a young woman in Eastern Europe, how different it was from America. Lacking words like 'conscientious', 'politically aware', 'genderisation', and 'dialectics', she had to make do with crude equivalents, and somehow her assertion that 'Here in America a woman can be not so free' ended up with her letting him take her to bed.

But he had been all right. By the time she had learned the language well enough to be able to judge whether he was really on her wavelength, he was so used to her that he seemed to be the sort of man she would have chosen anyway, even at the outset.

But then, it was hard to tell. If your man has already learned where on your butt to put his middle finger, how to disown patriarchy by handing over the newspaper, and what brand of shampoo your wiry black hair requires, you can't really size him up the way you would if he was new. And then of course, she loved him too. Loved him enough to want to kill him when he had an affair, four years after they were married: she'd thrown his clothes, meteorology textbooks, shoes et cetera through a closed window on to the street four storeys below, then slapped his face so that his glasses flew off, then punched him several times on the nose. Bleeding profusely, he had apologised to her energetically on the bedroom floor, and they had conceived the first of their three children.

That child, Lydia, was with them now, here in Bharatan. She was eighteen years old, and of course had no memory of her conception. The thought of her parents making love was like imagining Ron and Nancy Reagan engaging in *soix-ante-neuf*. Lydia was the only sexually potent one in her family, as far as she was concerned. Her own body was white and smooth, with jet-black hair, of which she liked her eyebrows and pubes best. Her legs weren't long enough, though: a genetic legacy from a short mother.

Cultural dissemination being what it is, an extraordinary variety of foreign spores had landed and failed to take root in Bharatan at one time or another. Ivan was not the first meteorologist to visit, nor Ivanka the first Hungarian woman. But Lydia was the first Gothic-style punk. Not one Bharatani, ever, had seen anything like this pale American girl dressed all in black, with black lips, black nails and a wayward nest of black hair.

'Lydia' wasn't her given name, which was Vanushka, another little joke between her parents, for old times' sake. Although 'Vanushka' was plenty exotic enough to satisfy the teenager's passion for individuality, it was still not her own choice, so she chose 'Lydia' instead. It reminded her of one of her role models with the same name, an avant-garde performance artist and musician who wore black leather and wailed poetry about killing domestic pets and being fucked in the ass by her daddy.

Ivan never dreamed of doing anything like that to his daughter, but she didn't consider herself lucky because of this or anything else. He had very little to offer her, and all her attempts to bridge the gap were failures. She had played him 'Harvester of Virgins' by Dead Souls through her CD Walkman, inserting the earpieces into his ears herself, and he had taken them out again after two minutes, pronouncing the music too monotonous. Monotonous?!? What a joke! When new acquaintances asked her what her dad did for a living, she relished replying, 'Oh, he watches clouds move, waits for snow to melt, stuff like that.' It was a delicious answer to be able to give, both because it was a swipe at her father's own tolerance for monotony, and because she could nevertheless impress her friends with the unusualness of his job.

This unusual job had brought the family to the edge of a desert whose name one army linguist had translated for them as 'the crust of Hell'. Ivan, Ivanka, and Lydia: that was the family. The other two children were dead, one in utero and the other in the men's room of a nightclub, his body's water supply poisoned by too much of the wrong chemical.

Lydia missed her kid brother Mike terribly, and hardly ever did drugs because of him.

Of course, she'd tried lat leaf within days of arriving in Bharatan – it would have been too great a shame to return to the US without knowing what it was like, even though she was disgusted by the mess it left on the teeth. Her verdict on it was damning: these people had to make do with shitty, primitive, underpowered versions of everything – food, water, clothing, equipment, housing, entertainment – and their drugs were no exception. Piss-weak! The real tragedy of the Bharatani's starvation Lydia saw as a direct result of several rectifiable mistakes: lack of education about contraception, lack of smart lawyer politicians who could demand the best at the bargaining table, and lack of information about the rest of the world, that is, TV.

Ivanka had a different view of the Bharatani's plight: their essential curse, she felt, was that they had no hope of leaving Bharatan, except as plumes of funeral flame. If only there were somewhere for them to escape to . . . But the whole continent was teeming with refugees already, all of them destitute, unskilled and feeble. The Somali fled into Ethiopia, and the Ethiopians fled into Somalia, but though there might be places where a refugee would not be beaten with axles left over from abandoned Communist agricultural machinery or forced to pound her own baby to death in a maize mortar, there was no oasis which offered freedom from despondency, diarrhoea, and death. The Bharatani were so far away from any city they could reach on foot (the scarce camels were for status, not for riding on) that their nomadism was confined to the same few hundred miles of desert, which they shifted across as mindlessly as the wind-driven sand dunes reclaiming their little plots of agriculture.

Ivanka hoped her husband could do something about this, but she had her doubts. But then, she had worse doubts about her own instincts to help, which were more along the lines of adopting Bharatani orphans.

She had raised this possibility with Ivan and Lydia only a few days after the family's arrival, and their response had been unenthusiastic.

'I know you're still very upset about that baby you lost,' said Ivan, 'but if you're dead set on adoption, why not adopt an abandoned American kid when we get back to the States? A life is a life, and a white kid would have more chance of being accepted and happy in an American environment than a transplanted Bharatani. There's not even any guarantee that our climate and bacteriological spectrum wouldn't kill one of these kids as surely as starvation and malaria.'

Lydia's response, though different, was the same.

'Look, Mom, I know you still miss Mike a real lot, and so do I, but adopting some, like, diseased black baby is not gonna bring him back, y'know? I mean, Jesus Mom, we've got our own problems.'

Ivanka wondered which problems Lydia had in mind, but she had a suspicion they were probably things like boy trouble and grief over short legs, so she didn't press the point. The last thing she needed was to lose her temper and yell another lecture about living in terror of an oppressive political regime, which meant nothing to Lydia anyway. So, she nurtured her secret empathy with the Bharatani and carried on cooking in her air-conditioned house, breathing deeply.

Apart from helping with the unloading and distributing of food from the aid trucks every morning, Ivanka didn't go out of doors all that often; the challenge of accompanying her husband on to the crust of Hell to look at sand all day was beyond the scope of her wifely devotion. Back in Seattle she was wont to give generously to hopeless and unselfish causes, but she had too much gypsy in her to die for such a cause herself. Nor was she so bored with her own company that sheer stimulus deprivation drove her out of the house, like Lydia, who loitered around the camps of Bharatan in her Goth gear almost every day. What must these destitute desert-dwellers think, seeing this mousse-haired, punk-blackened vampirella doing the rounds? Ivanka couldn't help smiling at her own responsibility for bringing such an outrageous incongruity into the world.

But for herself, she preferred to stay inside, listening to the short-wave radio, keeping the house neat, and reading books in case the telephone rang. In choosing to avoid the desert atmosphere she was also trying to prevent her chronic conjunctivitis getting worse, or even contracting the eye herpes which was epidemic here. The Bharatani all had bloodshot eyes, pus-yellow eyes, cataract-milky eyes, so Ivanka didn't feel as maladapted as she might have. She used to joke with Ivan that the only conditions under which her eyes could be white and healthy were in the heart of the Pest sector of Buda-Pest, with just the right chemical mixture of fresh Eastern European air, Trabant exhaust and alcohol. Away from Hungary she was never without her eye drops, and would come to a standstill in the oddest and most inconvenient places to administer them. In the exit lane of a supermarket car-park in LA once she had relived the fear of militia harassment during her last weeks in Hungary: the LA police sprang out of nowhere with guns cocked and yelled at her to lie down on the ground. It transpired they had mistaken her eyedrop ritual for some sort of drug abuse. Another time, during a job interview, she had abruptly thrown her head back, her mouth falling open with the pull of gravity, and squeezed the little droplets of medicated tears on to her eyeballs. 'Eshcuse me,' she had mumbled through her extended throat. But she'd got the job anyway, and not just because her extended throat was beautiful. She could get away with virtually any behaviour, because of her winning manner, her understanding of people, and her accent, which would always identify her as a foreigner deserving benefit of the doubt. At least in America. Here in Bharatan she was *m'geni* to the Africans, *infidel* to the Arabs; she was a guinea pig among warthogs.

She missed her girlfriends back in Seattle. Sometimes when Ivan was talking to some bureaucrat about the genetic make-up of cactuses or casuarina trees, she wished she were in a coffee-house with Winnie and Fran, hearing them talk about art or Welfare.

'It makes so much more sense to import something like ocotillo, which doesn't look that pretty but can survive drought, than to have millions of poppies blooming the day after a rainfall,' argued Ivan. 'The poppies look great in the *National Geographic* photos, but they don't fix the soil, mammals can't eat 'em and they're gone without a trace a week later.'

Yes, that's all very well, Ivanka thought, but how does the ocotillo feel about being transplanted?

Ivan didn't seem to mind where he was, even if it was nowhere, as long as he was permitted to use and improve his skills in his chosen area. That was one of the good things about him, Ivanka had found. Though he was highly ambitious, he wasn't fixated on the sort of success that requires a particular kind of house, make of car, brand of champagne, street of address. His ambitions were over a much farther horizon, their realisation barely glimpsed; while striving for them, he was quite content to make do and have fun.

At least, that was the way it had been back home in the States. Out here in Bharatan, Ivan seemed more obsessed with his research, less mindful of the other things in life, that is, less available for sex. With every week that went by, Ivan was more and more likely to spend all day and half the night out in the desert with his calculators and equipment, while she read books by bedlight. The arrival of crated consignments of new equipment from Japan (equipment for *what*, for God's sake?) she soon learned to equate with Ivan being AWOL for up to three days at a time.

'How about watering *this* little cactus tree once in a while?' she would tease him, and he would respond gladly, but only, of course, if he was there to respond.

As for Lydia, she didn't seem to mind the isolation and the lack of attention from her father. For the last two or three years at least she had demonstrated a preference for relationships that could be conducted by phone or shouted over the noise of a nightclub PA system. Her way of judging whether she could be comfortable socially with another human being was by deciding whether or not she could, on a given occasion, get away with wearing her Scraping Foetus off the Wheel T-shirt, which depicted a crucified Christ and the slogan 'If you're gonna get down, get down and pray!' Not many people passed this litmus test.

Ivanka, in trying to work out who and what was truly important to her deeply subcultured daughter, recalled that Lydia had left behind some sort of boyfriend called Stevo.

'Are you missing Stevo?' she therefore asked one morning

when Lydia was moping at the breakfast table, fiddling with a letter from him.

'I guess,' she said.

'Were you really close?'

'Oh yeah, sure,' said Lydia. 'We were a steady thing. We'd even listen to the same Walkman, like, one earphone in my ear and the other earphone in his. That kinda thing makes you, like, one person.'

'What was the best thing about him?'

'Oh, I don't know. I guess' – she smiled mischievously – 'he didn't ask too many dumb questions.'

One thing that was similar about Lydia and the Bharatani was that you could never tell if you had embarrassed them or caught them out in any way. The Bharatani were black, and couldn't blush as far as Ivanka could tell. Lydia used thick make-up to achieve her Gothic pallor, and blushes couldn't penetrate. A long walk outside in the blistering sun could do it, washing her pale topsoil away in a deluge of sweat, but then she would return with a flush that lasted until she disappeared for the evening into her bedroom.

Nobody in Bharatan took much interest in the Silbermachers except for Lieutenant Ralph Kravitz, an army interpreter who seemed to have been Heaven-sent to provide them with home-style social intercourse. Amazingly, he had also done a couple of years of a biology degree, so he had the ammunition to argue with Ivan: he relished the role of devil's advocate over the usefulness of Ivan's work, and Ivanka enjoyed nothing more than listening to the two of them argue because it reminded her, as her husband spoke more and more passionately, of why she still loved him. Visits from Kravitz always ended in particularly good sex when he was gone, and Ivanka had the added pleasure of dressing attractively to see if Ralph might, in another world and time, have been the one to take her to bed.

A typical night would find the three of them (Lydia preferred Nine Inch Nails remixes to Ralph) discussing the relative ascendancy of Death and Life. *How Eastern European all this is!*, Ivanka would think as she sipped her icy alcohol, and the men would go right on fighting.

'Life actually *wants* to take care of other life,' insisted Ivan. 'A fruit will struggle against all odds to be *useful*. Think about that! It could much more easily just grow up with no use to anything but itself: some thorny creeper with a texture like barbed wire and a taste like ash – just any old Life for Life's sake. But no: it goes through a million complicated biological changes just so it can be a fruit – juicy, delicious, beautiful, *edible.*'

'Usefulness is subjective,' objected Kravitz. 'You only think a fruit is so wonderful because we've taught ourselves to eat it. The fruit doesn't give a damn. Besides, it's only a temporary aberration – something that happens in the fly-speck millennia between lava flows. The Earth didn't support life to begin with and it's not interested in supporting it now. Have you noticed the increase in volcanic activity? Lava is the perfect life extinguisher. Have you ever been there when the sand dunes are on the move? They actually make a noise: they *boom* as they go, it's frightening as all hell. And you know what that sand wants to do? It just wants to roll all over the lakes, the roads, the human settlements, the eight per cent of the land that's arable – those sand dunes are just thousands of acres of Death on the move.'

'You're wrong, Ralph, you're wrong. Life wins out against all odds. The whole purpose of every organism is to survive and reproduce and prosper—'

'Yeah, so sand reproduces and prospers.'

'Life, Ralph, *Life*! If there's just the tiniest chance for something to grow, it will. Lichen will grow on the wreck of a car. Moss will grow on a lump of shit.'

'Maybe. But you can't feed a million starving people on moss and lichen. Especially if they have to scrape it off car wrecks and lumps of shit.'

Whether the tens of thousands of Bharatani in the refugee camps around the crust of Hell were really starving was a matter of debate. The international aid organisations claimed they were, and sent pamphlets all over the world imploring people like Ivanka Silbermacher to help, which she generously had, even before there was any hint that her husband's work would take her here. Other observers were more cynical, however. Lydia was of the opinion that the Bharatani males had a pretty easy life, lying around the camps chatting to each other, chewing lat leaf, drinking alcohol brewed in buckets from grain rations, and creating more little Bharatani.

'If they got off their ass and grew some food or, like, helped the women with the chores, the cooking, the gathering and stuff, there'd be more to go round,' she pointed out. 'I mean, they're not too weak to fuck, right?'

'Don't use that word,' sighed Ivanka. 'You know we don't like that word.'

'*Jee*sus, Mom, I'm being serious!'

'Well, you don't have to use that word to show you're being serious.'

But that was the word Fergie 'Fez' Shipley used in discussing the Bharatani problem with Lydia when they had their confabs behind the army barracks. The observation about the Bharatani men not being too weak to fuck was a direct quote from him.

'Those aid organisations, when they say there's a hundred thousand gonna starve, what's that mean? It means lots of people are real hungry, right, the way lotsa people in this part of the world've always been. And outta those people who are hungry, some are maybe gonna get weak and sick. And outta those, some are gonna get so weak and sick that the food they get ain't gonna do 'em any good. Those ones are gonna die, sure. But is that *real* starvation? I mean, like, is that people shrivellin' up and dyin' because they got no food to eat? I tell ya, there's more to it. I mean, there's pills these people should be gettin' that the pharmaceutical companies are makin' sure they don't get. There's an anti-malaria pill, there's pills to stop the runs. I mean, shit, these poor bastards don't see meat from one month to the next, and they don't even get a fuckin' iron pill!'

Shipley, for all that he impressed Lydia with his political analysis, did not impress her as a man. Her rendezvous with this chinless, bug-eyed, fez-toting army corporal were strictly business: he could get things she needed from across the border. The army's supply lines were like an impossibly long river snaking from Bharatan right to all those cool faraway places where drugs were made.

Shipley, for his part, knew better than to lay a hand on anything of hers besides her money.

'That's some allowance you get,' he whistled once.

'Hey,' she objected with a shrug, 'I'm wasting my life out here, just like you. You're getting paid for it, why shouldn't I? I could be in Seattle right now, seeing Godflesh.'

It wasn't such a big allowance really, for an American girl. It's just that it hadn't been adjusted to the Bharatani environment, where there were no expenses and almost nothing to buy. Apart from a trip to the army Christmas bash at the Cranfield Airbase near the Sudan border, where there was a glorious cool mist of outdoor air-conditioning fuelled by sixty gallons of water an hour, she hadn't really travelled anywhere, either. Her parents, insecure about the fairness of having brought her here, couldn't bring themselves to reduce her allowance as well, so it kept rolling in. They thought she must be saving it. And so she was, mostly, because Shipley was pretty cheap.

One thing was a big relief for Lydia about this time on the crust of Hell: no boyfriends. She had no need or desire for a relationship at this time in her life, but back home there was no getting away from it because teenage culture was powered by sex. She'd been worried about her nipples: were they too far towards the sides of her breasts, were the areolas too dark, would a guy even want to touch them? – even though she didn't want a guy to touch them, no guy she knew, anyway. She read about fellatio in glossy women's magazines, mouthing the instructions as she read, even though the thought of having some guy's hose down her throat made her sick. She worried about the way her naked abdomen wrinkled up when she sat and bent over – did that mean she could never sit on top during sex?

Even girl-to-girl friendships were difficult if there were no guy problems to talk about, and to go to a concert alone was more hassle than it was worth, both during and (especially) afterwards.

What Lydia had in mind for her time away was to relax and be celibate, and then to have a one-night stand (or better still, a close call) a few days before she was leaving, so that back in the USA she could receive a letter from the guy, some Aboud or Nusrat, saying that he would never forget the passion they had shared and that he was burning for her. Far out! What a letter like that would be worth!

She was storing up things all the time which would be more potent back home than they were here: objects, experiences, acquaintances. Things which were distasteful, inconvenient, even terrifying here would be the most precious cultural currency back in Seattle. Finding the bloated body of a dead baby at the aid truckstop, revolting though it had been at the time, was a recollection to strike awe into the hearts of her friends. Taking walks in 120-degree heat – 'Oh yeah,' she would say to incredulous friends, 'I'd get bored otherwise.'

Lydia's Walkman was a tape recorder, too, so she had the mourning songs of the Bharatani in the bag. She knew a couple of guys in Seattle who had a kind of a weird primitive industrial funk band going called Hybrid Spore, and these tapes she had of the Bharatani chanting were the sort of thing they would kill to sample. They might even let her join the band in order to get them – she could sing and play percussion, maybe even play one of those keyboards you just fed ROM cards into. Being a musician would certainly make a lot more sense than studying metallurgy and jewellery-making, the career her parents had most recently pinned her down to.

'It would be fun,' her mother encouraged her. 'All those strange metal wristbands and amulets and belt-buckles you're always looking for at the markets – you could make them yourself, and sell them to other people just like you.'

But if there was a way to sell Lydia on the idea of being self-supporting, this definitely wasn't it: she did not want to be deprived of a reason to frequent the markets, she did not wish to make jewellery for anyone but herself to wear, and she did not like the suggestion that there was a class of people 'just like' herself.

'Well, Mom,' she sing-songed, 'we'll just see how things pan out.'

She had only been interested in metallurgy originally because of the alchemy angle; the books on witchcraft she was always reading had chapters on alchemists sometimes and they sounded cool.

'Well you know, some of what *I'm* trying to do is a kind of alchemy,' Ivan had said to her once.

'Sure, Dad,' she'd replied.

Security was tight in and around the Silbermachers' house, because everything except the paraphernalia of Ivan's research was of some value to the Bharatani, even the atmosphere, which was air-conditioned to transform the infernal heat into something as easy and pleasant to swallow as chilled water.

'Lock up, always lock up,' Ivan told Lydia every time the girl was leaving. 'Who knows, they could take your Walkman.'

She would raise her eyes to her black, black fringe in despair at his pathetic attempt to make the danger real to her: why was he always so far off the mark! She never went anywhere without taking her Walkman with her.

Nothing ever went missing, anyway. Even Ivan had to admit that. The only items he seemed to be having to replace at an inordinate rate were ballpoint pens.

'Is it you who's taking them?' he asked Lydia on her return from one of her walks. She shrugged as she tore off her sodden shawl, revealing a black-corseted cleavage glistening with perspiration.

'I write to my friends in the States,' she said, extending her lower lip imbecilically to blow upwards into her sweat-matted hair.

'Well, you must have a lot of friends.'

'Not many,' she challenged him. 'I write heaps.'

Actually, Lydia didn't write at all, apart from the odd postcard. She hated writing, couldn't see the point of it; in fact, she admired the Bharatani for doing without it for so many thousands of years. When she missed her friends, she called them on the phone.

'I took, like, mountains of clothes, y'know,' she confided into the mouthpiece, cradling it between her chin and collarbone as she punctured blisters on her feet. 'Like I got stuff there's nooo way I can wear here, y'know, like gloves and fur-lined boots and stuff. But y'know, you may as well use up your luggage allowance. I mean, the Walkman and the CDs were, like, cabin luggage, y'know, so what else was I gonna take?'

'Well, it's real difficult to be, like, true to myself here. I go out in my black dress – the one with the long raggedy skirts and the lace-up bodice, y'know, that's real low-cut, and lace-up boots and my hair fluffed out like this, y'know, and then I gotta wrap a shawl around my chest, y'know, cuz of the religion here, and the weather is so *hot*, you wouldn't believe. In five minutes, I'm, like, plastered with sweat, and my hair's sticking to my face, y'know, and there's, like, a little stream of sweat running down between my tits, y'know, and I'm worried my inner soles are gonna, like, dissolve.'

' . . . '

'Yeah, well, I could do what Mom and Dad do, and wear light-coloured clothes. Cuz, like, black absorbs the heat a real lot. I mean, believe me, you don't see *any*body wearing black out here. But I mean, that only makes it more important to stand up for what you believe in, doesn't it?'

' . . . '

'Donna? Yeah, I've got her crucifix.'

' . . . '

'No, she didn't give it to me. She, like, sold it to me.'

' . . . '

'Well, not exactly. She came up to me in a club one night and started, like, insulting me? She was saying, like, I'd been hanging out with this guy Keith she was steady with, and like how she didn't want him anyway, cuz he was a real asshole, and I'm saying, like, "Hey listen, Donna, I don't even *know* this guy," but she's, like, "Sure, sure," and being, like, real un*pleasant*, y'know? So she reminds me about the crucifix and I say, "Yeah well, I don't have it with me, y'know, I mean, it's *nice*, y'know, but I don't, like, carry it wherever I go just in case I run into you." So I remind her about the ten bucks she owes me, and she says, "What ten bucks?" and all this kinda stuff, and then something about how this guy Keith's loaded, and I'm, like, thinking, "Well babe, looks like you just sold me your crucifix for ten bucks."'

'. . .'

'Oh yeah, it's real neat. It's big – big as a pizza sub, y'know. It's got, like, jewels all along it, that are supposed to be, like, rosary beads, and it's, like, so good to *hold*, y'know, its texture and everything, and it's always warm, y'know, cuz it's right there on my breast, y'know, real close to my heart. It's my most coolest possession. It's *wicked*.'

Lydia's crucifix had got her in trouble only once so far in Bharatan. A wrinkled old man in a loincloth and a threadbare flannelette shirt came up to her and smiled. He looked as if he had just about reached the maximum life expectancy of forty, and might fall dead at her feet any minute. 'You Christian,' he rasped, pointing at her bejewelled treasure. 'Me Christian. We pray.' And he went down on his knees, signalling her to do the same, which she did.

'O God Jesus,' the old man said, clasping his skeletal hands. 'We pray. Fadder witch art. Will be done. Earth same as Heaven. Give us day bread. Differ us from enemies. Fine is the kingdom. Amen.'

He looked to Lydia in case she had anything to add.

'Hey listen, Heavenly Father,' she said. 'Make it rain, will ya?'

The weeks of the Silbermachers' sojourn in Bharatan accumulated day by scorching day into months. There was no doubt that Ivan was working hard, but the original estimate of six to eight weeks was what Ivanka had planned for when she'd been packing, and now everything was running out. Not the basics, of course, like bread and ketchup and tinned fish and Pepsi, which were supplied by the army, but the little luxuries that make life in a harshly foreign place endurable.

'Where's the chocolate frogs, Mom?'

'We're all out of chocolate frogs, honey.'

'Chocolate cookies?'

'Out also.'

The army being a male institution, sanitary pads were not one of the basics they supplied, so when these ran out Ivanka and Lydia had no choice but to be philosophical.

'We'll have to wear strips of rag, like the Bharatani women,' sighed Ivanka.

'Cool,' said Lydia, for this too would be valuable cultural currency back home.

'Unless you want to try tampons.'

'No way! Toxic shock!'

'That was only one brand, I think, a long time ago. Anyway, I'm sure they researched it and it's fixed now.'

'They're not as bio-degradable.'

And so Ivanka and Lydia started cutting some of the extra bed-linen into strips.

Later when Kravitz got to hear about it he was pretty exasperated. 'You're crazy,' he said. 'What are you going to do when you're back in the States and it's freezing?'

'I guess we'll just have to buy more linen.'

'What a waste of resources!' Kravitz shook his head. 'You should have told me. The army's got hundreds of fleecy cotton blankets stockpiled up in the storerooms, that nobody's going to use and that we sure as hell aren't going to ship back where they came from.'

'Really?' said Ivanka. 'That's terrible! Why don't you just give them to the Bharatani? They're desperate.'

'For blankets on the crust of Hell?'

'It gets very cold at nights.'

'OK, I know, but there's still a problem. There's only a few hundred blankets and thousands of Bharatani. Who would decide who gets and who doesn't get? It wouldn't be like the food relief, which is divided equally.'

'It doesn't sound like an impossible problem to me. It sounds like the sort of thing that could be solved with a bit of common sense and a bit of sensitivity.'

'Common sense and sensitivity? From the army? Get real, Ivanka, and just tell me how many blankets you want.'

Three more weeks, and Ivanka began to realise that she couldn't stand to live here on the crust of Hell much longer. She really was beginning to feel like that poor transplanted ocotillo, except that she wasn't anywhere near as compatible with the environment as that . . . not frail exactly, but so unsuited: a winter flower pushed into sun-baked, salty soil in the hope that against all odds it would root.

The fetish for the exotic and the alien which had made her so enthusiastic about all things African and Middle Eastern when she'd been in America had been completely neutralised as if by chemical reaction: now she hankered after all things familiar. To open the last tin of cocktail frankfurters, a food she hadn't even liked in the past, provoked a mournful sense of loss. Her favourite bottle of mascara, left out accidentally in the sun, was baked so that the brush was fused with the contents. All her books had been read and reread, and there was nothing in the army library except short novels about men called Hank or Max or Ted who didn't mind getting the odd spatter of brains on their flakjackets. Perhaps worst of all, the fleecy cotton blankets were almost used up, and ever since the night Ralph had made a clumsy pass at her, she didn't want to ask him for anymore. She missed Ivan horribly; he was almost never in the house.

'I really *am* in Hell,' she said to herself, and to her mother too, in a letter. Complaining did her no good, though, because Ivanka's mother, a devout old crock living in a small Hungarian town, simply scolded her about using the word 'Hell' impiously. In a once-familiar language that Ivanka now found alarmingly difficult to read (was it her mother's hand-writing deteriorating with age, or was it her own mind getting poisoned by an overdose of foreignness?) the airmail pages of reply went on to remind her that this 'mission' in this 'primitive place' was a Heaven-sent opportunity to 'sow the Word of God' where it was most needed. Ivanka sighed and folded the letter up, utterly disheartened by the uselessness to her now of the mother who had once borne and nursed her. 'Sow the Word of God'? She no longer even had the energy to make a casserole, quite apart from the fact that all the possible ingredients were just about used up. She couldn't work magic.

She couldn't even feel sorry for the Bharatani anymore. The truck driver who worked for the United Nations High Commission for Refugees had a word for it: compassion fatigue. 'You've got compassion fatigue,' he said, as she helped him unload the food rations. Next day, she decided to stop going to the truckstop; she'd have to be crazy to go out in 120-degree dusty heat, with her eyes already sore from crying and infection, and a pounding headache.

'We have to talk,' Ivanka told Ivan at last, one night after he returned at 3 a.m. from a long spell under the vast cloudless sky, and tried to sneak past her on his way to the study.

'I'm very close to a breakthrough in my research,' he

pleaded mildly, his hands fidgeting up and down a sheaf of papers he was holding close to his chest.

'That's what I want to talk about,' she said. 'I can't understand what good anybody could possibly believe you're doing here.'

He laughed nervously, postponing anger.

'There's no need to insult me, just because . . .' He trailed off, suspecting he was about to make a mistake. While he believed very strongly that Ivanka resented his work because she was missing him sexually, he knew her too well to say so, and not just because he feared her exploding into a tantrum of aggrieved humiliation. He feared just as much that he might have misjudged her, as he had misjudged her often in the past, and that to his own shame he would discover she was thinking far more analytically than he; in short, that she would prove herself dead right and him dead wrong.

'Look, we're both tired,' he sighed, relieved to have so easily come up with a conversational emollient to neutralise what he'd begun. It worked, too – or perhaps Ivanka wasn't in the mood for a fight.

'The way I see it,' she said, 'even an idiot – well, any *Western* idiot – can see what's needed out here. The Bharatani need to stay on the land and make it good for things to grow, yes? Maybe they will, maybe they won't, who knows: *you* aren't the one supposed to persuade them either way, are you? And the weather, well, fact is, it doesn't rain enough, yes? You've done lots of tests, you've been very busy. I'm sure if there's anything the Bharatani need to know about what happens and doesn't happen when rain falls on their soil, you must have found it out for them by now. But what they *really* need is for more rain to fall, yes? The UN must know this, and the Bharatani sure must know this, and yet here you are after three months, still working day and night, and someone is paying for it all.'

'So?' One little 'So' wouldn't delay his capture very long, of course, but he tried it anyway, like a mouse uttering a peeplet as the mousetrap flips its trigger.

'So who's paying, and why?'

Ivan sank into an armchair, laying his papers down beside him. 'There's something I haven't told you,' he said.

'I'm listening,' she said.

'My work here isn't funded by the UN, beyond a few thousand dollars for military liaison. And it isn't funded at all by the Bharatani.'

'Yes,' she said, folding her slender arms dangerously under her breasts.

'It's funded by Fujumara-Agcor.'

'Yes,' she said, gently squeezing her biceps through the cotton of her blouse.

'They're a new conglomerate, the end result of a few mergers. They specialise in pharmaceuticals and fertilisers. They believe my work could be of use to them in the future.'

'What about now?'

'They're satisfied.'

'I'm sure they are,' retorted Ivanka. 'Because they're not paying anymore.'

'What do you mean?'

'They've stopped the funds. You're on your own now.'

'H . . . how did you know that?' He was grateful he was sitting down already, for he felt suddenly faint, dehydrated.

Ivanka spoke quietly, rocking on the balls of her feet. 'It's . . . a woman thing,' she said, the Americanism sounding odd in her still-heavy Hungarian accent. 'Women are born to receive certain phone calls. Something inside of us attracts them. A woman will always receive the call from her husband's mistress that says, "Is that you Ivan darling, when can

I see you?" A woman will always receive the call from a strange Japanese man that says, "Please tell your husband he's gone overtime, overbudget, whatever, and without results we can't send anymore machinery, chemicals, or money."'

Ivan gaped at her, aghast.

'Why didn't you tell me? An important call like that!'

'Oooh . . . I guess I must be the secretive type.' Her lips were pouting, swelling with anger. Her hands gripped her biceps. He could tell she was only a few seconds away from eruption.

'Well . . . uh . . . the same guy sent me a letter, anyway, telling me the bad news,' Ivan conceded, as if to retract his accusation.

'I know,' Ivanka said, tapping her fingernails on her folded arms. 'That was weeks ago. We're still here. Who's paying?'

'Well . . . *I* am, Ivanka,' he said, swallowing hard. 'That is, *we* are. I sold the house.'

'This house?'

'Our house in Seattle.'

'You *what?*'

'I'm very close to a breakthrough, Ivanka. When it comes, Fujumara-Agcor will pay me enough for a dozen houses. We can live anywhere we like, and leave whenever we like. Just think of that, Ivanka: summer in Budapest, winter in—'

She held up her hand to silence him.

'So what's the breakthrough you're waiting for?' she whispered.

Ivan drew himself up to his full height; permitted himself, almost shyly, to reveal his pride.

'I believe,' he said, 'I know how to make it rain.'

A terrible flush of red came up from the open neck of Ivanka's blouse, overtook her neck and face, and she erupted.

At the crack of dawn, Ivan was at the machinery, squinting

through a viewfinder at the clouds. He didn't need to squint very hard: one eye was already swelling shut with bruising. He'd tried to put a Band-Aid on his lip, but it wouldn't stay on. He hadn't even got laid this time.

The Bharatani were all smiles: they knew what a vengeful female was capable of. They even had a word for such a woman, but it was not a word which appeared in the first dictionary of their newly scripted language.

'Hai, boss!' they waved.

After an hour's work, the temperature started climbing, and Ivan decided to go deeper into the desert, the crust of Hell proper, before it was too late.

On the way there he passed the army barracks, where a group of young women were waiting for the daily delivery of food and water. Lydia was with them, her black dress and white skin the perfect reverse of their white dresses and black skins. They were all laughing hysterically, squatting around a large sheet of what appeared to be aluminium foil; Ivan tried to see what was going on as he drove past, but from his angle of vision the sun reflected blindingly off the foil. He waved uncertainly out of the jeep's window, ignored. He would never find out that his daughter was teaching the Bharatani women how to 'chase the dragon' – a game in which heroin is heated on foil until it turns black and wriggles like a snake or dragon, while giving off an intoxicating plume that is chased by a snorting device. Lydia and the Bharatani women were using plastic ballpoint-pen casings.

'Fak'n eh! Fak'n eh!' crowed the Bharatani, delighted with this American expletive Lydia had taught them. Lydia was learning their language, too, something that her parents never would. She was beginning to feel quite at home here.

The guide who accompanied Ivan to the desert was in a cheerful and energetic mood. He kept smiling, smiling all the time, and his teeth weren't even stained with lat leaf: the white powder the white girl had given him was better than anything he'd had before to get him through another hard day on the crust of Hell. He felt as if his body was made of a different clay that needed less water.

'Good day today, Boss,' he grinned.

Ivan didn't reply, didn't even hear. He was peering through the dust-opaque windscreen at the desert, trying to judge whether he was hallucinating or if he really could see a massive cloud formation just up ahead.

The Gossip Cell

[A]

ED JEROME'S wife was, at most, half a dozen thrusts away from orgasm when the bedside telephone rang.

'Don't answer it!' she wailed.

'It might be our Helen,' Ed suggested.

'It'll be Willie Spink,' his wife threatened through clenched teeth.

Ed disengaged himself gently, explaining that their daughter had promised to ring some time today, to pass on the latest news about the custody battle for little Fergus.

'Hello?' he panted into the mouthpiece.

'Hello! It's Willie!' gushed the voice at the other end of the line.

Ed's neck thickened while the rest of him slumped somewhat.

'I – it's late,' he growled. Behind him, Mrs Jerome was quietly metamorphosing from sex goddess to relationship troubleshooter.

'Never too late for a world-changing idea, Ed,' enthused Willie. 'By this time next year, you and I will be millionaires and people will be eating ice creams in the Gobi desert.'

'Ice creams in the Gobi desert?'

'Yeah, and going back to their cup of coffee six hours later!'

'Sounds brilliant, Willie. Call me back tomorrow after-noon, after work.'

'But you don't un—'

Ed hated to hang up on him like this; it was contrary to his generous nature, but, in the circumstances, it was the only way to earn points with Mrs Jerome. She was putting her bra back on, and it was a front fastener, too, which only she knew how to operate.

'Feeling cold, love?' he said nervously.

'Oh, I've cooled down considerably,' she remarked.

Two days later, Ed Jerome went to visit Willie at the labora-tory. It wasn't a dirty secret from Mrs Jerome: she'd given her blessing. She was not an unreasonable woman.

It would have been different if Willie Spink had been a no-hoper, a harmless crank whose discoveries existed solely in his own imagination. But Ed – and even Ed's wife – had to admit that there was much more to Willie than that. He was a genius, and a marketable one, at that.

His essential flaw (apart from a perennial inability to understand that other people went to bed at night) was that his vision of the practical uses of his inventions diverged from that of the average citizen of Earth. He was the sort of boffin who might have discovered nuclear fission and imagined it might be useful for garbage disposal or popcorn machines. Fortunately he had never discovered anything as dangerous as nuclear fission, but he had, three years ago, developed an eczema 'vaccine' in tablet form: the sufferer took the tablet, whose active ingredient was then sweated out through the pores, delivering constant, all-over relief. In truth, it wasn't the eczema vaccine as such that Willie had invented, it was the dispersing agent, based on a synthesised fusion of garlic and alcohol. Trying to imagine a suitable active ingredient, Willie had thought it could be one of those fancy perfumes like . . . erm . . . Chanel No. 5?

'Who would want to take Chanel No. 5 in tablet form?' Ed had challenged.

'I dunno,' Willie had said. 'Women who don't want to carry the stuff around, I guess. I mean, wouldn't the bottles leak into their handbags and so on?'

'Willie . . . Take it from me: women enjoy actually squirting themselves with perfume from a fancy bottle – it's part of the glamour.'

'Oh.' Willie was in awe of Ed, who knew so much about women – slept with one, even – and about the world in general. 'Well, I guess I've come up with another non-starter.'

'No, wait a minute,' Ed had said, becoming aware of Willie's dog frantically scratching itself in the corner of the lab. 'Wait just a minute.'

That minute had eventually translated into the Sperome Eczema Vaccine and a largish sum of money in the bank for Willie Spink and the Jeromes. Even now, there was interest from the deodorant industry which might mean more money in the future.

And face it: with poor Helen's ex-husband dragging the custody battle for little Fergus into higher courts, more money was going to be needed very soon, or that mad Cypriot bastard would ship the littlest Jerome straight to Nicosia and transform him into a little Papasidou there.

'So what have you got, Willie?' said Ed, looking around the laboratory, which resembled a failed amateur plumber's garage, as always. Willie wasn't a failed amateur plumber, even though he had the face and the habits of one. He was a failed pharmacist. He'd had his own shop and everything.

'What went wrong?' Ed had asked once.

'I dunno,' Willie had answered. 'I stocked all the usual

drugs. I gave my customers personal attention. I didn't over-charge. I stayed open late. People just stopped coming.'

'And your shop – did it look like this?' pursued Ed, waving his hand at the circumambient chaos of slimy beakers, test tubes, scribbled notepads, discarded packaging, old cups of coffee and trampled junk mail. Willie looked where Ed was waving, a frown materialising on his spherical forehead.

'Like what?' he replied.

Relieved of his duties as a pharmacist, Willie Spink was free to research the essential nature of chemistry. Some of his discoveries, like 'fugitive' gel (it shrank away from approaching spoons and flipped itself out of shallow containers) had not yet been paired off with a use. Others, like the universal odour-neutraliser which converted even the smell of cat diarrhoea or chloroform into a distinctive 'paradigm' odour suggestive of giant vats of burning curry, attracted the attention of the police and the fire brigade. But the Sperome Eczema Vaccine had been a winner, and enabled Willie to buy all sorts of hi-tech equipment which at last made it possible for him to experiment at a cellular level.

Now, proudly, he showed Ed Jerome an old cup of coffee, tipping it forward slightly so that the pond-scum of milk floated free.

'Have you ever noticed,' he said, 'how you make yourself a cup of coffee? And then you get engrossed in something, and by the time you remember your coffee it's cold?'

'Yes,' said Ed for the sake of argument. Personally, he drank his coffee fast.

'Well,' continued Willie, 'I've invented a substance – syn-thesised into a colourless, tasteless, odourless liquid – of which just one drop will maintain the temperature of that cup of coffee for many hours.'

'Uh-huh.'

'The work is done by a sort of . . . "gossip" cell,' elaborated Willie, putting the coffee cup down next to his densely scribbled notebooks with a slosh. 'Imagine the hot coffee is a community of cells. The ones in the centre are oscillating wildly, maintaining the heat. The ones further out are responding to the cold air, slowing down, losing interest. But introduce my gossip cell, and what it does is it zips around telling uninvolved cells what the central ones are up to, and persuades them to behave the same way – pulls them back into line, you might say.'

'For ever?'

'Nothing is for ever. Do you think I can overturn the principle of entropy?'

Ed combed his hands through his hair and tried to think, which was difficult for him on an empty stomach and without caffeine. Despite all the talk about hot coffee, Willie had, of course, not offered him any.

'Of course,' Willie went on, 'the gossip cell can incite cells to stasis just as easily as to frenzy. Which, in practical terms, means that you can buy a gossip-cell-impregnated ice cream at the beach, walk around with it for the rest of the afternoon, and then eat it.'

Ed was sweating now, but not because he was thinking of what, 'in practical terms', he could do with an ice cream at the beach. He was thinking of what, in practical terms, would be the commercial feasibility of central heating that only needed firing up once or twice a day. What about the electricity companies? Would they have him assassinated? Ed was a firm believer in the maxim 'Build a better mousetrap and the multinational mousetrap corporations will beat the shit out of you'.

'How much . . .' he groped, 'how much of this stuff would

you need to keep . . . ah . . . for example . . . a heated swimming pool the same temperature?'

'A ratio of 1:1000 is optimal – a drop in a cup of coffee, maybe a small bucketful in a swimming pool.'

'And how expensive is it to make?'

'It doesn't cost anything!' scoffed Willie goodnaturedly. 'I've got all the stuff right here!'

Ed breathed deeply; he was having a very clear vision of Willie Spink handing over the secret of converting base metals to gold in exchange for a box of clean test tubes.

'Willie,' he said. 'Make me a coffee. We've got things to discuss.'

[B]

Exactly six months later, Lindy Jerome was kneeling in front of an unfamiliar CD player, trying to figure out how to get sound as well as flashing lights, and wondering whether she should change her name from Jerome back to Witts, her maiden name. Now that she and Ed had been separated for almost a month and she had started a new life with Bryan, surely it was time to shake off the trappings of her old identity.

Trouble was, Lindy Witts was an awful name by any standards, and the lights on the CD player suddenly went off, which made her worry she'd wrecked something, which suddenly made her afraid that Bryan would kill her when he returned. The fear took her by surprise: only last night she had lain cradled in Bryan's arms, entrusting her most secret hopes and dreams into his care; she had spooned intimacy into his mouth like luxury ice cream, and he had murmured for more. But today he was away at work, and she realised that although she had already managed to get to the bottom of all his old relationships, she had no idea how he felt about his CD player.

'Don't stop now, you bitch,' she hissed at the machine. Mercifully, the random jab of another button abruptly caused loud music to blare out of the speakers: Joni Mitchell, but with electric guitars, computerised drums and synthesisers. Last night, Bryan had said he really respected her – Joni Mitchell, that is – for having the guts to change direction so radically, for refusing to conform to past expectations. 'Just like you, darling,' he had complimented her.

As Shiatsu therapist to the stars, Bryan had even met Joni Mitchell and been a backstage guest at one of her rare concerts. 'She was really good – better than I expected, even.'

What the hell had he meant by that?

Lindy noticed suddenly that the telephone was ringing.

It had actually been ringing for a while, but she'd taken it to be a sound effect on the Joni Mitchell song currently playing, a take on consumerism called 'Shiny Toys' which also included samples of people saying 'I love my Porsche' and suchlike. A ringing telephone hadn't seemed out of place, until she realised the place was right here.

'Hello?'

'Hi, it's Helen.' Not Ed, then.

'H – Helen? How did you know where to call me?'

'You gave me the number last week.'

'I did?' The notion seemed absurd, as if she had given her daughter the phone number of a supermarket she was nipping out to do a bit of shopping in, or a train she was catching to town.

'Yeah,' said Helen, sounding weary and tense and fed up. 'You said it was going to be your home from now on. You were talking about finally having a future and not just a past.'

'I was?'

'Listen, Mum, I've got a bit of a problem. I need to go away for a while.'

'Away?'

'All this media attention now that our family is rich – it's really getting me down. The newspapers keep calling me the Sperome Heiress; I used to be just an anonymous human being! The media all know where I live because of Fergus – they see the chauffeur driving him to school.'

'So?' Suffering the slings and arrows of outrageously good fortune had made Lindy unsympathetic: she herself had had to adapt to the new balance of energies in her life and find a way forward; other people should do the same thing.

'All these journalists . . .' lamented Helen. 'They want to know what I think of my father brawling with other members of the Sperome Corporation and buying a Monet when he can't pronounce "Monet" and getting arrested for drunk driving. They keep asking me if I know where Willie Spink has disappeared to, and . . . and how I feel about your separation from Dad. They hang around my house in . . . *clusters*, Mum, shouting through the doors and windows. I can't take anymore. I'm leaving Fergus with Dad, and going to Tunisia.'

'Tunisia? What about me?'

'Well, I'd rather you didn't come, Mum. The media—'

'No, I mean . . .' Lindy breathed deeply. What *did* she mean? 'How can you leave your little boy in the care of a man like your father?'

'Cut the crap, Mum. Dad loves Fergus. He needs someone to care for. He's just a lonely guy in his fifties who's lost all his old friends and has got far too much money. A bit of grandparenting will do him the world of good.'

'I . . . So when are you leaving?'

'It's happened already, Mum,' said Helen, breathing very deeply herself. 'I'm ringing from the airport. Fergus is at home.'

'Whose home?'

Lindy Jerome's only begotten child started crying then, her quavering voice vibrating the fibres of the telephone connection.

'I don't *know* whose home it is anymore,' she wailed. 'Are you and Dad divorced yet?'

When the telephone receiver was nestled back in its plastic depression, Lindy noticed that the house had grown rather chilly. She knew Bryan's central heating was Sperome-assisted (almost everybody's was), but she didn't know how or where to switch it on. Shivering in her bathrobe, she remembered the hot bath she and Bryan had shared last night, and how good it had felt. Only momentarily hesitating over her bearings to the bathroom, she found her way back to the now frothless tubful of adulterated water and dabbled her fingers in it experimentally.

It was still pretty hot, though: Bryan didn't spare the Sperome.

[A]

Exactly six months later still, Ed and Lindy Jerome were, at most, half a dozen thrusts away from simultaneous orgasm when the bedside telephone rang.

'Let it ring,' moaned Ed. 'It'll be Helen, with another change of plan about tomorrow.'

'No, no!' panted his wife. 'I know who it is. I just know it!'

She stretched one arm out as far as she could without leaving Ed, and flipped the telephone receiver on to the pillow where she could grab hold of it.

'H – hello?' she said.

'Hello! It's Willie Spink!' was the reply.

'Willie!' squealed Lindy. 'Where *are* you?'

Willie had been missing for the best part of a year. Newspaper articles liked to describe him as the first casualty of his invention's sensational success, and this was true enough. As soon as his gossip cell rocketed through the stock-market roof, his laboratory had been besieged by journalists of all kinds. Willie had lost all ability to concentrate on his research, quarrelled furiously with Ed, wept unconsolably on Lindy's shoulder, and disappeared in a cloud of media speculation.

Since then, the fortunes of Sperome had continued to rise, reached a peak, and then slipped into a dizzying decline.

When first abandoned by his partner, Ed had sought expert legal advice, the inevitable result of which was that Sperome became a limited company of which Ed, through the alchemy of boardroom manoeuvring, was soon not even the majority shareholder. After a while, the majority shareholders signed a deal with the electricity companies, which, under cover of a glossy publicity campaign about a glorious new era of customer service, effectively raised the cost of Sperome-assisted heating by 500 per cent.

Worse still, the company's overtures to the food industry provoked disaster when a leading fast-food chain, seeking an overheads edge on its competitors, decided to use Sperome in its coffee and ice cream. Almost immediately, customers were checking in to hospitals complaining that the piping hot coffee they'd sipped hours ago was still piping away in their tender stomachs now, or that a hastily swallowed mouthful of thick-shake had turned their innards to ice. Doctors prescribed drinking warm or cold water in sufficient quantities to dilute the Sperome; a simple, obvious and wholly effective remedy which nevertheless eluded the imagination of most people. Inexorably, litigation followed, with the earliest cases being sniggered out of court, but then finally an elderly woman in Duluth, Minnesota, got medical opinion to corroborate her claim that she had oesophageal incompetence brought on by the Sperome additive in her banana sundae, and after that the compensation jamboree was on. Universities which had been injecting rats with massive doses of Sperome for many months finally managed to rush some cancers through, and this story, more than any other, spread across the media like a nuclear reaction.

Sperome virtually vanished from the market, and the Jerome family disappeared from the newspapers, except in sober fine-print analyses in the financial pages. There was no more talk of the Sperome Heiress, or headlines like 'Bags of Monet' and 'Ed sees red!'.

Of course, having already been pushed to the periphery of his company, Ed was not as severely affected by its collapse as he might have been. Even more felicitously, a private deal he'd made with a livestock firm, a sort of experimental 'gentlemen's agreement' before the gossip cell was even patented as Sperome, had remained binding despite all the brouhaha, providing Ed's family with a steady income based on temperature-controlled bull semen.

An acceptable version of normality had returned; now, so had Willie Spink.

'I'm back in my old place,' he enthused over the phone. 'There's no media people here at all now.'

'Oh, Willie, good for you!' Lindy was almost crying.

'There's some squatters here, though,' elaborated Willie. 'Two girls, a young man and . . . somebody I'm not too sure of. But we've come to an arrangement. I don't tell anybody about them, and they don't tell anybody about me.'

'Good for them!' sobbed Lindy as Ed wrestled her for the phone.

'How's little Fergus?'

'He's adorable, walking, talking – learning to swim, even!

He lived with me and Ed for a while, but now he's back with Helen and her new man, in Tunisia. Except they're visiting us tomorrow.'

'Wonderful,' chirped Willie. 'I might come. Only I'm working on something: a new synthesis. Plant tissue grown on the same principles as yoghurt from a culture. My lodgers gave me the idea. But there's something I need to check with Ed.'

'Ed?'

'He knows about these things.'

Ed, cheek to cheek with Lindy, had heard everything, and wrenched the receiver from her grasp.

'Willie?'

'Ed? Is that you?'

'Yes,' said Ed hoarsely.

'Ed? Is cannabis legal yet?'

'No, Willie.'

'Oh.' There was a pause. 'Oh, well then, let me know when it is. Bye!'

The bedroom was quiet and dark, and tropically balmy despite the sleety weather outside. The kitchen clock chimed a muffled midnight, and Ed, almost as a reflex action, reached behind the bedhead and squeezed the little rubber thingummy to deliver another drop of Sperome to the central heating. When he turned again, his wife hadn't moved.

'Is it too late to get back to where we were?' he asked.

For answer, Lindy took his arms and wrapped them around her naked shoulders, to show him she was still warm.

Accountability

GROWING OUT of her childhood on the farm that wasn't a farm anymore, Margo was never allowed to forget the wolf at the door. By the age of three she'd already known that money didn't grow on trees, and her father filled her in on the rest as soon as her little mind was big enough to hold it: no detail too dull or too disheartening.

By the age of thirteen, Margo was painfully aware that everything in her life depended on three fortnightly arrivals of money from the Government: an invalid pension for her grandmother, a single-parent allowance for her father, Frank, and an unemployment benefit, also for Frank. Margo wasn't owed any money by the Government, it seemed. To make up for this, she worked, doing just about everything that still needed doing on the farm which wasn't a farm anymore. Schooling was out of the question, because her grandmother developed pressure sores if she wasn't repositioned in the bed at least every two hours, and because her father couldn't be expected to go eight hours without a meal.

She'd always called her father 'Dad', but lately he preferred 'Frank' because he said she wasn't his, and she was doing her best to change. Frank described Margo's mother as a pig-faced slut who was better off dead, and said if he ever met the black bastard responsible for Margo, he'd kill him. 'There's no way it was me,' he argued. 'No way. I was always ultra-careful with the birth control. This world can't afford children. Children are a bottomless pit.' By this he meant, of course, that children cost a lot of money – Margo understood that – but she'd heard the phrase from such a young age that it had a powerfully literal sense for her: sometimes in her sleep, she really did imagine herself to be a bottomless pit, feeling nothing but the occasional clod of earth falling into her, and the odd gush of rain.

Awake, she wondered how her father – Frank – could be so sure her sire was a black fellow. Did he have someone particular in mind? Margo never saw any Aborigines: they just didn't seem to live anywhere near Milwullah, despite its very Aboriginal-sounding name. But Milwullah wasn't outback anymore: the city had spread out so much it had roped Milwullah in, making it a kind of outer outer suburb. The Post Office even had a computer in it (so Frank said, anyway; Margo had never been there), there was a Chinese take-away next to the pub (Frank had brought some of its food home one Christmas when she'd crushed a finger and couldn't cook; at $7.95 for a small plastic tub of it she had better not complain) and the grain-feed merchant had half his shop given over to video hire (no VCRs in Frank DeVoort's house, thanks very much). None of this was anything like the outback Margo read about in the *Australasian Post*.

Maybe an Aborigine had visited once long ago, and her mother had fallen in love with him, if only for a few minutes. It was hard to imagine, though. Margo looked at herself in the mirror, and couldn't help observing that even at her most tanned, she was still, well, *white* – pale, even. Maybe it was her shape that had given Frank the idea: big head, flat nose, big chest, pot belly, long thin arms and legs. But there again, the evidence wasn't conclusive. She had been thrown flat on the floor once, for doing things wrong when she was a toddler; her broken nose might have lost some of its natural shape then.

And as for the round belly, well, that was Frank's doing. Frank's.

Despite her lack of formal schooling, Margo knew a lot about a great many things, including the facts of life. Her father – Frank – had provided for her, by giving her an almost complete set of *How and Why Wonder Books*. Not that he'd handed over the whole lot all at once, no: they lived under his bed in a big pile, waiting for birthdays, Christmases and other celebrations, when he would fetch one out and present it to her. Of course, she knew how many he had left, because she'd lain on the floor and peeked under his bed many times, counting them; she even knew some of the as-yet-ungiven titles (only *some*, though: she was too terrified to disturb the pile). And she knew for sure that her father didn't hand them out at random from the top, that he must have some kind of unguessable selection criteria, because she'd received *Comets and Meteors* only a few weeks after noting its position near the bottom of the stack, whereas *Coins and Currency*, which had been topmost then, wasn't given to her until three years later. Half the fun was the fervent hoping for a particular volume, an experiment of sorts to see if she could beam messages at her father to influence him in this one small way.

As for the *How and Why Wonder Books* she'd already been given, she'd read them so many times that they were committed to memory. She could have recited them in front of a class at school, if she'd had a school to go to. But a woman from the government had come to see her father – Frank – about school once (Margo had to keep out of sight) and afterwards Frank said that there was no school around here for girls with Aboriginal blood. It was a State regulation, he said.

Nanna used to be a great help with Margo's education, because she answered questions not covered by the books. Over the years, however, Nanna had developed some sort of gum disease, related probably to the cancer, and stopped wearing her teeth. Understanding her had become difficult then, and she'd started speaking softer and softer, and after a while preferred just to point or roll her eyes.

Television wasn't much of a teacher for Margo, because it was never hers to choose. Her father didn't allow her in the room while he was watching it, and when he'd finished watching it Margo would carry the still-warm machine carefully into Nanna's bedroom and set it up there for the night. By a process of elimination Margo would find the pleasantest most inoffensive programme, preferably a very old American movie or a documentary about animals, and curl up to sleep on the flaccid old bean-bag in the corner. It was ideal, this bean-bag, because it was exactly uncomfortable enough to wake her up every two hours, and then she could turn Nanna over, and reposition the television, too.

Another lucky thing was that her father didn't mind the TV being on all night: he had a newspaper clipping pinned up on the kitchen wall which rated electrical appliances according to how much power they used up, and televisions were among the least costly. Mind you, if he'd never found that article, he might not have got angry about the electric fan, and instead of it being exiled to the toolshed it might still have been in the house, helping to make Nanna more comfortable in midsummer.

There wasn't a *How and Why Wonder Book of Cooking*, but Margo soaked the labels off soup tins and sauce bottles and cut the little recipes out for filing in a little notebook called 'FOOD'. Pies and pasties were her speciality, because the pastry was cheap and could be folded around just about any old thing, and the cooking time was so short. (At 65c an hour for oven use, speed was essential, at least if her father was watching.) How grateful she was that her father had agreed to buy a meat-tenderiser at her request: before that, she had always gone limp with despair every Saturday afternoon when he'd come home with the week's shopping, because the meat he bought was always the kind that needed stewing or baking for hours, and Frank would not allow that. Now she pounded it, pounded it to mince if need be, and what couldn't pass for steak she was able to use up in pies.

The washing machine was dumped in the toolshed too (48c an hour), so a lot of Margo's day was spent at the laundry sink, scrubbing away at Nanna's bed-linen. Her father's overalls got very dirty, too, even though there were no more animals on the farm. There was a ute that Frank was always trying to repair, which despite being dead for years was still juicy with grease, and then there were the fences to maintain, despite the fact that there was nothing and no one escaping or intruding.

Toilet paper was a dangerous topic of conversation: at 52c a roll it must not be wasted on old women who could no longer discipline their bodily functions. Margo's conscience would not allow her to take more than her fair share: that would be stealing. Instead, she developed a mathematically exact system of exchange, whereby she would use strips of newspaper on herself whenever she went to the toilet, and then tear off the equivalent amount of toilet paper for Nanna.

Once, in a newspaper she was about to tear into strips, Margo had read about nursing homes, and how well looked after old people could be. She had dared raise the subject with her father – with Frank. Frank had become very angry. But afterwards, he spoke with a quiet and reasonable intensity.

'As long as she stays here with us, with things just the way they are, she'll be all right,' he said. 'Do you think the State would buy her all these pills, every day of the week?' (Panadeine Forte, $5.95 for twelve, one every eight hours, so $1.48 a day, $10.36 a week.)

'She's old and useless,' Frank pointed out. 'She doesn't work anymore. The State can't afford to keep her alive the way we do. They'd put her in a hospital, give her a big injection of morphine and then she'd be off their hands. The morgue, Margo – you know what a morgue is?'

Margo shook her head, grateful in advance for the rare gift of knowledge from him.

'It's where they take dead people from hospitals. They put them in fridges with no clothes on, just a tag around the ankle. If nobody comes to collect them after twenty-four hours, they get used for pet food.'

Margo's earnest struggle to come to terms with yet another example of how money made the world go round must have been misinterpreted by Frank, because he got a little angry again and said, 'You think I'm lying? You think they bury everybody that dies? Thousands of people die every day – where's the room for them all in the ground? Think about it!'

Margo thought about it. She remembered when drought had killed off the last hundred sheep, back when she was about five, back when Mum was alive. The farm was already on the skids then, and a hundred dead sheep was nothing compared to what there might have been once upon a time, but still there had been too many to bury. From her window Margo had looked out over the barren paddocks, watching the gasoline-basted sheep burn, smelling the wholesale roast mutton on the air.

Mum had died so soon after this mass immolation that Margo always associated her death with the smell of roast mutton, but perhaps that was for the best, because nowadays she almost never got to smell roast mutton or roast anything, because of the 65c an hour. The police had come and taken Mum away, and Dad had gone with them, and stayed away for four days. Then he had returned, without Mum of course, although the 'of course' was something Margo could add only with hindsight, because at five years old she hadn't understood that the mess in the bathtub meant she wouldn't be seeing her mother again. Living on Vegemite sandwiches and raspberry cordial, she had waited for her parents to return.

Early on the fifth morning, he – her father – Frank – had walked in the front door. She'd left the porch light on for him, her first mistake in this new motherless phase of her life. He had made sure she would never dare to do anything so wasteful a second time.

How and Why Wonder Books aside, it had been a fairly unhappy life for Margo after that.

But now Margo was thirteen, and her life was changed by the arrival of two more bits of printed fact, neither of them in a *How and Why Wonder Book*.

Firstly, there was the article on abortion in a toilet copy of the *Sun-Herald*, which described how, in the bad old days, many women used to die as a result of unsterile operations performed by persons with no medical qualifications. A quick check of the *How and Why Wonder Book of Medicine* confirmed the need for sterility and surgical expertise in all operations. This led Margo to the conclusion that Frank must be mistaken when he said that there was nothing to fear from the 'little operation' he was planning to perform on her soon, to get rid of the baby that was growing inside her.

She accepted without question that the baby must not be born, because Frank had made enquiries and apparently there was some reason why the State would not grant Margo a single mother's pension. (For a while there, Frank had been in favour of the baby idea, because it would mean an additional fortnightly benefit of $148. But this was not to be, so the baby must die.) The problem was, it seemed quite possible that Margo would die too, and that was out of the question, because whenever Margo was out of action even for a day due to illness, Nanna would get pressure sores, because Frank didn't bother to turn her.

So, therefore, Margo must not have the abortion Frank had planned for her. And that meant getting herself and Nanna away from Frank.

The other bit of important information was delivered by the Melbourne *Age*, on its front page, and Margo lost no time in writing away for the mailing address of NASA in the USA.

In view of the fact that she never received letters, it was just as well that Frank was never at home when the postman did his round, because when *The Age* sent her NASA's address, she would have to intercept the letter, as well as the money that NASA would send her later.

In the meantime, she had many calculations to make, in order not to offend Fate by asking too much.

Then again, money was in some ways the least of her problems. Getting Nanna to the bus stop would be very difficult. As far as Margo knew, it wasn't possible to order a taxi by mail (no telephones in Frank DeVoort's house, thanks very much), and in any case the money from NASA would probably be in the form of a cheque, which she didn't think taxi drivers would accept.

She could maybe try to drive the ute, but she wasn't sure whether the work Frank was always doing on it had affected it sufficiently to get it moving. Besides, she might have an accident and kill Nanna or herself. Of course, if they were merely injured, they would probably be taken to hospital, which would get them out of Milwullah to Albury-Wodonga probably, but then Nanna might be given that fatal injection of morphine, and besides, the ute would be traced back to Frank and he would come to get them.

There seemed no alternative to wheeling Nanna to the bus stop in a cart; at least it wasn't uphill *all* the way. The bus ride into town would cost $2.40 for the both of them, unless the driver mistakenly assumed that Margo was over sixteen, in which case he might charge $3.60, or unless the driver also insisted on Nanna producing a pension card (always in her son-in-law's safekeeping), in which case the trip would cost $4.80. Accommodation was the next hurdle, since it would take three days for the cheque to be cleared after Margo opened her bank account: three days during which she and Nanna must stay somewhere, but nowhere that Frank would think of looking for them. A flash hotel would cost $105 a night for a twin share and was less likely to be investigated by her father, but it was also less likely to accept a sighting of her cheque from NASA as a guarantee of payment. A shabby $40 hotel might have slacker regulations, but might also be Frank's first point of call, since he himself would never pay anything but the cheapest rate for accommodation.

Most likely of all would be that no hotel of any kind would take in a thirteen-year-old girl and an incapacitated old lady on credit. What was it to be, then? Sleeping on the streets? Margo couldn't accept that this would be her only option, given that she had a $20 bill to spend. (She'd found the money in a cardigan of her mother's, which she'd only recently grown big enough to wear.) After the bus trip into town, she might have as much as $17.60 left; $15.20 at the least. For that, there must be some way of avoiding the street.

At last she found the answer, again by studying the toilet newspapers: there was a cinema just outside Milwullah which showed movies about love all night long. She and Nanna could stay there, sleeping in their seats or, if that wasn't allowed, they could watch the movies, just like they did at home. There was a pawnbroker in town, too, so Mum's jewellery would surely raise enough for two nights' cinema admissions. (Margo was sure Mum wouldn't have minded this, since it was for Nanna's sake, and anyway Margo would redeem the jewellery as soon as NASA's cheque cleared.)

Once she'd withdrawn the money from the bank she would catch the coach to Albury-Wodonga ($26 for two) and then book a sleeper train to Melbourne (another $126). In the event that they arrived in Albury-Wodonga too late for the Melbourne train, they would need to spend the night (up to $105) and leave in the morning. A travelling alarm clock cost $15.95.

Nanna's nappies would need washing; a laundromat would probably wash them for $2, dry them for $1. Then again, disposable pads might be easier to organise, perhaps even cheaper; she would have to check how much disposable pads cost. Certainly on the train there would be no laundromats: she would either have to buy a bucket and some Napi-San ($4.99 + $3.95) or take enough nappies with her to be able to throw some of them away.

Food was a tricky proposition, as Nanna could no longer tolerate many things. Rice cream (85c per tin) and baby food (99c each for the small ones) seemed the safest bet, with baked beans ($69c) being perfectly adequate for Margo. The opening of the tins would require a can-opener, and she didn't know how much those cost, but it surely wouldn't be more than $5. For a moment only, she considered taking the one from home, but this was unjustifiable, since her father couldn't cook and would have no choice but to open a can of something when he got hungry.

In Melbourne she would need to get a taxi to the nearest hotel, and in city traffic this might be expensive: $10, even. But there was no way around it, because she would be dependent on the driver to know where a hotel was and to take them directly there. Accommodation might be as much as $120 a night, and there was no guarantee that Margot would be able to find a flat to rent that was ready to be moved into the next day. If she was unlucky (it was perhaps best to assume she was unlucky) she might have to wait a whole week, going through $840 in the meantime. But then once Nanna was settled in the hotel, Margo would have an opportunity to explore the city and find a cheaper one; they couldn't *all* be $120 a night, surely. Margo knew there were flats, even small houses, to be had for $130 a week.

Once she and Nanna had a home, Margo could enrol in a correspondence course and learn a trade. She'd decided, after some heart-searching, that she couldn't ask NASA to pay for her education on top of everything else. Their cheque would have to cover the costs of everything up to and including the first month in Melbourne. By then, Margo would simply have to have found herself some sort of job, preferably something like delivery work or door-to-door sales which would allow her to stop off home at regular intervals to turn Nanna.

So many things she would need to do in that first month! A refrigerator ($149, reconditioned, if she was lucky, with perhaps $30 delivery on top of that), a television ($95 for a little black-and-white one, or rental for $9 a month), pots, pans, crockery, cutlery (say $40 the lot, second-hand).

And then, if the *How and Why Wonder Book of the Human Body* was to be believed, after nine months Margo would be too fat to move, and she'd most likely have to go into hospital to have her baby. But that was far into the future: her life would be unrecognisable by then.

The expenses she would ask NASA's cheque to cover, according to her most careful calculations, came to $2376 (she resisted the temptation to allow for 'unforeseen expenses' and round the figure off to $2400). NASA would be less suspicious of her if she could give an exact figure justified by an itemised list.

NASA's mailing address was quick to arrive, which was just as well, since Frank had made her strip naked again yesterday evening, and pronounced that the operation would have to be very soon.

Margo wrote her letter as soon as she had somewhere to send it. On a fresh sheet of pure white paper (extravagant, but she could not risk her message being ignored) she neatly printed:

Dear NASA officials,
I inclose the article about you in the Melbourne Age. Disposing of human waste is very important, especially in Space, I am sure. Many people may not understand how important it is, and thats why they get angry at how much it costs. Please try to not be too hurt by their critisism.

However, I believe I have the solution to your problem. I have done a lot of study in the field of Comets and Meteors, which perhaps you havent, being experts in Rocketry. Really it is very simple. Meteors mostly burn up before they get anywhere near the Earth. Even if they are enormous to begin with, the friction created by the speed at which they travel vapourises them in the outer atmosphere.

What has this got to do with your problem? I will tell you. You simply make some valved openings in the hull of your space shuttle, for the astronauts to do their number 1's and number 2's in. The vacuum outside sucks the waste into a net. When the net is full, it is attached to the craft the astronauts use when they are returning to Earth.

All the waste simply burns up during re-entry, like a soft meteor.

I know this idea would save you millions of dollars, but I am not asking you for millions of dollars. I am asking for $2376 ($1661.92 American) which I need desparately for my grandmother who is very sick with cancer, and myself who am in danger.

An itemised list of expenses is attached, and the address for you to send the money. Please hurry, and best wishes with the space programme and expanding the frontiers of human knowledge,

Sincerely,

Margo DeVoort.

O D D S P O T

NASA officials have been blasted for allowing the cost of a new space shuttle toilet to blow out to $A23 million.

Pidgin American

KATARZYNA was doing London.

By night, she sampled dance clubs and slept with strange men; by day, she waitressed at her uncle's restaurant; during spare hours and weekends she combed flea markets and charity shops for cheap T-shirts. White ones mostly, though pale grey, bright yellow and fluorescent green were acceptable too.

'What, more T-shirts?' her uncle challenged her in Polish when she rolled up to work at the Café Kraków.

'I want to stock up,' responded Katarzyna in the same language. 'Once I'm back in Poland...' She shrugged and mimed fruitless searching.

'You trying to tell me there's no T-shirts in Poland?'

Her uncle had left Poland in 1980, and such letters as he still received from disapproving relatives had degenerated lately into lists of things you could buy in the shops of Poznań.

Katarzyna tossed one of her new T-shirts into the air and deftly penetrated the sleeve-holes in free-fall with her sharp little hands.

'The ones in Poland have all got stupid messages on them,' she complained, muffled as she pulled the big white garment over her head, over her waitress's uniform. 'You know: "San Tropez", "Ultra Sport", pictures of Ninja Turtles, "I'm Too Sexy For My Shirt" – junk from five, ten years ago. Plain ones are hard to get. Especially for 95p each.' She pulled at the hem of the T-shirt like a frock, and did a mock curtsy. 'What do you think?'

'Are you crazy? Two of you could fit into that.'

'Sloppy is fashion, Uncle. You should see the T-shirts they sell in the trendy shops. Large and X-Large, that's all they stock.'

'Craziness. Your father could have sewn you a dress out of that T-shirt.'

'I'll grow into it, Uncle, I promise. I'll become one of those enormous old hens.'

'Is there anybody there?' called a testy female voice from inside the restaurant.

'It's that old whore Halina Kozłowska,' muttered Katarzyna's uncle. 'Time to get moving, Kasia.' He made a purposeful gesture towards the stove, and Kasia pulled her T-shirt off again. But before walking out into the restaurant she had to adjust her disordered hair in the oven window, because Mrs Kozłowska was as potent a bratwurst of Polish bitch juice as nature ever cooked up.

In fact, when you're dead, thought Katarzyna as she hurried out to take the old woman's order, *they'll make stock cubes of the stuff from your ashes.*

Then she thought, *I must write that down*. She was always writing her thoughts and impressions down, getting ready to be the latest literary sensation from Eastern Europe, her face smouldering on a million paperbacks.

'Well hell-*oh* there sweet child. You see: I hadn't given up hope!'

'Mm?' responded Kasia, ready to write on her order pad. In fact, she was writing already, because Mrs Kozłowska always ordered the same thing. A week from now, after

Katarzyna was already back in Poland, her uncle would find
a slip of notepaper lying around the kitchen listing:

HAM+GHERK SW
COFF
POP SEED CAKE
BITCH JUICE BRATWURST/ASHES/STOCK CUBES

'Very funny,' he would frown to himself before binning it.

Next day, a Saturday, Katarzyna fronted up to the Virgin
Megastore and asked who was the Next Big Thing.

'I'm from Poland,' she explained with a much thicker
accent than she authentically had. 'The record shops there,
it is only Phil Collins and Dire Straits.'

As expected, she came away from the Virgin Megastore
(and HMV and Our Price and Reckless and Sister Ray and
Vinyl Experience) with armfuls of promotional material –
posters, postcards, stickers, flyers, display sleeves – without
actually having to buy anything: she'd paid with her exotic
accent, her smile, her musical refugee status. The young men
behind the high counters, so blasé to everyone else, smiled
down on her and her cleavage, and leaned forward to rescue
her from Phil Collins and Dire Straits. A girl so beautiful
must not be condemned to ignorance of the forbidden fruit
of novelty; she must experience it now, in these few precious
months before it was discovered by Woolworths, overmark-
eted and stale.

'What's all this junk?' Kasia's uncle wanted to know.

'It's free, Uncle,' she shrugged.

'Nothing's free,' the old man said. 'Here or anywhere. I've
learned that much.'

Katarzyna tied on her apron, disinclined to argue. Her air
fare from Warsaw to London had been paid by her uncle: in

return, she had this apron to tie on and this job to do. The only pity was that she had no uncles in America, because that was the real centre of the world, the control centre. She would have to end up there some day, not because it was so wonderfully different from the places she knew, but because the places she knew were insufficiently different from it.

Out in the restaurant, the expatriate Poles flipped through Polish magazines, then tossed them back on the pile. The topmost one, Kasia had noticed, was always the one which had a colour picture of the crazed-looking bimbo who was accusing the President of the USA of sexual harassment. It bore the legend 'CLINTON – WINNY ALBO NIEWINNY?'

America was the only authentic country in the world now; all the others were copies and derivatives. Maybe somewhere there existed a country that was still proudly and distinctly itself, but it was probably hidden in a volcanic valley some-where behind Lapland and populated by starving halfwits wearing sealskin loincloths. Everywhere else was either an American colony or a crude imitation. As a young teenager she'd read, in Polish, Arthur C. Clarke's novel *2001: A Space Odyssey*. At the end of the story, the astronaut ends up in an alien spacecraft furnished with what seem to be all the comforts of home, including a refrigerator full of packaged food. On closer inspection, this food proves to be fake, an array of 3-D approximations reproduced as if from blurry television images. That's what the whole world was like now: a shoddy facsimile of the USA. A few years ago in Eastern Europe Levi's jeans had been unavailable, and instead they'd had denim pants (farmboy pyjamas, Kasia called them) with all sorts of labels and slogans sewn on to them – on the pockets, on the butt, on the knees – misspelled American mottos or just plain nonsense – anything to pledge allegiance to the empire of brand names. You didn't see those pants so much now. Levi's had become available in Eastern Europe at last: she could buy a pair in Warsaw for the same price her great-grandfather might have bought his linen factory for. Or maybe a bit less, if she had American dollars.

'Well, I say the son of a whore did it,' one of the regulars was saying in Polish. 'I just hope they make him show his dick in court, the dirty fucker.'

'Shut up, Andrzej.' These two obese, tufty-browed old farts came to the Café Kraków almost every day. They were superannuated Silesian oilworkers who had not yet reached that stage of alcoholism where food is unimportant.

'Hey, there's that little whore again – look at the tits on her!'

'Shut up and look at the menu, Andrzej. She's coming over to take our order.'

'My order is pretty fucking simple, I can tell you. Just bend over . . .'

Katarzyna had learned that there was no point hanging around near the desserts waiting for them to run out of gas. They could keep this up for half an hour, then complain about the bad service.

'So, gentlemen, have you decided?'

'Yes, young lady, we have. Clinton should show his dick to the world, and then they should send the fucker to the electric chair.'

'So that's your order, hm?' deadpanned Kasia. 'Fried Clinton?'

The Silesians wilted. Wit from a female always nonplussed them.

'Soup and a roll, please,' coughed Andrzej.

'Same for me,' said his companion.

'Uh-humm,' murmured Kasia as she scribbled. She'd already written down their order, which was always the same. Now she was writing, *Barbered gorillas, buttoning tufts of black fur into bulging shirts.*

Back in the kitchen, her uncle had been examining the promotional material Kasia had blagged from the music stores.

'These people look like escapees from a mental institution.'

'I know. But I've made up my mind not to say bad things about your customers. Two soups.'

'Very funny. I was talking about these pop musicians here. They're evil-looking.'

'That's the image they want, Uncle. They want to look mean, like in an American crime movie. They're probably very nice boys really.'

'These fellows look like the Mafia. I'd rather have Phil Collins.'

'Really, Uncle?' said Kasia evenly, tossing a couple of minuscule foils of butter into the wicker bread-basket.

'Yes, that Phil Collins is all right. Are you sure he's not Polish? He looks Polish to me.'

'He's from London, I think,' said Kasia, frowning as she shifted the typically brim-full soup bowls around on her tray, preparing for take-off. 'He lives in America now.'

'Funny . . . Go to Łódź, and every third guy looks like Phil Collins, right down to the hair.'

'Is that why you like him?' smirked Kasia, turning, raising her eyebrows to encompass her uncle's bald forehead.

'No, I think he's got talent.' Startlingly, her uncle began to sing in heavily accented English, imitating Phil Collins's antiseptic whine, complete with ersatz American vowels. ' "One more night, give me just one more night" . . . "Another day in Paradise . . ." There's a tune to his songs, he's not like these long-haired screamers.'

'Obviously not.'

'He's rich, too,' Kasia's uncle persevered, 'but I read in one of those magazines out there that he still plays darts in his local pub. Also he runs all these businesses – trout farms and God knows what else – at a huge loss, just because he enjoys it.'

'Well, Uncle, maybe you can do the same with this restaurant.'

'Very funny.'

But one evening, Kasia's uncle confessed to her that his restaurant was not doing so well. He wasn't in dire straits yet, but every year he slipped closer. Kasia's mother, her uncle's sister, had already told her this, of course.

'The old Poles are dying off,' he sighed. 'The young ones are eating fast food, or they've gone back to Poland to make a killing. The old Poles quarrel with one another; one starts avoiding my restaurant just in case "that scumbag" is there again, and finally "that scumbag" stops coming too, because he misses his friend. That's how I lose them, mostly. That, and death.'

Awkward in the face of her uncle's uncharacteristic gloom, Katarzyna left the kitchen and fiddled with table napkins and dried bouquets.

'Look at the arse on that little whore,' muttered Andrzej to his familiar.

'Put your dick away and eat.'

After work that night, Kasia decided not to go to a dance club; she was tired and would probably accept more Ecstasy than was good for her. Also, she didn't want sex tonight, particularly with some shaven-haired big-eared lunatic with pop-eyes.

Instead, she went to a live gig at one of the many venues her friends in Warsaw venerated like shrines of pilgrimage. She caught a tube to Shepherd's Bush, where there were no shepherds and no bushes: only a foreigner can thoroughly appreciate how much of its heritage a country has lost. No saints or woods in St John's Wood, no knights or bridges in Knightsbridge, no black friars in Blackfriars.

England's Englishness was tourist brochure stuff, history book stuff, like the fairytale palaces of Kraków surrendering to acid rain and Kodak flashes, like Queen Anna Jagiellonka, buried ever deeper by wars and ideology. The English Queen was only good for putting on tea-towels and coffee mugs for Americans to take home, and all those castles were just crumbling to rubble, waiting to be used as backdrops in Hollywood movies about Robin Hood. Kasia had seen Hollywood's latest Robin Hood movie in Warsaw. Robin of Sherwood was played by New Yorker Kevin Costner, and he'd brought his own black sidekick to medieval England, just to give all the black moviegoers back home somebody to root for. If that wasn't colonisation, what was?

The band she'd come to see tonight was Spiritualized. They were, according to the Virgin Megastore, one of the Next Big Things; the tardiness with which the music papers reached Poland would ensure that by the time Jan, Krzys, Alicja and her other friends read the feature articles on Spiritualized in the *NME* and *Melody Maker*, Kasia would be on hand to describe having seen them play. She'd better reread the articles herself first, though, to help her remember.

In the magazine articles, the godly Kraftwerk were invoked as influences, the Balanescu Quartet, My Bloody Valentine, ancient Sufi music, Terry Riley. In the confines of the club, Spiritualized were none of these things, of course. The sounds they made, hosed at high volume through an oversized PA, achieved the shimmering din of anonymity. Labouring intently at their guitars and keyboards, they projected beautiful and intricate arcs into an Elysian field of their own imagination, while all around them the distorted thicket of decibels walled them in, as private inside there as prisoners in an exercise yard. Kasia had been to gigs in

Germany, in Hungary, in Poland of course: all different flavours of groups, all sounding much like this: Sisyphean chord progressions never scaling the cacophonous haze, a ringing in the ears, a turgid rumble of bass and drunk people braying, 'Mind my drink!' 'D'you want another drink?' 'Is the bar crowded?' 'Fuck, I've spilt it!' 'No, it's all right, I'm just tired': the language of rock'n'roll.

Spiritualized T-shirts had been on sale before the band started playing. Kasia hadn't even looked at them: she wasn't going to pay £14.99. Even £2 for a drink was a bit much: she paid it just once, before attracting a guy to buy the rest for her.

She'd been through this *pas de deux* many times before, in Germany, in Hungary, in Poland, at other gigs in London: the stumbling ballet of nightclub courtship. The ritual was played out in semi-darkness, in a claustrophobic bunker toxic with cigarette smoke, alcohol and body odour. Why here rather than somewhere airy and open? Because here all communication must be shouted straight into the ear-hole, in hoarse abbreviated sentences. A truce on all nuances, then; an amnesty on any finer expectations; the struggle was to be merely heard rather than understood.

'Poland!' she yelled into his ear, giving his Concorde nose a clear flight path to her luminous bosom.

'Holland!' he confirmed, nodding semaphorically.

'Poland!' she yelled again.

'Gotcha! Gotcha!'

His name was something she would not remember a week from now, and he lived in a hotel called the Delta. Katarzyna had thought that in England only wealthy people or tourists lived in hotels, but when she arrived at the Delta with her man, she found that there was room for the poor as well. Not much room, though: her man lived with five other men in a rabbit hutch five floors up, an attic used not for stashing broken sinks, toilet cisterns and other dubious prostheses, but for superfluous humans.

'Kasia, this is Dougie, Tim.'

'Pull up a piece of floor, babe!' A crewcut white man and a fuzz-headed black man raised beer cans in greeting.

The floor was indeed the only place to sit, as the bunk beds claimed most of the room, three squat stacks of old wood and bedding like monstrous oblong Big Macs. A chest of drawers drooling socks and shirtsleeves claimed much of what was left; on top of it a portable CD player rattled out the Manic Street Preachers and Nirvana. Dougie and Tim were hunched in a litter of beer cans and cigarette butts, their eyes plexiglassy under sweaty brows. Kasia's man began to explain that Pete, the occupant of the bunk nearest the washbasinette, was missing, whereabouts unknown; Dougie explained more succinctly: 'He's a fucking nutter!' The other two were out buying more beer and had better not drink it all before coming back, the cunts.

Katarzyna decided she would not be sleeping here tonight after all, and gave her man a casual, reassuring hug around his midriff, to let him know that he could relax, sit down, open a beer for her. She wasn't anxious about her safety: the smell of impotence was so pungent here that it cut right through the miasma of alcohol, smoke and unwashed T-shirts.

'Where are *you* from, Tim?' she enquired, settling her back into the bony sofa of her man's parted thighs.

'Papua New Guinea,' the black man grinned. 'You?'

'Poland.' He looked a bit confused, so she added, 'Home of Solidarity, you know?'

'You speak Poland language?'

'Sure. Of course.'

'Speak us some Poland language, babe.'

'*Ja rozmawiam po Polsku i ty mnie nie rozumisz.*'

'Far out.'

'How about some Papua New Guinea language?'

'I speak only English. English and Pidgin. Pidgin's not a language. You know Pidgin?'

'Who says it's not a language?'

'Everybody knows that. Pidgin's just shit English, know what I mean? It's imitation English but . . . just shit. *Bipo mi kam singaut na yu no i stap. Yu go we?*'

'Sounds like a different language to me.'

'Bull-shit, bu-u-ull-shit! *Bepo* – that's "before", right? *Mi kam* – "me come", right? You see what's goin' on? English is the real thing. Anyone thinks I'm better off in fuckin' New Guinea needs their fuckin' head read. This is the place for me. Right, Dougie?'

'Right, Tim.'

The other two men arrived with the beer reinforcements. They had been delayed by one of them falling victim to a mysterious exhaustion which made him attempt sleep on every public bench and shop doorstep. He now crawled into his bunk, pleading for the music and the light to be switched off.

'Fuck you, man!' jeered Dougie. 'I have to put up with your fucking snoring *all* fucking night, *every* fucking night, right? So you can put up with my fucking music, right?'

These men had been living with each other in this toiletless toilet of a room for two years. They were the guinea pigs of endless unemployment, subsisting half insane in their vertiginous pen.

Kasia and her man were almost horizontal now, their heads propped up on pillows dragged off one of the beds. His arms were around her breasts, from behind, loosely. His wrists pressed vaguely down on her nipples through the fabric of her top; he lacked the courage to use his hands, except to open cans of beer for her and light cigarettes.

'You shouldn't be drinking,' he crooned teasingly. 'You're still a baby.'

'Yes, a very big baby,' she teased back, stretching against him. 'One and a half metres.'

He pressed his face momentarily into her hair, with no noise of a kiss, then tipped his head back and let the alcohol drain into his palpitating throat. Kasia turned and looked up at him indulgently, maternally almost. Her own country was a morass of drunken male despair; she was used to it. She realised now that it must be the same the world over: the nominal countries demarcated so distinctly on maps were in fact covered over by an ocean of alcoholic male despair. It was Kasia's mission to sail on that ocean, keeping her feet dry and her eyes open for every little Ararat.

I must write that down, she thought.

'You got a pen?' she asked her man.

'No,' he said. Kasia looked around the room from where she lay, but didn't really expect to see a pen. Apart from anything else, the pall of smoke could hardly have been thicker if some over-zealous militiaman had thrown tear gas into the room. It was even difficult to make out if the life-size *Baywatch* poster of a topless Pamela Anderson was misty by itself or through poor visibility. Kasia blinked and squinted at the elusive nipples.

Dougie asked: 'You here on holiday or what?'

'I'm working in my uncle's restaurant. The last waitress he had, quit very suddenly.'

'How come?'

'It was sexual . . . sexual ha – harassment?'

'Your uncle a sleazebag?'

'Maybe. I didn't ask him. I think it was the customers. I don't know.'

Her man was sort of touching her now, the alcohol having calibrated him to that magic notch just short of comatose sleep where he had the confidence to cup his palms over her breasts. She rubbed her head gently against his neck.

'I've got some applications in,' Dougie was saying. 'I'm on the shortlist in a couple places.'

'Jesus Christ, please, can you turn the fuckin' lights out and let me sleep!' came the voice from inside the layers of Big Mac.

'You got to be super-mobile these days,' Dougie elaborated, 'for the top jobs. If they can smell on you that you got anything holding you back, they don't wanna know. You gotta be prepared to live inside a car with a mobile phone, sleep where they put you. That's why I'm biding my time in temporary accommodation like this. I've got this girl that wants to settle down with me, fucking beautiful girl, but short on brains, you know? She works part time in a What Everyone Wants store. She don't understand you need more than that to make it in this world . . .'

The caresses of Katarzyna's man seemed to come from far away, remote control commands which lost strength and clarity as they travelled through a million miles of alcoholic space. *We bring you greetings from the planet Cygnus*, his fingers seemed to be saying as they fumbled a purchase on the damp hillocks of her bosom. And yet, for all that, it was nice to get some greetings from a distant planet.

All he wanted from her was sex. His clubfooted inability to vault over the language barrier and his typically British fear of deep waters rendered him harmless compared to her friends in Poland, who all wanted much, much more from her than mere sex, and had ways of punishing her for not surrendering it. She was used to feeling her soul under scrutiny from all angles; boys intent on disclosing the meaning of human existence snapped her back to attention if she let her eyes drop momentarily; girls did the same, while also taking note of that extra centimetre of fat on her thighs, those dark shadows under her eyes, that tense exchange she'd just had behind closed doors. Friendships poked around for the vein in her heart, trying to find a way in so they could fix her up – infusion, exfusion, transfusion. No one could resist the urge to tamper. This English guy just wanted to fall asleep next to her, or on top of her. Nothing could be simpler.

One of the men who had gone out for more beer was asking her questions, trying to verify his conviction that capitalism had turned Poland into as bad a place as England. He meant the divide between the haves and the have-nots: like many Western foreigners, he was getting a bit nostalgic about communism, a system he'd never known.

'Yes, things are bad in Poland now, if you're not very rich,' agreed Kasia. She was sleepy: a meaningless stock response was easiest. 'People stand in front of shop windows, looking at all the goods they can't afford to buy. The goods are like things in an art gallery . . . or no, like in a movie. Like a big Hollywood movie.'

'Wow: that's pure capitalism, right?'

'Right,' she yawned, but she didn't really think so. It was human nature to look in shop windows; it was the eternal way of the world to be too poor to buy what you wanted most. Pure capitalism was something which hadn't reached Poland yet, but it would soon. She could see it everywhere here. It was when people had less interest in what was available than in what might soon become available – when they hankered only after the things which would make what they already possessed obsolete and undesirable.

'At least turn the music down, for Christ's sake.'

'Tim, turn the music up for our little snoring friend.'

'I'm not your fuckin' slave, man. Leave 'im alone.'

'Aaww, don't be like that, Timmy-boy.'

'I'm not your fuckin' boy.'

'Aaww . . . have another beer.'

'There's no more fuckin' beer.'

'Well, let's go out and get some, then.'

'Too fuckin' drunk, man.'

'The shops are shut now anyway,' added the other man who had gone out before.

'Give up!' moaned the man swaddled in his bunk. 'Today is over. It's tomorrow already.'

Tim the Papuan was collapsing into a compact bundle, his head and arms slipping out of sight between his updrawn legs.

'Penis, penis,' he seemed to be mumbling, making Katarzyna snort involuntary laughter and cigarette smoke.

'He's saying, "*Pinis, pinis,*"' her man murmured in her ear. 'It's Pidgin for "finish" – the end.'

'I need to go to the toilet,' yawned Kasia. Her man shifted sluggishly beneath her; Tim was hauling himself into his bunk; Nirvana had stopped playing all by themselves; a snore started up in one corner of the room and Dougie said nothing. By consensus, then, it was bedtime.

'Down one flight of stairs,' said her man, squinting up at her as if trying to fix her features in his mind. 'There's a big trolley of linen outside, you can't miss it.'

Kasia pulled herself up on her feet by a beam of bunkbed. Her back was instantly cold, the perspiration in the fabric of her top cooled by the cross-current of air from the single window and the opening door.

'See ya.'

Downstairs, sitting on the toilet, Kasia refreshed her make-up and made sociopolitical analysis while she pissed. She could see certain differences clearly now. In Poland since long before she was born, society had been something that existed independently of its citizens. Indifferent to the needs and desires of everyone living, it lumbered ever on, carrying out the instructions of long-dead Frankensteins. No one can truly love a monster, especially a dangerous one, but they can exploit it, and this was what the Poles had always done – and still did, even now that the monster was flailing around aimlessly, its instructions revoked. They exploited it in every possible way, grey-haired dignitary and green-haired punk alike, united in disdain for the system. It didn't seem to matter what you wanted, you weren't supposed to have it, whether you were an old codger hankering after fluffy slippers, a would-be Psychick Youth dreaming of a nipple ring, or newlyweds wanting off-white curtains – only by breaking the rules could such basic treasures be had. In fact, the corruption of the Poles was so unanimous it was almost ideally communist.

What was going on in England struck her as essentially different. Society here was more like a religion to which all its citizens belonged, or at least imagined they belonged. But not a focused, evangelical religion, no . . . a McDonald's kind of religion, ubiquitous and watered down. People might complain about society, but it was like people making disparaging remarks about the size or nutritional value of a McDonald's hamburger – while eating one. English society offered what English people wanted, and they stood in the queue for it, more patiently than any Eastern Europeans could have managed. But of course, no religion, no fast-food restaurant, no matter how universally welcoming its slogans, can offer a pew or a cheeseburger to everyone. There had to be some losers, some *biedaki*.

London seemed to be crawling with these losers: they might even be the majority. Society had taken them in, found them bitter-tasting, spat them out, and now they were human garbage. A moat of human garbage eddying around every McDonald's, disqualified from sharing the Happy Meal.

But oh, the shame of their exclusion! The stigma of their failure!

No one in Poland could ever have felt that way, because society there had always been designed to make criminals of everyone anyway. It was difficult to feel like an outcast in a society where your basic humanity put you and everyone else at odds with the ideals of inclusion. Cunning risk-takers at every level managed to attract all that was officially unavailable; the rest lived safer lives of envy, minor pilfering and despair. But nothing like this English shame . . . no, it wasn't even shame . . . it was something more desultory and cringing than that. It was embarrassment.

On the main street not more than a hundred metres from the Delta Hotel, homeless beggars were wrapped up for the night in shop doorways, little parcels of grey wool and Sunday supplement. Neon slogans beamed messages down at them, such as, 'YOU WANT IT? YOU'VE GOT IT!' and 'TO THE MAX!'. Messages from another galaxy, from the planet America. At that distance, the message-senders couldn't be expected to notice if these sleepers were dead or just resting.

A Turkish restaurant was still open. Kasia ordered a coffee and drank it slowly.

'Yawwah-yawwah-yawwah-yawwah-Tom Cruise-yawwah-yawwah,' said the Turks around her.

'Yawwah-yawwah-Sylvester Stallone.'

When Kasia got back to the Café Kraków, it was about three o'clock in the morning and her uncle was still up, an unusual thing. He had never yet made any comment about her nocturnal escapades, and he made none now, though her clothes and skin brought into his kitchen a heady aroma of tobacco, 100 per-cent-proof alcohol and male armpit.

'I couldn't sleep.' He gestured. A small pot of soup burbled on the stove, an old-fashioned paperbound book which might have been a cheap Polish New Testament was balanced in the empty breadbasket, and on the cutting-board O. J. Simpson's story lay open, headlined *Sprawozdanie z Ameryki*.

'Neither could I,' brazened Katarzyna.

'Very funny,' sniffed her uncle. Without actually ignoring her, he went about his business of stirring soup, buttering slices of bread. She fell into rhythm with him naturally, filling the kettle for coffee, clearing away vegetable peelings.

'You know, Kasia . . . this girl Zofia, that's starting next week . . .' He paused to taste the soup, blowing on it gently. 'She can take or leave this job, you know what I mean? She wouldn't be heartbroken . . . I mean, it's not written on tablets of stone that she has to come.'

'Thanks, Uncle. But it's all right. I *want* to go back to Poland.'

He nodded, frowning. Outside, a car alarm began to whoop irrepressibly.

'Write and tell me what it's like,' he said, raising his voice to a clarity and intensity unusual for him. 'All I get from my sisters is lists of what's in the shops. You're a sharp kid. Write to me. About Poland. The Poland that *you* see.'

Kasia blushed, for the first time since she could remember. 'Sure,' she replied. 'Of course I will, Uncle Jarek.' Then, 'Can I have some soup?'

They ate soup together. In time the car alarm stopped and let the silence return. Kasia tried to imagine herself sharing with her uncle the perceptions she had had tonight, on the toilet in the Delta Hotel, in the arms of the already nameless man from the Spiritualized gig. She could almost imagine it. The words were not far away.

After another little while, out of the blue, her uncle said, 'You know, my father, your grandmother's kid brother, wasn't the loser he's made out to be.'

'I hadn't heard anything about him,' said Kasia.

'He never made any money. Making money didn't suit him. The family never forgave him for that.'

'I hadn't got that impression,' said Kasia, peeking over the rim of her steaming coffee mug.

'My father was a poet. He died in Buchenwald.'

'I didn't know that,' said Kasia, putting the mug down, cradling her hands around it, attentive.

'One of your great-aunts had a stroke a few years afterwards and it knocked out the part of the brain that stops people speaking what's really on their mind. I was there for dinner once, and the subject of my poet father came up, and she said: "Trust him to die in a concentration camp nobody outside Poland ever heard of."'

'That's not very funny,' said Katarzyna.

'What she didn't say, what nobody ever mentions, is that my dad is buried in the Avenue of Meritorious Persons in the Powązki cemetery in Warsaw. That was for his poetry, that was. Not for making shoes or hubcaps or battleships or . . . or . . . soup, but for *poems*.' Uncle Jarek picked up the old book from the bread-basket. '*These* poems.'

'Cool,' said Kasia, her eyes lighting up. 'Can I have one?'

'What do you think I am?' protested Jarek sharply. 'A Hare Krishna bookshop? Free poetry books with every meal? You think I've got a crate of these upstairs?' He held the book up to her face like a mirror, firmly gripped. 'This is *my* copy of Bolesław Szajna's poems.'

'So how can I get one?' challenged Kasia.

Jarek smiled condescendingly. 'You go to a good bookshop in Poland. You ask them if they've got a copy of Bolesław Szajna's poems.'

'And if they haven't?'

'Do I have to explain the principles of capitalism to you? You ask them to order it. If they can't help you, you try somewhere else. Eventually, somebody will get hold of one.

You hand over some money, they give you the book. Maybe the week after, somebody else asks for the same book. That's the way books survive, yes?'

'I just thought . . . with things in Poland the way they are . . .'

'Well, you check it out. Write to me about it. My sisters tell me you can get car phones and Reeboks in Poznań. You tell me what you can get in Warsaw, as far as Bolesław Szajna books are concerned.'

'Yes, but—'

'People never want to pay money for the really valuable things in life!' exclaimed Jarek in exasperation. 'They save up for years to buy a car from the assembly line, but the unique poems of an individual man they want to be given free.'

'OK, OK, I'll look, I'll look,' placated Katarzyna. 'What's the book called?'

'Easy to remember,' said Jarek, tossing his empty soup bowl into the sink so emphatically that he had to check if it had smashed. 'The first line of the Polish national anthem.' He sang sweetly and accurately, '*Jeszcze Polska nie zginęła . . .*'

'Poland is not yet lost,' Katarzyna repeated after him.

'That's another thing that pisses me off,' continued Jarek, as if there were a hotplate under him that no one had yet managed to turn down. 'He wrote that poem, the title poem, a few days before he was carted off to Buchenwald. He was already under house arrest. People read that poem nowadays, and they assume that my dad was either a crazy man, living in a dream world, or else he was being *ironical.*'

This last was not a word Kasia knew in Polish, but it seemed wrong to ask her uncle to explain it.

'That's the main way this world has changed, you know,' he sighed, running out of steam at last. 'People can't imagine anymore how somebody can hope for something beyond his own life.'

Kasia opened her mouth to speak, but, helplessly, yawned instead. So did her uncle. They both laughed.

'Bedtime,' Jarek declared. 'For me, anyway. You'll do as you please, as always.'

'Wake me in the morning,' said Kasia earnestly. 'You shouldn't have to face Halina Kozłowska on your own.'

In the morning, however, her uncle Jarek let her sleep in. When she eventually arrived in the restaurant, showered, spruce, and rather sick in the stomach, Halina Kozłowska was long gone and two of the other regulars were there instead, already served and eating.

'This soup was sucked out of a pig's arse-hole by a toothless whore,' pronounced Andrzej.

'Shut the fuck up, there are people eating.'

'Well, they're eating shit sucked out of—'

'They're eating *all kinds of stuff*, Andrzej; they didn't *all* choose the soup. *You* chose the soup because it's the cheapest thing on the menu.'

'In the old days I could buy a Volkswagen for what this soup is costing me.'

'You must have got your Volkswagens cut-price from the Nazis, then.'

'Don't get me started.'

'Eat your soup. You're drunk. The soup will help.'

'Pouring booze into it would help.'

'Eat the bread roll, then.'

'It's stale.'

'It's not stale. It's fresh Polish bread. It isn't pumped full of damp air like buns from McDonald's.'

'Here – *here* – call that fresh?'

'Just eat the fucking thing.'

'Jesus, look at the tits on that little whore.'

'Gentlemen, a little respect, please!' bawled a fearsomely loud voice from the kitchen.

Katarzyna took a deep breath and stepped forward.

'Anything else?' she enquired coolly.

Two days before she left London, Kasia lugged her suitcase of T-shirts to the U-DESIGN-IT T-shirt shop in Notting Hill Gate. There, according to pre-arranged agreement, she paid an Asian man to take down her precise instructions as to which designs were to go on which T-shirts. The promotional material from the music stores came in very handy for images and logos; so did the full-page advertisements she'd selected from music magazines. There were only a couple of images she'd brought with her from Poland, just in case she had trouble finding them in London: the ones of Phil Collins and Dire Straits. Those would sell like crazy back home, especially to older types with lots of money, so she could experiment with what she could charge. She would probably have to charge less for Spiritualized, Future Sound of London, Tricky and the rest, but their uniqueness would be on her side: no one else would be filling this niche. She could even guarantee her customers that if they found her T-shirts on sale cheaper anywhere in Poland she would give them double their money back. The Poles were pushovers for that sort of thing: it was *so* American.

She did the rounds of the bureaux de change and selected the one offering the best deal on converting her unused English pounds to American dollars; she was in no hurry to clutter up her purse with złotys, and left herself with only a few pound coins to last her through the next couple of days. The tube fare to the airport, a McDonald's milkshake maybe: anything else, other people could take care of, both here and at the other end. As if on a mental notepad, she checked a list of the things she needed to remember: American dollars, yes . . . black plastic bin bags, yes . . . roll of adhesive price tags, yes . . . passport . . . sanitary pads . . . the crap House of Windsor tea-towel for her mother . . . her folder of notes . . . oh yes, and . . .

Bolesław Szajna . . . *Jeszcze Polska nie zginęła* . . .

The Tunnel of Love

HAVING READ THE signs carefully, I confirmed that I was over eighteen and that explicit nudity didn't offend me, so I walked into the Tunnel of Love to find a job.

As an unemployed advertising executive, I had no previous connection with the sex industry, unless you want to claim there was something phallic about my roll-on antiperspirant commercials. What my previous career had left me with, however, was a habit of seeking out gaps in the market, no matter how tacky. I figured that whereas there must be thousands of out-of-work executives trying to to get into show business, academia, the public service, or, failing those, politics, there wouldn't be many people queueing up for a job in a porno-cinema-cum-dirty-bookshop.

Anyway, it was a last resort. Even before my old job had been hosed down the drain, I'd already done all the right things, like applying for positions with other ad agencies from Perth to Pennsylvania, but none of that had come to anything, so here I was, trying to sell myself to the manager of the biggest 'Sinema' complex in Melbourne.

'So, what do you think you have to offer us?'

It was that same old job-interview question, coming from a man who looked the same as any other employer might look: well-dressed without tie, slightly overweight, on the ball, faintly suspicious. In his neat air-conditioned office not one penis reared its ugly head, and if there were any vulvas they must have been in his filing cabinet.

'I want to work for you as a spruiker,' I said. (Better to be that, I'd decided, than be the guy who has to mop out the coin-op cubicles.)

'I've already got a spruiker,' the manager pointed out.

'You're thinking of getting rid of him, though,' I guessed. 'Because no one takes any notice of him whatsoever.'

'True,' he admitted. 'But what makes you think you'd do any better?'

'My experience in advertising,' I said, leaning back in my chair, unfazed by the startling creak. 'Most spruikers, and the one you've got is no exception, obviously have no experience in selling a product. They stand out there and mumble things like, "Great show, great show, come on down, don't be shy" – that sort of rubbish. They sound bored to tears. In advertising, I learned that to sell a product, you've got to convince people it's the best – in fact, you yourself have got to *believe* it's the best.'

'So, do you believe our show is the best?'

'I don't know, I haven't seen your show.' Observing his torso starting to expand with a deep sigh of annoyance, I added, 'Which just goes to show you need a better spruiker, doesn't it?'

'OK,' he grinned, leaning forward. 'How about you convince *me* our show's the best – right here and now.'

'Oh well,' I said hastily (I had nothing prepared), 'I don't think I can perform, you know – until the time comes.'

'Jesus!' he scoffed, rolling his eyes up. 'One day I'm gonna meet somebody who doesn't think like a prostitute.'

As a way of winding up the interview he said he'd ring me, and I left his office convinced I'd blown it. But then something happened that changed my mind. As I walked out of the luridly flashing entrance/exit of the Tunnel of Love, I had to squeeze past the spruiker.

'Excuse me,' I said, briefly establishing eye-contact with him, and he let me through. Out on the footpath I walked a few steps, then realised I was heading in the wrong direction and walked back; the spruiker immediately called out to me in a voice that was equal parts blasé and forlorn:

'Come in 'n' see the show, top girls, top girls, do y'self a favour, hottest acts in town.' I looked back at him: obviously, as far as he was concerned, he'd never seen me before.

That's when I thought: I've got the job.

And indeed I had.

I started work at the Tunnel of Love four days later, long enough for me to receive another two rejection letters from advertising agencies in Toronto and Auckland. One letter explained: 'Our staff has already been cut from twelve to eight. The reason is a simple sign of the times: nobody wants to buy anything.' Except sex, I added silently. At the railway station news-stand near my new workplace, the covers of all the bestselling magazines promised me bonking secrets of the stars, S&M, better orgasms, and sex that lasts all night. Even computer magazines had digital babes inviting all comers into the playstation. Clearly, I had landed on the horn of a growth industry.

So: I had a job, in a business that was thriving. My only concern was therefore, would I get along with my workmates?

Well, my fellow staff members at the Tunnel of Love were decent people, all of them – at least comparatively. By this I mean that I didn't have an overwhelming impulse to wash myself after meeting them, the way I used to have after dealing with some of my advertising agency's clients.

George was the boss, hard-headed, reasonable, rarely seen. Dennis ran the cinema and tended the machinery in general, a sleepy-looking man in his late fifties, rousable only by disgruntled cries of 'Focus!' or the challenge of a coin-op booth that refused to switch off the action after the statutory sixty seconds. Fortyish Karen ran the bookshop with a cool, sexy efficiency of her own that promised unbearable humiliation to anyone caught shoplifting. Mandy and Kelly performed erotic dances during the intervals between movies. They sometimes did a double act in which they sucked on opposite ends of a salami, subject to availability of salami and of Mandy, who was often away in search of heroin. At her best, though, Mandy was talkative and friendly, a country girl who had once been a vet's assistant and whose happiest memories were of watching cats wake up from anaesthetic. Kelly used to be a taxi driver. She didn't say much. Andrew was the guy who mopped out the booths, the guy I had decided I didn't want to be; he also fetched lunches, unpacked boxes and was trying to get a driver's licence so he could be more useful.

Initially, I got along best with Mandy, because of her air of being an out-of-towner suffering a harder welcome than she'd hoped for. Despite the fact that she'd been dancing naked and sucking salami for almost two years now, she talked as if she, like me, was still a newcomer. This place which employed us both seemed somehow connected, in her mind, with a carnival her parents had taken her to when she was eight, in Bathurst.

'The carnival had this thing – this sideshow – called the Tunnel of Love. You remember that?'

'I've never been to Bathurst.'

'I thought Melbourne might've had a sideshow like that, at Luna Park.'

'I've never been to Luna Park.'

'No kidding . . . Neither have I. Funny, isn't it? It's so close and everything. Anyway, I never went into the Tunnel of

Love – I was too young – not interested. I went on the Ghost Train, though. Things would spring out at you from the dark. Ugly faces – hairy paws – slime everywhere.'

We looked at each other and at our surroundings.

'What are you two laughing at?' yelled George from his office.

In the long run, though, it was Karen I became friendliest with, because she proved to be an amazingly smart lady. Her strong point was analysis, and this came in very handy when I was struggling to establish myself as God's gift to peepshow spruikers. I had done a bit of analysis myself, and rethought every aspect of the job. Levi's, pullover and dressy leather jacket replaced the white shirt and baggy dark suit of the classic spruiker: why look like a guest at a Greek wedding waiting to get to the booze? Making myself heard in the busy street, right next to the traffic, was a challenge too: I got myself a microphone, and wrapped its shaft in a dildo, to attract anyone who might have a sense of humour. My script was advertising copy of the most calculated virility.

'Sex acts close enough to touch!'

'We've found a loophole in the law, folks, so we can show you what's always been banned.'

'Your most explicit fantasies happen in here, for real!'

'Yes, this is the place where you'll experience women doing everything you've always wanted.'

Nobody unexpected came in.

Oh, the regulars: Japanese tourists, sales managers, the odd drunk. But certainly no influx of new blood or indeed any other bodily fluid. Across the street, a fat lady stood in the doorway of a clothing store, explaining in a barely audible, faintly desperate monotone that there were opportunities too good to pass by. Passers-by trotted meekly into her shop, one after another.

'How's it going, hotshot?' It was Karen, on her lunch break.

'Not so good.' I pointed out the success of the clothing-store spruiker, who was silent just then, staring down at her shoes as if embarrassed by the customers' enthusiasm.

'I don't understand it,' I said.

Karen smiled, her big lips revealing eccentric teeth. Out in the daylight I noticed how real she was: the wrinkles at the corners of her eyes, the softness of her hair, the stitches in the seams of her jacket.

'Sure, people go into that shop all the time,' she conceded. 'But they go *out* of it all the time, too, usually after about thirty seconds. That's the secret.'

'What do you mean?'

'In a clothing store,' explained Karen, 'you go in, you have a peek at the gear, maybe pick up a shirt and put it down again, and if you don't see anything you like, you just leave. Easy. A place like ours is different. Once somebody makes the decision to go in, he *knows* he's going to pay for something. I mean, he knows that the other people on the street who watched him go in are thinking, "Look at that slimeball going into that sex shop." Then once he's inside, he knows everyone in the shop is thinking, "Look at that loser, he's got a hard-on and nowhere to put it, poor ugly bastard, no wonder he can't get himself a girlfriend." Then when he leaves, there's more people out in the street thinking, "Look at that slimeball coming out of that sex shop – what's he been doing in there? Probably just finished wanking!" Now, do you think a guy's going to go through all that for nothing? No way! He's going to spend a heap of money on a dirty movie, maybe a stripshow, magazines – *anything* to make it worthwhile coming in. And all the guys you're calling to *know* that. That's why they don't come in!'

'So what should I do?'

'Same thing prostitutes do. Look them in the eyes.'

'Is that all?'

'That's all.'

I noticed as she said this that she herself was looking straight at me the whole time, and that I was beginning to find her very attractive.

I didn't want to just take her word for it, though, so I asked Mandy too, she being a prostitute as well as an erotic dancer.

'Oh, it's true,' she said. 'Once they've looked into your eyes, nine times out of ten you got 'em. There's just something about eyes. It's not that guys are more attracted to you once they've really looked at you – it can go the other way sometimes. But it's as if, by looking into your eyes, something's already happened between you. Like a relationship, you know? It's harder for them to look away from you then – it would be like rejecting you in some really outrageous way, like married people making a big scene in public or something, and like the woman's got the right to break down and cry and hit the guy with her fists and stuff. It's weird, but it works. On the phone, I tell ya, it's completely different. They go over you like you're a used car. I've had guys trying to find out exactly how tight my fanny is – like, I thought I'd have to measure it for them. But I'm dead sure if I saw those same guys in the street and I could look them in the eyes, they'd just ask the price and then tag along like little lambs.'

Next day, I repeated what Mandy had told me to Karen over lunch. I was hoping to get to know her better by sharing some terrible café food with her, and telling her she was probably right.

'Of course I'm right,' she said, brushing her long hair away from her mouth as if to prevent herself eating some of it along with her meal, though that might have improved it.

'The thing is,' I went on, 'how does it apply to *my* job? I'm male, and so are the customers.'

'It doesn't matter,' mumbled Karen, mouth full. 'Once they've stopped and looked you in the eyes, there's a relationship there. If they break away, they almost give you the right to follow them down the street yelling, "What's wrong with you? I thought we were friends? How can you do this to me?" and so on.'

'That's pretty frightening.'

'Are you kidding? What about people who are *really* friends? What about people who are *really* married?'

I looked at her face to read how serious she was. She was deadly serious. In fact, she was suddenly in a bad mood – with me, it seemed.

'Do you know what *I* think?' she said, leaning forwards across her plate of crap and fixing me with a narrow-eyed stare. 'I think advertising is shit.'

'Oh, I agree,' I smiled, hoping this would save me, but it didn't.

'Advertising,' she pressed on, 'is a cowardly, namby-pamby, make-believe way of selling things. It's all a lot of theory, guys in suits wanking in boardrooms. Nobody ever has to go out into the real world and grab somebody and say, "Hey, buy *this*." You people have no guts. You win awards and you don't know the first thing about persuasion.'

'Well, I don't know, Karen,' I said, roused to irritation. 'All I know is that my ad for Softsan made an extra four to five thousand women per year buy that brand of sanitary pads, and it made them do it so promptly that six weeks after the ad came out we got a letter from the Softsan comp—'

'*Bull*shit!' exclaimed Karen, her voice loud enough now to draw the attention of the other diners. 'Why don't you try to sell *me* a sanitary pad, right here and now? Go on: I'm a woman – it should be easy!'

'Karen, keep your voice down,' I hissed, agitating my out-stretched palms over the table between us as if to magically return a dangerous genie to its bottle. 'People can hear you!'

'So what! Isn't that what your dildo microphone is for?!'

Awed by her outburst, I tried to beat an inconspicuous retreat from the café but she had more surprises in store for me. Grabbing my hand in hers (I wasn't so awed I couldn't notice how small-boned, how delicate, how startlingly *female* her hand was) she pulled me out on to the street and towards a destination of her own choosing.

'Let me show you something, Mr Ad-Man,' she said as she strode along. 'Mr Hidden-bloody-Persuader. Let *me* give *you* a little demonstration of persuasion.'

She led me to a second-hand bookshop which always had bins of worthless or near-worthless books outside on the footpath. Some of the bins were marked '$1' or '$2'; the outermost was marked 'FREE'. Karen rummaged through this bin for a few seconds, selected ten books, and walked into the store.

'Excuse me,' she said to the girl behind the counter, a fey-looking lass with glasses and blonde hair tucked behind her ears. 'I need to sell some books, please. You *are* buying, I hope.'

'Well,' said the girl, 'it depends on what they are.'

'Oh, they're in very good condition,' replied Karen, and then suddenly craned her head forward to get a better look at the girl. 'Oh hey, that's such a lovely jumper you've got on. Did you knit it yourself?'

'Thanks,' blushed the girl, looking down at her own breast and then straight into Karen's waiting eyes, which were bright and warm. 'It's just from a charity shop, you know.'

'Oh wow – that's what I call a find. You know it's a real art to be able to look good without spending a lot of money. What's your favourite charity shop?' By now the books were on the counter and so were Karen's folded arms, the better to narrow the distance between her and her new friend.

'Well,' hesitated the girl, 'there's one in Richmond, in among all the Vietnamese grocers. They have a lot of stuff there. Jeans as good as new for, like, five or six dollars.'

'You're joking! Wow, I must go there. I really need some new clothes. Nothing fits me anymore. You know, I lost a baby just recently and I got really depressed afterward. I just ate and ate and ate. You know how you eat when you're depressed?'

'I . . . sure. Now, about these books . . .' The girl was sorting through them now, pink in the glow of Karen's stare.

'I thought I might be able to buy myself a pair of jeans that really fit me, you know. It would make such a difference. Lately I open the wardrobe and look at what I used to wear and I just want to cry.'

'That's awful,' grimaced the girl. 'But these books . . . Ah . . . We can't really use them.'

Karen's face dimmed, subtly, horribly.

'Can't really use them?' she echoed.

'I'm really sorry,' squirmed the girl, 'but they're not . . . up-to-date. I mean, I think we might even have a couple of them sitting in a bin outside, for free.'

'You mean, you won't even buy *any* of them?' Karen stepped back a little from the counter, but not too far. She had the look of someone who has just been told the cancer is too far gone.

'Maybe you could try somewhere else,' pleaded the girl.

'No, no, I couldn't,' said Karen. 'I almost didn't have the courage to come in here. I – I just can't cope with people being nasty to me right now. I mean, *you*'ve been nice, but . . . If I had to . . . Oh God . . .' Karen took a deep breath and smiled bravely. 'Couldn't you give me *something* for some of them? You can have the rest for free.'

'Well, what I really meant was . . .' The girl caught a glimpse of rescue. 'What I really meant was you might get more for them somewhere else. I could only offer you a dollar each – maybe three dollars for this one.'

'Oh but that's fine, really. That's just fine.'

And that was that.

Walking back towards the Tunnel of Love, Karen seemed much calmer. Her bad mood had caramelised into a sort of sassy good humour, and she kept looking at me as if she were a bit concerned that I might not be feeling well.

'So, how did you like that?'

'Not very much,' I confessed. 'It was like . . . I don't know . . . begging . . . or rape.'

'Of course it was! A rapist is only a beggar turned nasty!'

I thought that one over when I was back in the entrance of the Tunnel of Love trying to establish eye-contact with the world at large. The way she'd said it was so neatly controversial, so smartly pretentious – so cut-and-dried!

Maybe, with a mind like that, she could have been hot stuff in advertising. I tried to imagine her in that world, but realised it was all wrong. What she seemed suited for, despite all the smartness of her argument, was not so much convincing people they liked something, as convincing them they *didn't* like it. That wasn't advertising, it was literary criticism.

'Are you a university graduate?' I asked her when I next had the chance.

'Sure I'm a university graduate,' she smirked, sorting the anal from the oral as she extracted it from the box. Tuesday was the day when new shipments came in: latest-issue pornography from around the globe. Customers who would have had difficulty locating Denmark on a map knew that the most glistening vulvas came from there.

'So what are you doing in a pornography bookshop?'

'I'm not qualified for anything else.'

'Oh, come on.'

'I was assistant manager of a feminist bookshop for a while – I did the ordering, stock control, layout, you name it, I did it. The manager just put up the money and gossiped with the customers. The shop went bust during the recession, nobody else was hiring, so I ended up here.'

'Wasn't it kind of a big change, from feminism to pornography?'

She shrugged, got out the pricing gun. 'Not really. In both of them there's this terrible, pathetic *wishing* that people would cast off their actual lives and feelings and behave according to some amazing sex fantasy. You're not allowed to point out to the customers that in the real world, nobody's going to let them do it. You have to let them buy their fantasy so they can sneak it home and get busy pretending.'

Was she aware how ideologically mischievous she was being? I couldn't tell, despite the faint smile on her face, because Karen was always cheerful on Tuesdays. Sorting through the new arrivals seemed to please her as no other aspect of her job did; she was never more content than when she had magazines to sort, shrink-wrap and find niches for. Mondays were often too slow for her, as clientele was hardest to come by then. Theatrically she would describe to me the agony of keeping sentinel duty behind her desk, watching a lone pervert to make sure he didn't slip a copy of *Milk-Squirting Mamas* down his trousers, and nodding off to sleep thirty times an hour.

'Roll on Tuesday,' she would sigh.

Thursdays and Fridays were red-letter days for the Tunnel of Love's homosexual clientele, because these were the days when the bookshop was presided over not by Karen but by Darren. (In a world where fake names like Cindy Sheer and Brad Hardman abounded, Karen and Darren were a bona fide coincidence.) Though Karen knew the shop's stock well, she didn't have that certain something that enabled gay customers to ask her questions like, 'Have you got anything with dicks with very thick veins on them, stroking against pierced nipples?' Darren was the man to ask. Shaved from the ears down (ah, but how *far* down?), bleached and permed on top, he had a face whose focus was nevertheless his startlingly attractive eyes, which exerted even on heterosexual men an allure so potent that his receding chin and wine-bottle shoulders couldn't dim it. He was a man who wore his gayness so proudly, so insouciantly, that I was convinced he must have a mum somewhere who didn't know yet.

Still, he was stimulating company when we went out to lunch together. On one occasion, he pointed out all the billboards, posters, magazine covers and real live females offering aggressive heterosexual stimulus during our 200-metre walk to the sandwich bar and back. Sure enough: there seemed to be a jostling, pouting universe of vacuum-packed rumps, crotches, uplifted cleavages, kisses, promises of climax.

'And you know what would happen if just one little shop had one little magazine in the display window showing a guy kissing another guy? Or if even one guy in the middle of this crowd was walking around with a big dong bulging through a pair of tights and a torn T-shirt on? The police would get called in!'

'So what you're saying is that homosexuality should have equal representation in shop windows and in the tights and T-shirts of pedestrians?'

Darren sighed, his extraordinary eyes half closing.

'Actually, I'd be happy if the heterosexuals would just tone it down a bit. I think sex should be more private.'

'Are you having me on?' I was beginning to think Karen and Darren might have more in common than their jobs.

'Of course not.'

'But what about the pornography you sell?'

'What could be more private than some guy coming into the Tunnel of Love, buying a magazine and taking it home in a brown paper bag?'

Through talking to Karen and Darren, I was becoming more confused every day about what I thought of pornography, the sex industry, and . . . Karen and Darren. I couldn't tell if I was being corrupted or redeemed: old prejudices were melting away, yet at the same time I was letting go of permissive values I'd once claimed to hold but which had never really been tested.

My old friends were no help. I made the mistake of telling one of them what my current line of work was; I might as well have told him I was kidnapping babies for use in the pet-food industry.

'But I'm just inviting people to buy something, same as I was before.'

'Oh come on – don't tell me you can't see a difference between antiperspirant and pornography.'

'Sure I can: people don't actually need to stop sweating, but they need to release sexual tension.'

That's what I said, but I don't know if I really believed it.

I certainly didn't seem to have any sexual tension in need of releasing, at least not since I'd started working at the Tunnel of Love. In fact, nobody who worked there seemed to have much interest left in all the pinky-orange activities in the magazines and movies and strip shows. The recurrent motif of swollen nipples on the walls exerted all the fascination of Christmas bells or polka dots. The word 'fuck' inspired the same excitation in us that the word 'carpet' might inspire in a carpet-seller. Kelly was reading a book on sports injuries, a very technical text, to figure out how she could perform her erotic dances with less muscle strain.

Mandy spoke wistfully about going back to the country and finding a nice boyfriend. 'I might even have sex with him,' she speculated dubiously, as if that would be an untried experience she mightn't have a taste for. Darren, who used to work in his father's greengrocery, told me that at times in the Tunnel of Love a customer would ask him a question and he would almost call out over his shoulder, 'Dad, do we have any Asian anal?' Even Andrew, a red-blooded young male who might have been expected to be most vulnerable to the stimulus, was more concerned with finding exactly the right chemical to add to his bucket of water, so as to neutralise the smell while mopping out the cubicles. He didn't know the word 'neutralise', though, so he used 'antidote' instead – not a bad choice to sum up what we all seemed to be hankering after.

To be honest, what I grew to crave most, working in the Tunnel of Love, was innocence, particularly sexual innocence, though innocence of any kind was fine. In the world of pornography, people were always pretending to be out in the woods for a picnic or to be employed to mend the stove, when really they were just hot for a fuck. In time, I came to feel the attraction of a world where people really did want to have that picnic in the woods, and where the stove-mending man mended the stove, tipped his hat to the lady and drove off in his van with maybe one friendly toot of his horn.

I discovered that Karen and I shared a love of children's books, and this brought us closer together. I'd mastered the spruiking by this stage and knew what times of day to go out there and herd them in: George was satisfied to see the extra people shambling through the door and so he didn't begrudge me the time I spent talking to Karen.

'Just don't block her view of the shoplifters,' he cautioned.

'Some of these guys have got secret pouches down their fronts.'

Not wishing to spoil my chances of seeing such a marsupial being caught red-handed, I did as I was told, but even though I stood to one side of Karen, she always turned to look me straight in the eyes whenever we were talking, as if to prove she lived according to her own theories of communication. Or maybe she just liked me.

I certainly liked her. There was something very charming about this intelligent unglamorised woman enthusing about children's books in a room filled with depravity of the most deceitful kind. She spoke affectionately of moles, mice and Marsh-wiggles to a background murmur of robotic cries filtering through from the cinema. She laughed her smoker's laugh and was beautiful.

Looking back on one of these conversations one evening after work, I saw her as if she herself were a character in a classic children's book: eccentric, delightful and yet dignified at the same time. I wanted more, and was suddenly inspired to take her out to dinner. I had her telephone number, though Karen had warned me she didn't like telephones. In fact, 'hate' was the word she'd used. Once when Darren had needed to know something only Karen could have told him, I'd suggested ringing her, and he had smiled and shaken his head in such a way as to say, 'Out of the question: I know better than to do that.'

I still phoned. Maybe it was the advertising man in me: I just couldn't believe there wasn't a way to sell someone an opportunity. Maybe I was in deeper than I thought.

I dialled, she answered.

'Hi, this is Mike,' I said.

'Who?'

'Mike.'

'Who? Speak louder, there's a lot of noise around.'

'It's Mike!' I barked. 'From work!'

'Oh. Hi.' She sounded testy, as if I'd woken her up in the middle of the night or interrupted her five seconds before orgasm. (Now why did I think of that? I *never* thought about things like that in the Tunnel of Love.)

'Listen, I really enjoyed talking to you today. It was the best conversation I've had in years. I didn't want it to end. I still don't.' I could have gone on for a bit longer, but I left it there, hoping she would break the uncomfortable silence with an invitation.

'Look,' she said, 'what am I supposed to do about it now? Whatever you want, can't it wait until we see each other?'

'Well, it's just that I was thinking about you right now – I mean, tonight.'

'Fine, that's very interesting. Come and see me at work and we'll discuss it, OK?'

And she hung up.

Next day I couldn't bring myself to discuss the incident with her, so we talked about other things, in a friendly, even playful way, and I contented myself with that. I found Karen no less attractive than before, but now I had to remind myself that she wasn't a simple deal, that there was more to her than met the eye. Like a character in Lewis Carroll's Alice books, she wasn't going to behave the way I'd expect her to, and would keep me guessing. But she only had to smile, showing off those eccentric teeth of hers, or shrug, calling attention to her finely shaped shoulders, for me to be charmed.

Good though our conversations were, I did find Karen rather difficult to challenge, though. Everything she said was either invincibly logical or so intensely felt it was dangerous – or both. To disagree with her was to risk either looking foolish or offending her irreparably. In fact, I already felt I must be offending her often, for she had a way of just walking off when a conversation had gone as far as she wanted it to go, and anything I might add as she was walking away she would ignore as if she hadn't heard it.

And yet, in other ways, she was unusually easy-going and even suggestible. If I said I wanted to have a Chinese meal, she would stop what she was doing and say, 'Sure.' If I changed my mind half-way to the restaurant and said I wanted Italian instead, she would shrug and say, 'Fine with me.' If the Italian place proved to be shut and there was only enough time left to buy a stale doughnut from a snack bar, she would grin and say, 'Never mind.' Though she had the air of someone who is cynical about everyone and everything, she didn't seem to have any need to lay blame. Even the Tunnel of Love's bookshop she ran with the same tolerance that a farmer who has come to loathe pigs runs a piggery. Customers who were bamboozled by the hundreds of shrink-wrapped, unperusable magazines on display would ask her what made an $11.95 one different from a $24.95 one. 'Colour quality,' she would reply, or, 'Better grade of paper.' When accepting money, she would always say, 'Thanks,' or even 'Have a nice day.'

One day when I happened to be there, she sold a gro-tesquely overweight, slightly mongoloid-looking man a magazine emblazoned BIG BLACK SLUTS BEG FOR IT.

'This must set some new standard for politically incorrect transactions,' I quipped when he was gone.

Karen shrugged. 'He's not going to rape anybody,' she said. 'He's probably got a job as a crate-unloader at the back of a supermarket or something. Almost embraced a woman back in 1992 but lost his nerve. Gets ordered around by the checkout girls.'

'All the same—' I began.

'Look,' she said warningly, 'in the feminist bookshop, I once sold a book called *Life in the New Clear Age* to a woman with a couple of black eyes so bad she looked like a panda. The book was all about sensitive, artistic people living in communes of seven to eleven members, caring for each other in a semi-rural environment, taking turns to work. Of course I knew perfectly well that the woman who bought this book was probably living in a mortgaged slum with her abusive husband and a kid who's hassling her to buy him a commando video game. There's no *way* this woman was going to use this book to make any changes in her life whatsoever. She was just going to . . . *wank* all over it. If I was going to worry about "politically incorrect", I would have worried about it then.'

Brave words, sharp thoughts, but still something didn't quite add up. I sensed there were times when the job did get to her after all, and at the end of the day she would look drained of everything except tears as she emptied the cash register.

'What's the matter?' I dared to say on one of these occasions.

'Scumbag overdose,' she sighed.

Desperate to get closer to her, I asked her about her childhood. It's funny, but asking people about their childhood is often an irreversible move towards sexual intimacy, much more so than talking about sex. In my horny bachelor years before my marriage and divorce, I found that I could discuss multiple orgasm with a woman over drinks and at the end of the evening she could still look at her watch and say she had the 10.37 to catch, but if I could get her reminiscing about the long-lost family home or looking for the old photograph album, it was almost a sure thing we'd end up in bed.

So, I asked Karen about her childhood. She responded promptly and at some length, but it was only afterwards that I realised she hadn't actually told me anything about her parents or her past, and instead had steered the conversation to one of her pet subjects.

'You know,' she mused, 'one of the hardest things for me to cope with when I was a kid was that all the characters in my favourite children's books were male.'

We were talking in the corridor near the cubicles, and Karen was trying to persuade the cigarette machine to surrender a pack of Marlboro Lights.

'I didn't go for Cinderella and all that. It was too obviously make-believe. I liked to think that somewhere, the things that happened in books were really going on. I loved *The Black Stallion*, *Catweazle*, the Winnie the Pooh books when I was younger, and especially *The Wind in the Willows* – all that enchanted forest, wild wood, riverbank kind of stuff.'

She jabbed the machine's buttons in what she hoped was just the right, not too rough, not too gentle way, and stepped back, her black hair defined sharply against a yellowed advertisement for *Cocksucking Co-eds*.

'I would have given anything to be Ratty or Mole, or even Eeyore, you know. They were just so *there*.'

'There?'

'They never had to justify their existence. Everybody accepted them for who they were. They had a space that was just naturally theirs, they didn't need to hustle for it, and they were free to be happy, or miserable, a loner, a party animal, whatever they liked.'

'What about the stories with female characters in them?'

'I never liked them as much. As soon as there are females, things get tense. Everybody in the story has a much harder time, especially the females. Have you noticed that? It's weird.'

I hadn't noticed. It sounded like the premise behind a lit. crit. thesis, the sort that Karen herself might have written.

'I think,' she went on, 'one of the main reasons I learned to read and write was so I could make up my own *Wind in the Willows* stories, with my favourite characters turned female. I'd print them very neatly on paper the same size as a real book, and I'd do drawings. It was, like, "Ratty woke up one morning knowing she simply must go exploring" – that sort of thing.'

'It's a wonder you didn't grow up to be a writer of children's books.'

A flash of pain reshaped Karen's face: innocently, I had touched a nerve. Too late, I knew we *had* achieved the intimacy I'd hoped for, but that it was gone now. Ripping the cellophane off her new packet of cigarettes, Karen scowled, 'There's no point writing children's books anymore. There aren't any children left to read them. Little girls are worrying about whether their tits are big enough. If there was such a place as the Wild Wood, they'd use it to lose their virginity in.'

She stumped off with her cigarettes. The conversation was over.

Afterwards, she was cooler towards me, more distant. It was as if we'd been to bed together and she considered it a mistake. I hung around the bookshop whenever I could, hoping things would get better, but I only ended up learning something that put rather a big dampener on any plans I might have had for our lives together.

One afternoon a gay customer said to her, 'Darren's got the latest issue of *Hot X Buns* laid aside for me.'

'I can't see it,' said Karen, rummaging under the counter.

'He definitely told me it would be here. And I need it by Wednesday. I'm flying to New Zealand Wednesday afternoon.'

'I'll see Darren tonight,' said Karen, 'and ask him about it.

If not tonight, I'll definitely see him in the morning before I leave for work.'

'So,' I said when the man was gone, 'is Darren staying with you just now?'

'You might say that. We live together.'

'Just good friends?'

'Very good friends. We've lived together for eight years. In actual fact, we're thinking of getting married.'

'Ha ha,' I smirked, sweat breaking out everywhere.

'No, seriously,' she insisted. 'It would make a lot of things much easier – bureaucratically, socially. I think I could go on just living with Darren for ever; he understands me. But there are certain things marriage comes in useful for . . . home loans . . . prospects overseas . . . children . . .'

'Children? With Darren?' By this time I was wondering how I could sit down in a hurry without it being obvious I needed to sit down in a hurry.

She shrugged. 'Who knows? Homosexual men make good fathers. Good fathers are hard to find. We'll see.'

I didn't sit down after all, I walked away. I couldn't recall ever being hurt so much by something a woman had said to me, not even during my divorce. I went outside and spruiked for all I was worth, roping them in with a cajoling good humour and merciless eye-contact.

'Yeah, come on, bring your girlfriend too, yes, come on love, don't be shy, this is the nineties, you're a big grown-up girl.'

The next couple of days weren't easy for me, but, funnily enough, I noticed that Karen was much warmer and friend-lier again, now that she had told me about her plans for the future. She thought I looked unwell, was worried I wasn't eating properly, wanted to go out to lunch with me. She was willing to argue as animatedly as ever, but there was a queer new affection there, a protectiveness. Glad of the opportunity to spend more time with her, I followed her on to a train on the way home, and she let me follow.

'Everything's much cruder nowadays,' she was saying, 'than people like you would like to think.' (She was talking about books again, and how the time for them was long past.) 'People communicate on a much more basic level. There's no use for the written word anymore except as padding for sexy pictures.'

'What about letters?'

'You mean like A, B, C . . .?'

'No, no: letters that you write to people.'

'I don't write letters to people. Who needs letters? The only important things happen face to face, eyeball to eyeball. You can write to someone for ten years and then when you finally meet them face to face, in five minutes you realise the relationship's a non-starter. The fact that you filled them in on all the trivia for the past ten years makes no difference.'

'You don't have to write about trivia. You can write about your feelings.'

'Letters don't contain feelings. They contain ink. Do you know how many women have written long, articulate letters to a guy saying it's all over, and then the next time they set eyes on him they smack together like magnets!'

'So you believe the only way people can understand one another is by talking face to face?'

'No, that's bullshit as well! What really goes on is even cruder than that. Language is just a way of keeping people's attention. If you don't keep talking, they stop looking at you, and if they stop looking at you, you can't make them do what you want.'

'Karen, Karen,' I said, shaking my head in bemusement, '*I'm* the advertising man. *I'm* supposed to be the cynical one.'

She pulled a face, and unexpectedly removed her jumper,

yanking it up over her head in a single irritated motion. When I say 'unexpectedly', I have to admit it was a stinking hot afternoon and the train carriage was jostling with peak-hour passengers radiating extra body heat; I was sweating too in my spruiking jacket. Karen's action was unexpected only in the sense that I had never seen her wearing just a bra before. Maybe it wasn't a bra, maybe it was some kind of fashion garment with a similar design to a bra: I couldn't tell, except that it wasn't see-through, and no one on the train seemed to think she had done anything outrageous. Me, I was electrified. Months of constant exposure to explicit sex acts and the naked flesh of strangers had not prepared me for the shock of Karen's soft bare shoulders, her bare midriff with its downy, sweat-sheened belly rising and falling under the ribs.

'Just look at the people on this train,' she was saying. 'There's too much noise for you to hear any of them in particular, but you can easily tell what they really want from each other. That toddler' (she was pointing, so I had to take my eyes off her glistening skin) 'is crying because his parents won't do something he wants. Who needs to know what it is? It's not important. Maybe he's upset because they won't let him keep throwing his toy on the floor. It doesn't matter. He's not really upset about the toy, or about the weather, or his shoes, or going to the zoo or not going to the zoo. What he's really saying is, "I am God and if I'm not feeling perfectly happy every second there must be something badly wrong with the universe, so you'd better fix it up right now or I'll destroy you." And those teenage girls huddled together over there – they're probably talking about how somebody behaved at a party, or whether a certain guy is cool or gross. The details are irrelevant. They won't remember any of it a year from now. The essence of what they're saying is, "Hey, you're my girlfriend, I'm your girlfriend, and here we are, on this train, having good times together." And that old pair of drinking buddies over there – see them? – they're saying to each other, "Life's been a bastard to me and as a result I'm a loser, but I know I can rely on you to show me a bit of respect because you're even more of a no-hoper than I am." You see? That's what it comes down to – it's *that* crude.'

'And us?' I enquired, blushing. 'What do you think *we're* really saying to each other?'

She turned away then, and blushed herself, though of course there was no way of telling whether it was in defeat at having to admit our conversation was too complex and meaningful to dismiss generically, or in embarrassment at the generic crudity of our attraction to each other.

'This is my stop,' she announced, as the train slowed into a station. 'Bye.'

Falling in love: how does it work? Over the years we gather the odd clue, but nothing adds up. We'd like to think we have a picture of our future partner projected in our mind, all their qualities recorded as if on film, and we just search the planet for that person until we find them, sitting in Casablanca waiting to be recognised. But in reality our love lives are blown around by career and coincidence, not to mention lack of nerve on given occasions, and we never have respectable reasons for anything until we have to make them up afterwards for the benefit of our curious friends. A cynic once said that people fall in love with somebody liking them. Was that what I found so loveable about Karen, that she liked me? Of course, there was no forgetting that she'd treated me very coldly at times, especially on the phone – which only made me all the more fascinated. Maybe that was explained by a different theory of love: that we're fascinated by the challenge of hostility, and strive to persuade the unwilling lover's eyes to focus on us and twinkle their approval. Then again, perhaps it was Karen's body that was attracting me? There was no denying I was charmed by the beauty of her breasts as they shifted about gently under her favourite grey sweater, or that a subtle hint of her nipples through a T-shirt excited me more than the erect and naked ones all around us. On the walls of the bookshop was displayed, from every angle and in every imaginable state of protrusion and lubrication, the hole that Karen, too, must have between her legs, yet to me it was a mystery as potent as the afterlife.

I was less nervous with her than I'd been with women in the past, in that I felt no need to dress better, or practise looking self-assured in the mirror, or agonise over my choice of aftershave. Did this mean Karen meant more to me than they had, or less? Perhaps the casualness of her own dress and grooming was making me feel more relaxed. Now that summer was here and she wore lighter clothing, I noticed she didn't even shave her armpits.

'A legacy from your days in the feminist bookshop?' I teased.

'A legacy from a terrible rash caused by roll-on antiperspirant,' she pouted mischievously. That pout immediately entered the legend of her attraction, and lent the underarm hair, by association, a quirky expressiveness. After that, all underarm hair I saw reminded me of hers.

'I think I've fallen in love,' I confessed to Mandy. 'I don't suppose you think there's such a thing.'

'Sure I do,' she said dreamily. Then, after a pause, 'Not in this world, though.'

'You mean, in the sex industry?'

'No, planet Earth,' she replied, still dreamily. I noticed her pupils were dilated by recent heroin infusion: she really did look like an alien with phony contact lenses for eyes.

Deep down I knew that the only appropriate person to discuss this with was Karen herself, but that was difficult, because I was overwhelmed by her presence at work, couldn't write to her, given what she'd said about letters, and couldn't ring her because of her incredibly off-putting phone manner.

However, one Wednesday evening, when the prospect of the coming two days without her seemed too grim to bear, I decided to give her phone manner another chance.

'Hello, Karen?'

'Who is this?'

'It's Mike.'

'Who?'

'Mike!'

'Oh, right. Look, you'll have to shout. Darren's got his music on.'

'Couldn't he turn it down?' (I felt queerly unreasonable saying this, because though I *could* hear some dance music in the background, it didn't sound that loud to me.)

'Never mind that. What do you want? Why did you ring?'

'Well, I . . . uh . . . I wanted to tell you . . . I wanted to ask you . . . damn it, I want to have a relationship with you. I mean, be your lover. I mean—'

'Look, there's no point talking about it on the phone. Can't it wait? I'm at home now, I'm off duty, I want to relax and not have to think about anything to do with the Tunnel of Love. Can you understand that? Good, I'll see you tomorrow – no, Saturday. Bye.'

And she hung up. I went to bed three hours earlier than usual, and masturbated for the first time since starting my new job.

The next day, my spruiking went badly. I felt universally rejected, and passers-by avoided me for the lowlife I was. Fearing to venture out too far from the anonymity of the Tunnel of Love's entrance, I was unable to look anyone in the eye. Darren was visited by a gay friend from interstate, so they went out to lunch together. I just stayed in the doorway, on duty but totally ineffective, avoiding George's raised eyebrow.

At the end of the day, I went home exhausted and humiliated, and found a letter in my mailbox with a Philippines postmark and stamps. It was a job offer from an advertising agency in Manila, the biggest one there. Accommodation and car were thrown in.

I thought about it long and hard, then decided to leave the Tunnel of Love without notice. After all, I didn't want a reference, and it wasn't as if my unannounced departure would seriously inconvenience anybody. I wrote my letter of acceptance to the advertising agency, and immediately felt so godawful I didn't know whether to weep, smash furniture or masturbate again. Finally I decided to phone Karen one last time.

As soon as she picked up the receiver and said, 'Hello,' I didn't waste words: I told her about the job offer, and that I'd be mad not to take it, but that I was in love with her, and I didn't want to go. She said she couldn't see what it had to do with her, that she was on her day off, that if I had a problem I should just make a choice and see it through. With a pathetic show of bravado, I said I would have to go, then.

'Fine, fine,' she said. 'You do that. See you around. Bye.'

The next day, I travelled into town to buy my ticket to Manila. The ad agency wanted me as soon as I was ready, and I was ready now.

I had no intention of setting foot in the Tunnel of Love again, but on the way back from the airline office I literally ran into Darren, who must have been on his way to work. Much as I would have liked to run away, we'd already established eye-contact, so it was too late. Besides, what eyes the guy had! I was so mesmerised by them that within fifty seconds, standing there in the street, I'd confessed everything to him.

'I really don't want to go,' I said. 'I was hoping there could be something between me and Karen, but it's obvious she doesn't want me in that way.'

'Have you talked it over with her?'

'I've tried to. She's happy to talk to me as a workmate, and she wants to keep it that way.'

'I'm surprised,' said Darren, gesturing that we should sit down together. 'I got the impression she was growing kind of fond of you.'

'Yeah? Well, Karen gave me to understand that you and she were "kind of partners",' I retorted, giving in to masochism.

Darren smiled and stretched his thin legs out from the bench. 'Karen and I take turns cleaning the shower recess and making toast in the mornings. I'm not sure if she under-stands that I've got slightly more romantic fantasies of partnerhood myself. Besides, she *is* the wrong sex for me.'

'She kind of implied that didn't matter.'

'Yeah? Well, you know, the sign of a really intelligent person is that they can make you believe something that's totally stupid.'

I checked his face to make sure he wasn't making fun of me. He wasn't, but I blushed anyway.

'Anyway,' I said, 'Karen doesn't seem very susceptible to any romantic ideals of love.'

'Are you kidding? *Everyone* is susceptible to those. We just have different ways of expressing it, that's all.'

'You can't know that for sure.'

He laughed and zipped open his attaché case, pulling out a magazine called *Well Hung*. 'It's the *only* thing I know for sure. Look – look,' and he flipped through the pages cursorily until he found what he wanted to show me. '*Look*,' he said, pointing out a man with biceps the size of motorcycle saddles, a prick like a crowbar and an expression that seemed to say, 'Come here, boys, and I'll tear you apart.' Darren waited until I'd had a good look, and then put his face very close to mine and murmured, 'I can promise you that even this guy, in his little heart of hearts, stored deep inside all that beef, is *yearning* for someone to love him truly, tenderly, exclusively, permanently. That's what it's all about, God help us.'

I chuckled nervously, and out of the corner of my eye noticed two pedestrians stopping near us and whispering to each other. I caught the word 'disgusting', but whether it referred to the copy of *Well Hung* fluttering on Darren's lap or to the spectacle of two homosexuals almost kissing on a public bench, I couldn't judge.

'I got the impression Karen isn't very interested in sexual love or affection,' I went on.

'I know what you mean,' sighed Darren. 'I think with all this fake passion all around her, she's become very inhibited about showing any of her own. You know, we were in a bank together once and two other people in the queue were snogging really enthusiastically. Karen got this awful expression on her face and said to me, "Who do they think they're fooling?" Maybe the couple heard her. Anyway they started giggling and smooching and squealing like a couple of happy dogs. Karen looked as if she might be sick, and left.'

'That's sad.'

'Yes, well, her childhood can't have helped: being sexually abused and watching her parents beating each other up. But really, I think a lot of it is probably caused by her deafness.'

'Her what?'

'Her deafness. You did know she's almost completely deaf?'

'*What?!* No!'

'Sure. Her father beat her around the head with a ping pong bat when she was eight, and that was more or less the end of her hearing. Oh, she reads lips very well, but I think tone of voice is *so* important, and she misses out on all that. Sincere people and complete bastards can say exactly the same thing, after all, and if you can't hear them speak I guess it's tempting to just decide *everyone's* insincere.'

'Deaf . . .' I echoed dazedly, leaning closer to Darren as if for support. Another couple of passers-by stared at us, assuming with disgust and pity that I had just learned I'd got AIDS.

'She's so proud, though,' Darren went on. 'She just carries on as if there's nothing wrong. She even has a little routine worked out for taking telephone calls that's basically one-size-fits-all, if you know what I mean.'

'Oh Darren,' I exclaimed as the full implications filtered through to me. 'I'm so grateful you told me all this. This changes everything!' And once again we were, in the eyes of yet more passers-by, two homosexual lovers on a bench, sharing a tender moment.

'So, what are you going to do now?' asked Darren.

'You go to work now,' I advised him. 'I'm not sure how this will end. Maybe you'll see me later, in the Tunnel of Love. Thanks for everything.'

Poised as ever, he embraced me and left.

I went straight to a quaint old-fashioned bookstore and bought a pad of *Wind in the Willows* notepaper. In the inside breast pocket of my jacket I found the essential tool of my old career, a felt-tipped calligraphy pen. Establishing eye-contact with the lady behind the counter, I explained that I had an important letter to write, for which I needed just a little corner of her counter to rest this beautiful notepaper on, which I was so happy she had been able to sell me. I continued to look at her and smile, and as soon as it was all right to take my eyes off her I put pen to paper and began:

Dear Karen,

Sheep

IN ORDER TO get to the Alternative Centre of the World, the five chosen artists did not set off together; they set off individually, in their own peculiar ways.

Their plane tickets were pre-paid, courtesy of the curators of the Alternative Centre: all they had to do was get to JFK international airport on the day, which shouldn't have been very difficult, given that all five of them lived in New York City.

Come the time, however, only Gerrit Plank did the conventional thing of packing his suitcase the night before and catching the bus into JFK the next evening. It would never have occurred to him to do anything else.

Morton Krauss, immediately upon receiving the tickets, sold them for half their value to a student at the university where he was artist-in-residence, and used the money to buy more drugs. Then, near the departure date, he telephoned an old lover in the north of England (reverse charges) pleading that he had an invitation to speak at a symposium in Scotland (what a chance to get his career back on course!) but couldn't afford the air fare. The university had thrown him out on his ass, he said, after a controversial exhibition of homo-erotic photographs including, you know, *that* one of *us*.

June Laboyer-Suk incorporated the tickets into one of her shows, called 'Trust', whose centrepiece was a small windowless cubicle like a photo booth. Her airline tickets were pinned up inside, along with many other personal effects; also on offer were scissors, felt-tip markers, a cigarette lighter, glue, ketchup, and a sanitary towel disposal unit. After failing to tempt any of the audience to destroy, mutilate or steal the tickets (not to mention her birth certificate, passport, credit card, family photographs, keys, private letters and so on), June resolved to go to Scotland after all, but drove to JFK a day early, so she could get twenty-four hours' worth of work done: in this case, close-up photographs of the expressions on people's faces as they stood at the luggage carousel, waiting for theirs to appear. With an hour to spare before her own flight, she handed the camera and completed films over to her usual courier.

Nick Kline's tickets had to pass through his agent first, a startlingly horrible woman called Gail Freleng. She faxed the Alternative Centre of the World for 'clarification' on a few points because 'frankly, I've never heard of you'. Days later, she received a fat parcel of brochures and leaflets of the Centre's previous exhibitions. Enquiries to the airline also proved that the tickets were fully paid for and legit. More faxes confirmed that Nick Kline would not have to share accommodation with any other artist or person and that at the symposium he would speak last. His name was spelled K-l-i-n-e and would appear on the promotional material first, or biggest or as part of a strictly alphabetical list. All this achieved, Ms Freleng tried to call Nick himself to tell him he was going to Scotland, but he was out at the scrapyard again, looking for Ford hubcaps.

Fay Barratt persuaded the airline to change her destination to Ottawa. She told the airline that her mother had come home from Scotland to Canada because she was dying of lymphatic cancer, and that the airline was surely not going to stand in the way of this last reunion. She wept uninhibitedly at the ticket counter, mentioned attorneys and Oprah Winfrey, and got her way, to Ottawa. She was sort of hoping that once she was reunited with her ex-boyfriend he would decide to come with her to the Alternative Centre of the World, and they could share the cost of the air fares. Instead, she ended up getting a lift back to New York with a woman she met in the YWCA hostel, and getting a loan for a new plane ticket from a gallery owner in exchange for her next three paintings.

At the airport on the day of departure, none of the artists met each other. They had no interest whatsoever in each other's work and had never bothered to attend any of each other's shows, preferring to read about them in reviews. They also had no hope of recognising each other because, having all been spiky-topped and gel-slicked during the '80s, they had all grown their hair long and fluffy for the '90s. (Long and greasy in the case of Morton Krauss.)

At Edinburgh airport, a special minibus was waiting to take them to the Alternative Centre of the World. The time was seven o'clock in the morning, a bad time of day for all the artists except Gerrit Plank, and they barely acknowledged each other as they stumbled into the vehicle. The driver was a uniformed employee of a chartered taxi company; he claimed to know nothing about the symposium except how to get there.

'Everyone all right?' he called over his shoulder as he revved the engine. There was a murmur of grunts and mumbles, and a 'Yes' from Gerrit.

The minibus pulled out of the airport, made straight for the M9 motorway, and drove north for a very long time.

Morton Krauss, Fay Barratt and Nick Kline slept soundly through most of the journey, the darkly tinted windows shielding them from the spring sunrise; Gerrit Plank was awake but saw no point in asking questions; only June Laboyer-Suk spoke up.

'I don't think we're in Edinburgh anymore,' she said.

'No, indeed,' agreed the driver. Outside, beyond the highway boundaries, the countryside was getting short on buildings. In time, there were mountains.

'I don't believe this,' said Fay Barratt, who had been woken by Morton Krauss's head falling into her lap. 'There's snow on those mountains. Where am I gonna get warm clothes?'

'It's like a packet of Alpine cigarettes,' blinked Morton. 'It's like the logo at the start of Paramount movies.'

After five hours, the minibus pulled in at a small village. The artists piled out of the vehicle, assuming that this was a fuel and toilet stop, but to their surprise the driver wound down his window, tossed out a large parcel, and, without warning, drove away.

'Hey!' yelled Morton, always first with paranoia. 'Come back here! Come back here, you dumb fuck!'

It was the first time, without a doubt, that this particular form of address had been uttered in the little village of Inver, possibly even in the entire Scottish Highlands.

What the artists did not know, but would learn as soon as they read the typed letters inside the parcel, was that they were the victims of an elaborate hoax by a man who identi-fied himself only as 'An Art Lover'. This man had spared no expense to bring them here, though he had spared some expense in the opposite direction: their return plane tickets had been rendered null and void. However, to compensate them for this, he had bought each of the artists a copy of *The Glory Of The Highlands*, a book of high-quality repro-ductions of Scottish paintings, mostly from the nineteenth

century and all vividly figurative. On the title page of each
copy of the book was written in ink:

*I am very pleased to introduce you to the world of real Art,
and the environment that inspires it.*
                                            Yours

                        An Art Lover.

The letters were personalised.

Gerritt Plank's was a diatribe against abstract art in general
and Plank's large coloured slabs of concrete in particular.

June Laboyer-Suk's was a diatribe against conceptual art
and audience manipulation, in particular Laboyer-Suk's
shows which, in the opinion of 'An Art Lover', showed no
skills of any kind except an infantile urge to pester and goad.
He singled out her 'People Factory' exhibition, in which a
succession of well-built young men in cubicles masturbated
constantly, producing syringe after syringe full of semen,
which were piled up on a table outside another cubicle,
where female gallery visitors were invited to help themselves.
This show, as far as 'An Art Lover' was concerned, repre-
sented some sort of low point in twentieth-century culture
so far.

Nick Kline's was a diatribe against installations. 'An Art
Lover' was deeply disgusted that the gallery space which
could have been used to display the work of talented and
dedicated painters should be 'cluttered with a literal obstacle
course of junk'. He suggested that there was something fundamentally dishonest about giving a lofty, allusive title like
Metamorphosis of Infinitesimals to a heap of sand. (Actually,
the title of that work had been Gail Freleng's.)

Fay Barratt's was a diatribe against incompetence hiding
behind sociopolitical flavours-of-the-month, which was all

that 'An Art Lover' considered Barratt's highly praised paintings of women in sexual crisis to be. He discussed in particular a picture called *You may as well have this, too*, recently purchased by the Guggenheim. He suggested that its idea, of a woman cutting her vulva out of her body with a penis-handled kitchen knife, was questionable enough to begin with, without adding the clogged mess of botched and murky impasto that arose out of basic ignorance about oil paint.

Morton Krauss's was a diatribe against Morton Krauss, especially his notorious 'Fistfucks with Extra Pepperoni' exhibition of 1989. This show, Morton's biggest brainwave, had offered people unframed original 8 × 10 pornographic photographs for $50 apiece. There were twenty copies of each photograph, all more or less identical (allowing for imperfections resulting from Morton's famous 'dishwash' method of bulk developing). Anyone who bought one had to point at it, then a gallery assistant would tear it off its nail in the wall and hand it over to the purchaser inside a pizza box. Then another copy of the print would be nailed up, until they were all gone. They all went very quickly – Morton's last major success. Since then, he'd had trouble thinking up something to top 'Fistfucks', especially since the 'take-away' angle had really been sort of someone else's idea anyway, and *she* wasn't talking to him anymore since he'd sold her camcorder for drugs. However, 'Fistfucks' had assumed almost legendary status, and had certainly made an impression on 'An Art Lover'. In his opinion, no one had ever managed to squeeze so much nastiness, bad faith, poor workmanship and exploitative cynicism into one exhibition.

'Yeah?' said Morton to himself when he'd finished reading his letter. 'Well, fuck *you*!'

'Baah!' responded a nearby sheep.

A minute's silence followed, as if to commemorate their

official status as suckers. In the far distance they could see a military jet climbing into the clouds.

'Somebody should call Gail – I'll give you her number,' said Nick Kline. 'She'll know what to do.'

All five of the artists struck off in different directions to look for a telephone booth, but the village of Inver did not appear to have such a thing. Behind the village hall, which was closed and offered Bingo, there was an expanse of shallow water and wasteland. Swans sailed in the deeper parts, and a small tethered rowing-boat fidgeted in the shifting sands. To the left, a sign said SCHOOL, but nothing resembling a school could be seen: no basketball courts, no car-parks, no crowds of teenagers, no cops. The air was so quiet they could hear the swans rustling their wings. To the right, Inver's street had a narrow strip of rocky beach on one side, houses on the other – modern little bungalows, not picturesque old cottages.

'Someone in one of those houses may have a phone – that's if there's any telephone connections at all,' said Fay Barratt doubtfully, wondering whether she should knock on some doors and try to win the sympathy of the natives. The problem was that that sort of thing was best done when she had only herself to plead for – all these other artists were just a millstone round her neck. Besides, she was only confident of getting her way with fellow Americans – years ago in France she had gone spectacularly to pieces in a railway station café and no one had taken any notice of her except a Polish upholsterer with no money.

'I see telephone wires,' observed Gerrit Plank. 'Every-where.' He pointed upwards with one eyebrow and one finger, a calm and economical gesture.

'We're missing someone,' said June Laboyer-Suk. 'The installation guy.' She wasn't talking about telephones now: Nick Kline was nowhere to be seen.

'*Village of the* fuckin' *Damned*!' concluded Morton Krauss. '*Texas* fuckin' *Chainsaw Massacre*!'

Nick Kline was, in fact, inside the Inver pub, sipping a beer. He had no intention of asking anyone anything, except for more beer, and the publican accepted this, having recognised him instantly as a serious drinker with a deep, undiscussable pain.

As he sat at one of the tables in the Inver Inn, Nick studied the menu on the wall, wondering if he was hungry enough to risk something that wasn't the pastrami-and-pickle-on-rye he was used to having every day at Juanita's Bar & Grill. Alone of all the artists, he had plenty of Scottish money on him, organised by Gail Freleng and the First National Bank, but his problem was that he couldn't guess what 'stovies' were. He was pretty sure he didn't want a Scotch pie (68p), a beef- or cheeseburger (£1.20), a smoked sausage (£1.70), lasagne or chicken curry (£1.85). That only left 'stovies' (£1.70).

Nick sipped his beer some more, half closing his eyes. Maybe somebody in the pub would start talking about stovies some time soon, in such a way as to reveal what they were.

The pub was bright and unpretentious, with decor reminiscent of a Boy Scout hall. A pool table and a pinball machine stood waiting to be touched. There were no other customers except for one old man whose dog slept at his slippered feet. Behind the counter, hemmed in by inverted whisky bottles, ornamental coasters and foil-wrapped crisps, the publican cleaned glasses and his wife made racing bets over the telephone.

'Number 5: Captain's Guess,' she said. 'Number 6: Eve's Pet. Fifty pence each way.'

Nick noted the strangeness of her accent, wondered how long he would be in Scotland. Somebody else would have to call Gail: he didn't like talking on the phone. If nobody called Gail, she would probably find him anyway: she always did. But if he waited too long, he might run out of money.

'That Fiona's a nice wifey – you know, the niece of that joiner from Kildary.'

'Pettigrew.'

'Aye, Pettigrew.'

No one seemed about to raise the subject of stovies, and Nick had almost finished his beer. On the wall opposite him there was a petition pinned up, saying, *'We the undersigned demand that the government reduce British beer tax'*. It was signed by eight people so far, all from Inver. It occurred to Nick that he could sign it too, since beer was something he believed in. On the other hand, Gail always told him never to sign anything without consulting her. He really ought to call her. The telephone was free now.

'Excuse me,' he said.

'Yes, sir?'

'Another beer, please.'

A little while later, three young men in overalls walked into the pub, followed by the four other artists. Nick wondered if any of them would remember his suggestion that Gail Freleng should be phoned, but instead they started asking questions about public transport – well, the women did, anyway. The little guy with the long greasy hair just stood there, whispering to the big Dutch guy, and the big Dutch guy was frowning with the effort of trying not to listen.

'You've just missed the bus,' the barman said. 'It was going to Portmahomack anyway – opposite direction to where you're wanting to go.'

'Won't it come back?' asked Fay Barratt.

'Well . . . yes and no,' replied the barman. 'On the way back it takes a different road, past New Geanies, Mackays, Loch Eye . . .'

'When's the next bus that stops here?'

'School bus, about half past four.'

This answer evidently did not please the artists, and after a brief exchange of murmured opinions they seemed about to leave. Nick Kline got up hastily and paid for his drinks, resolving to stick with the others now in case they ended up some place where Gail could be phoned. Morton Krauss, who had a policy of never travelling with foreign currency or, indeed, more than about $5 American, observed Nick Kline's handling of the strange-coloured banknotes with interest.

'We were worried about you, pal,' he said. 'Thought you'd got yourself lost.'

'I was just . . . here,' said Nick, fumbling the strange golden change into his pocket.

'Stovie and pint, please,' said one of the overalled men as Nick followed his fellow artists out of the pub.

After half an hour or so, it began to look as if June Laboyer-Suk's plan to hail a taxi at the side of the road might be impractical. One red Toyota fuelled by adolescent testosterone, one Volkswagen van full of children and one tractor with mysterious attachments had passed by. Overhead, a jet plane screeched back and forth like a giant insect, worrying at the bombing range near-by. Machine-gun fire rattled dully across the boglands.

'We maybe should have asked at the inn,' said Nick. In his mind he could see the three overalled men sitting at the bar, eating piping-hot stovies – though he couldn't picture the stovies themselves, of course.

'I'm not going back there,' declared Fay. 'Bunch of dumb-assed yokels.'

'What about you, Gerrit?' suggested June Laboyer-Suk. Her pronunciation of his name was precise; she had even, when they'd been talking earlier, managed to remember what kind of art he produced. Nevertheless, he was unmoved.

'I don't think so,' he said.

'Dumb-assed yokels, huh?'

The sarcasm seemed to perplex him. 'I couldn't make such a judgement,' he frowned. 'I know nothing about these people. I just don't like going backwards once I have made a decision to go forwards.'

June Laboyer-Suk looked to Nick Kline, but he had wandered off a few yards, apparently to study a squashed rabbit on the road. She looked briefly to Morton Krauss, considered him for a fraction of a second, then walked over to Nick.

'Nice rabbit,' he commented, pointing it out to her. She looked down at the perfectly squashed pelt.

'Maybe you should take it back to the States with you,' said June, wondering if maybe this Kline guy was 'challenged' in some way.

Nick shook his head. 'I got in trouble once in Fiji. At the airport. Customs. I had a heap of squashed frogs in my suitcase. They were dry as autumn leaves. I showed the customs people how dry they were. It didn't make any difference.'

'Gee, that's a pity,' said June. 'Listen, we'd better go back into that village together.'

'You and me?' He blushed. 'What do you need me for?'

June sighed and hugged the padded shoulders of her leather jacket in frustration.

'Come on, Nick: in a tiny village, in the middle of nowhere, you want me, a lone woman, to walk into a bar full of strange men? I could get raped, murdered, dumped in a field – nobody would know.'

'So how will being with me help?'

'This is a very sexist society, can't you tell? If a woman's alone, they think she's easy. If there's a guy with her, they think she belongs to him.'

'Well . . . OK . . . as long as I don't have to do anything.'

So June and Nick walked back into the village, and a while later they returned. The stovies were all gone, but Nick had bought himself a smoked sausage, which he'd already had to throw into a field on the way back to the roadside. First of all the artists, he had lost his innocence about Scottish take-away food. June had asked for something vegetarian and had been offered a packet of potato crisps; she'd declined, confident there would be a health-food restaurant nearby.

'There's no taxi companies here,' she told the others. 'What you do is, you phone a guy called Henry, and he drives you to the nearest town for four pounds.'

'So . . .' began Fay.

'So I've already phoned Henry's wife, and she says he'll come soon.'

Henry did indeed come soon, his last fare having been nothing more than the delivery of roast chicken to some dedicated pool-players in a local hotel. He delivered the artists into the Royal Burgh of Tain, a small town near the shore of the Dornoch Firth. Tain was pretty much closed for lunch when they arrived. The travel agency, tucked away above the pharmacy, was closed for the rest of the day.

'Fuckin' neanderthals,' fumed Morton Krauss, squinting in the sunlight reflecting off the sea.

Tain was built on high ground, with panoramic views not only of the sea but of miles of farmland. Near and far there were sheep, nibbling the grass at the edge of the road, their faces Ektachrome vivid in the sun; sheep milling about in the middle distance; more sheep dotting the unkempt horizon. The artists had never seen so many sheep; indeed,

Morton Krauss had never seen *any* sheep, except in other people's photographs.

Morton had his own camera with him, mounted with the world's most powerful telephoto lens. Peering through the viewfinder, he could be eyeball to eyeball with a black-faced sheep, or get a fix on the licorice torrent of turd-balls falling out of its asshole. He glimpsed the murky genesis of a new photographic exhibition, his follow-up to 'Fistfucks' – naked guys – no, naked babes – shitty-assed sheep with black faces – horns – the whole black stud/white virgin bit – he could do the sheep here, the girls back in New York – sandwiched negatives, cut-ups, whatever was easiest – or Kozinski could print them for him . . .

Somewhere behind his left shoulder, the other artists were discussing the immediate future. He didn't need to know what they were planning, since he had borrowed £20 from Nick Kline. That would probably last until he could get more sent to him from Charles in Newcastle; then again, the fact that Kline had lent him this much already probably meant he'd buy Morton any necessary bus or train tickets. Even better would be if the bus and the train proved to be a no-go; then somebody would end up hiring a car and he could just go along for the ride.

Eventually, the artists reached the limit of what they could finalise, given that Tain's four banks were still shut for lunch and that both Gail Freleng and Tina Golem (June Laboyer-Suk's agent) were in Ansafone mode. Predictably, none of the artists possessed an internationally valid credit card except June Laboyer-Suk, and she had left hers behind in the States, packed away in a bundle of other stuff from the 'Trust' exhibition. She had known from the outset that she didn't have her credit card with her, but had argued herself out of going back to the gallery to look for it because the invitation from the Alternative Centre of the World had taken such pains to stress that everything would be provided.

As for the others, Nick Kline didn't need a credit card because he had Gail Freleng, Fay Barratt and Morton Krauss had once had credit cards but weren't allowed them anymore, and Gerrit Plank was ideologically opposed to credit.

All things considered, it was agreed there was no point in the artists sticking together every minute. They would explore Tain individually, and meet in front of the post office in an hour or so. By that time, refreshed, with a clearer sense of priorities, they could exchange whatever they had managed to learn about how they might get back to New York.

Nick Kline, knowing that Gail Freleng never left her answering machine uncleared for longer than a few hours, parted company from the others in a state of perfect serenity. It was as if some tide of trouble had rolled dangerously close to him and then had gone out again, never reaching the rock on which he was standing. Now, free to roam, he had his eye on an ancient-looking graveyard down near the firth; there were stone steps and a narrow path from the High Street right through the fields down to those ruins, nothing could be simpler.

Gerrit Plank disappeared into a church, where he sat quietly in the warmth as if praying. He didn't even have to look at his watch, because on one of the walls there was a clock much larger than his own.

June and Fay, having forged a rudimentary intimacy from needing a female toilet, found one together, and sat in adjacent cubicles, listening to each other piss. Earlier on, Fay had shown June her letter from 'An Art Lover', in order to vent her wounded feelings about its accusations. She had, she said, sweated blood and tears over the painting singled out for derision, *You may as well have this, too.* Its apparently crude technique was totally deliberate, she said, suggesting the rawness of the emotion and the unresolved pain and confusion of women who did not have a voice. Even the clogging of the paint was to show physically the frustration of impotence. June Laboyer-Suk had tried her best to comfort Fay, even though she was fundamentally indifferent to painting, whether good or bad. Coming from a circle of powerful, successful women and thoroughly feminised men, she did her best to respect Fay's rage, but the respect felt sort of . . . anthropological. And sitting in the toilet cubicle next door, June couldn't help thinking that the sound of Fay's pissing was exactly what she would have expected: forced, fitful, hitting the bowl at an acutely deflected angle. Fay, for her part, simply couldn't believe how much piss June Laboyer-Suk seemed to have inside her: it went on forever. There must be parts of her missing, to have room for so much.

Still together back in the High Street, June and Fay ran into Morton, who had found a sort of mini-supermarket open and was brandishing his booty.

'Look what I got!' he grinned, happy for the first time since leaving New York. Out of his white plastic bag, bulging with milk, canned beer and cigarettes, he whipped a packet of Kellogg's Variety, eight tiny boxes of different cereals shrink-wrapped together.

'Want some?' he crowed, as if he were offering high-quality cocaine.

'We don't have any bowls,' June pointed out.

'We don't need any,' beamed Morton, tearing the cello-phane off the cereal boxlets. 'I have these all the time. The

boxes kinda *turn into* bowls. The cardboard's got kinda . . .
kinda . . .' He punched the air inarticulately.

'Perforations?' suggested June Laboyer-Suk.

'Yeah. Each little box is like a total art statement. It's like
the total opposite of eating at the family dinner table, or a
restaurant. It's *more* than just anti-social, it's . . . it's . . .'

'Sub-social?'

'It's . . . *beyond* social.'

Enthusiastically, Morton poked at one of the packets with
the handle of a spoon, searching for the familiar perforations.

'Fuck!' he announced in incensed bewilderment. 'There's
no . . . there's no little holes!'

'Well, Morton,' smiled June Laboyer-Suk, 'we *are* in a
different country.'

'They shouldn't fuck around with the cereal packets,' he
retorted.

'The Scottish maybe don't think they *need* perforations in
their cereal packets,' Fay chipped in.

Morton was offended, as if morally, by this insinuation.
'Some things,' he declared, 'should be like . . .'

'Universal?'

'Yeah.' Profoundly crestfallen, he replaced the cereal
packets in the plastic bag and slouched away.

'I'm surprised he had a spoon, actually,' said June.

'He probably needs it for melting heroin in,' said Fay.

This slur on Morton Krauss's drug life was undeserved, as he
had not regularly taken heroin, at least intravenously, since
the early 1980s. He always carried a spoon around with him,
and a can opener, because he had a weakness for cold cocktail
frankfurters and tubs of 'gourmet' ice cream. He had never
melted heroin in a spoon anyway: other people had done it
for him, with heroin *they* had bought. An inveterate needle-
sharer in the pre-AIDS days, and as promiscuous as oppor-

tunity allowed, Morton had somehow never become HIV-positive, a stroke of luck that chagrined art speculators who had bought up lots of Morton Krauss works in anticipation of his death. A recent interview with Morton in an art magazine had captioned his photograph with the quote: 'HIV-positive? I'm a negative kind of guy.'

Morton was indeed a negative kind of guy, and he found plenty in Tain to be negative about. The mini-supermarket suggested he buy himself a bowl for 10p at the St Duthus charity shop rather than giving him a refund on his Kellogg's Variety, and they had never heard of peanut-butter chocolates. When the other shops finally opened, none of them had anything that Morton wanted. The streets were full of pudgy young women in lilac anoraks with babies and toddlers, and old people who looked like the Queen of England on a rainy day. At one point, a group of teenage schoolchildren converged on the Café Volante, the local fast-food shop, and Morton hung around near them for a while, but nobody offered to sell him drugs of any kind. Instead, the kids ate pale-yellow batter in various shapes and agreed that Mr McLeod was 'fuckin' mental'.

The news from June Laboyer-Suk, when the artists met up again, was bad. International electronic transactions in foreign currency were not the order of the day here, and it might be up to thirty-six hours before the money came through. There were no car-hire companies. Between them, Nick Kline, June Laboyer-Suk and Gerrit Plank had enough British money to bus all five artists to Inverness and accommodate them in a cheap hotel for one night, but this would not solve the problem of air fares back to the States. Possibly the wiring of money from the USA could have been achieved faster through an Inverness branch of the bank, but in her relief at getting through to her agent June had specified Tain as the point of contact, and now Tina was in Ansafone mode again. Gail Freleng's Ansafone, strangely enough, was still giving the message that she was not in the office right now.

Gerrit Plank's agent, whom Gerrit had telephoned himself, had been philosophical about his client's plight.

'These things happen,' he'd said.

'I hadn't actually heard of them before,' Gerrit replied.

'A lot of things don't get publicised.'

Gerrit's agent suggested that Gerrit get himself down to Glasgow, where there was a gallery owner who owed them $3000, or approximately £1900. The gallery owner could either pay Gerrit's fare back to the USA or give him free accommodation, maybe even a studio. In three weeks, Gerrit's agent would be in Amsterdam arranging a Plank retrospective there; Gerrit could catch a ferry to Holland then. There was no use wasting money.

Fay Barratt didn't have an agent anymore, after David had left her, so she was dependent on the kindness of strangers.

Whether Morton Krauss had an agent or not was a matter of legal debate, since he and Konigsberg were still involved in litigation and the hearing for the counter-suit was not until November.

'It looks like the best thing all round is for us to stay here until my agent wires the money through,' announced June Laboyer-Suk. 'I've found a Bed & Breakfast on the edge of town which will put four of us up in two rooms for a special rate. I'll write the address down for you. The lady's name is Mrs McAlister. She asks us not to turn up after eleven because her husband's on special sleeping tablets that wear off after midnight. Also she says the dog is nervous too.'

'Wait just a second,' interjected Fay. 'You said "four of us". Does that mean one of us is out in the cold?' In Fay's world, of course, there was always someone out in the cold, the weakest, most vulnerable one: Fay Barratt. One of her best-known paintings, in fact, was called *Out in the Cold*, and it depicted a dead (drowned?) naked woman curled up in foetal position inside a toilet bowl.

'Gerrit here doesn't believe in hotels,' explained June. 'Or debt. He's bought himself a sleeping bag, and he wants to say goodbye.'

'Goodbye,' said Gerrit, and, with a minimal flourish of his military-green bundle of independence, he strode off down the road.

'Even if it takes the full thirty-six hours for the money to get here and be cleared,' continued June Laboyer-Suk. 'Nick and I have enough between us to pay for two nights' accommodation, so we're going to be okay.'

Morton Krauss was glad something was being organised, cash-wise, but the thought of spending two days and nights in what he called The Town that Time Forgot was almost too much to bear. Judging Fay Barratt to be the closest to himself in personal values, he muttered his frustrations to her as the group were parting ways again.

'I can't stand it,' he said. 'There's nothing here, nothing. No nightclubs, no pizza joints, no movie house . . .'

'It's not so bad,' demurred Fay half-heartedly. 'It's pretty. The air is clean. The people seem friendly.'

'Friendly?' scoffed Morton. 'They're just going through the motions, Fay. *Stepford Wives*-burg, that's what this is. Robot City. People here – they're so hung up, so stiff. I tell ya, I'm going crazy without the street culture of New York – the blacks, the Hispanics, the gangs, the ghettoblasters, people leaping around, rollerblading, singing, yelling, hustling . . .'

Fay cast her mind back to New York for her own experience of these things, but her apartment was in Queens and anyway she didn't get out much, spending most of her time painting and watching TV.

'Come on, Morton,' she challenged. 'I bet you don't do any of that stuff yourself. You probably just stand and watch.'

'Get real, babe,' he protested. 'In *my* neighbourhood, a white guy can't *afford* to stand and watch. You keep moving or you get wasted.'

'Sounds just wonderful.'

'I don't think of it as good or bad. I *need* it for my work. I thrive on the tension!'

'Well, you're tense *now*,' Fay pointed out. 'So thrive!'

It was this exchange with Fay that convinced Morton he had no allies. He was stuck at the end of the world among people of unlike mind. He had better try to phone Charles again.

At five o'clock, Tain closed down, at the beginning of a long, luminous twilight. Motley bands of teenagers loitered near the fast-food shop, smoking cigarettes and swearing ostentatiously. They were complaining about exactly the same things Morton Krauss had complained about, but with Scottish accents.

'There's fuck-all to do here,' they said.

'Can't wait to get out of this fuckin' hole,' they said.

'Dingwall might be getting a Burger King,' they said.

In the distance behind them, the surface of the Dornoch Firth turned gold and hundreds of sea birds wheeled over the ancient rooftops. June and Fay were standing on the edge of town, looking down at the ruined graveyard. They could see Nick Kline perfectly clearly, though he was hundreds of yards away; the clear air and uncluttered landscape seemed to foreshorten perspective like a medieval altarpiece.

'He's not moving at all,' said Fay.

'He looks happy, though,' said June.

Nick was sitting among the stones, facing out into the fields. He'd been there for hours.

'Let's go for a walk,' said Fay.

'OK,' said June. 'But not to where Nick is. He's enjoying being there alone.'

The two women set off together without another word, down the steep road leading back towards Inver. A few steps took them beyond Tain's abrupt outer limits into open pasture; scale shifted almost instantly to dwarf the two women against the hills. They themselves were aware of being dwarfed, of their aerial-view tinyness, and it made them feel queerly less alone, more genuinely companions. To someone catching sight of them from a far-off hilltop, they would appear that way: not adjacent by chance, the way they must have been last night at JFK, but together by choice.

June looked at Fay as they walked, noted she had a widow's peak of fine grey hair under the dark-brown dye, a scar like a ghostly knife-slash on her long neck, a beautiful mouth and yearning eyes. Fay was marvelling at the almost supernatural clarity of everything in the early twilight: the way every pebble on the road, every clump of grass seemed distinct as if outlined with black, as if the entire landscape were a vast painting executed with impossible skill. Then she looked aside at June, and saw the same degree of detail in her face, all the wrinkles present and future, the mischievous humanity, the imperfectly suppressed idealism, the pain of too much energy.

These were small and subtle intimacies, but there was more. They were also noticing at exactly the same time the mountainous silence, the undivided sky, and their own bodies' common response to these things. It was as if their brainwaves and bloodstreams were releasing contamination invisibly, all the effluvia of New York's lethal atmosphere, the noise of traffic and TV and ten million angry people, all of it expressed into a pathetic little cloud of ions, disappearing into the immense sky.

After walking for an hour or so, they passed a field which had been ploughed dark brown. Sheep stood ankle-deep in outsize turnips, munching the glowing white pulp. Their fleeces were luminescent. June and Fay stopped for a while, looking.

Two other people walked by, on their way up to Tain, a young mother and her daughter. The little girl ran up to the barbed-wire fence and plucked a wisp of fleece from it.

'You've collected loads of these already,' chided the mother, adding the fleece to the bulging pocket of her lilac anorak. 'What are you going to make out of them?'

'A sheep, of course,' said the little girl.

This little interaction got June Laboyer-Suk thinking, as she and Fay continued to stare into the fields. She hadn't thought about art since early this morning, but now she began to have an idea for a new show, called 'Reconstruction' . . . no, 'Reclamation' . . . no, 'Reconstitution of a sheep'. She would collect all the different cuts of lamb from a butcher, and put them together again, with sheepskin car-seat covers and lambswool slippers wrapped around them. Or maybe it would be better just to lay the bits out loose, with a text inviting the audience to assemble them. More confrontational that way. She could probably dispense with the text as well. Leave it to a critic to spell out. She'd have to be careful – a lot of stuff had been done already with dead meat – she'd have to avoid comparisons with the 'stinking-carcass-in-your-face' brigade. Maybe get the meat coated in plastic . . . liquid perspex . . . neutral to the touch . . . like Lego for kids to assemble . . . DIY kits . . .

Her thoughts were interrupted by the conspicuously unnatural sound of Fay weeping.

'What's wrong?' she said.

'I'll never be a painter,' mourned Fay, staring into the phenomenal sunset. 'Never in a million years.'

June turned back to the sheep, at a loss for what to do or say.

'Baaaaahh!' said one of the sheep, and June realised all at once that her idea for the 'Reconstitution' show was much less interesting than the fact that these animals were here alive, a different species from her, existing on a part of the planet she might easily never have seen: an alternative centre of the world.

'Come on,' she said, folding one arm around Fay's shoulders. 'Let's go and get something to eat.'

An hour later they were sitting in a hotel, marvelling at the inedibility of Scottish food and pining for New York.

Next morning, there was good news at the bank. The transaction which the bank manager had warned June could not simply be 'rushed through' had been rushed through; an irregularity for which the manager seemed almost to be apologising. The money had arrived. One day and night in the Scottish Highlands was all they were going to have after all. A bus would take them to Inverness in an hour; they would reach Edinburgh by evening.

June and Fay had had a really good night's sleep, each having a room to herself at the Bed & Breakfast: Morton and Nick had never shown up. The men reappeared next morning, smelling of alcohol and (in Morton's case) sheep-shit. Nick explained that he had walked all the way back to the Inver Inn, 'for stovies'. Stovies, he declared with an authority unusual for him, were easily the most vile food he'd ever tasted. But the people of Inver were real friendly and he might go back there again today, if there was time, even though it was raining just now. There was one lady there in particular, a woman whose husband had left her with a young daughter, who seemed to really like him. She had a big dilapidated farmhouse near Loch Eye with all this really neat metal junk lying around the yard.

'It's got possibilities,' he said.

'Shall I try phoning your agent one more time?' suggested June.

'You do that. You do that,' murmured Nick, deep in thought.

June watched him wandering off, then went to the phone box and dialled the number.

'Gail Freleng here.'

'June Laboyer-Suk here, in Tain, Scotland.'

'I know. Miss Golem has helped me with some of my enquiries. Is my client with you?'

'Er . . . no. He's gone for a long walk.'

'He's been taken for a *ride*, Ms Suk. You *all* have. As soon as your plane took off, the Alternative Centre of the World stopped answering my faxes. Of course I investigated. The brochures were fakes. The office that sent them was in a building due for demolition. There *is* no Alternative Centre of the World.'

'We already figured that out.'

'Excuse me for boring you. Are you in a position to say if my client can return to Edinburgh by six forty-five p.m. tomorrow evening, that is Wednesday twelfth?'

'I guess so. I don't see why not.'

'Good. A business-class ticket is reserved for him at the British Airways desk. Please make sure my client understands that this ticket is valid for tomorrow Wednesday twelfth and tomorrow Wednesday twelfth *only*.'

'Well, I'll tell him . . .'

'Fine. I understand Miss Golem is handling the arrangements for your own return.'

'Would you happen to know . . .?'

'I've been too busy to assess her progress, Ms Suk. I suggest you call her.'

'Not a problem, Ms Freleng. Shall I give Nick your love? Best wishes?'

' . . . Just the information will do fine. Have a nice day.'

By the time the Inverness bus was idling in front of the post office, June and Fay had managed to get the gist of Morton's night, and had persuaded him that he would be refused a seat on the bus if he didn't seal his malodorous jacket in a plastic bag. To save him from shivering in the wet breeze, they had followed the advice of some helpful people in the queue and dashed into the St Duthus charity shop, where they bought Morton another jacket for £1.85, a glossy purple one with I ♥ LAWN BOWLS emblazoned on the back.

As far as Morton's night went, the gist of it was this: Morton had been unaware that in the Scottish Highlands, the word 'crack' meant an enjoyable social experience, not smokeable cocaine. Standing in a telephone booth yesterday afternoon, making another attempt to phone Charles in Newcastle, Morton had overheard some teenagers agreeing to meet each other that night at the village hall in Balintore because, they said, there would be 'plenty of good crack' there. Was he hearing them right? Yes, definitely: one of them said it again: 'The crack's brilliant down there.'

So, that evening, Henry the taxi driver had driven Morton to Balintore and dropped him off at the village hall, where there was a ceilidh in full swing. Rosy-cheeked girls in Highland dress were doing the fling, a rock band called the Reelin' Creels were playing raucous versions of old Scottish tunes, and everyone was well on the way to dancing and drinking themselves into a stupor. Morton just sat there for hours waiting for a dealer to appear and offer him something.

'You should have got drunk, instead,' said Fay, making

conversation across the aisle of the bus while they waited to see if Nick would show up.

'I *did* get drunk,' he retorted. 'I got so drunk I spent the night sleeping in a field. I got so drunk I lost my camera. My special one with the telephoto lens. The film had all the pictures for my new show on it.'

'Pictures of what?'

'Sheep.'

'Well, can't you take more pictures of sheep?'

'Through the fuckin' bus window?'

A Japanese tourist, seated next to Morton, was alerted by this camera talk, and called Morton's attention to his Minolta compact.

'State o' ze art,' he beamed.

'Real impressive, pal,' grimaced Morton.

Encouraged, the Japanese tourist set out to reassure Morton that it was possible, after all, to take good pictures through bus windows, as long as we don't try to do it with a normal, run-of-the-mill camera.

'Noh-mal camerah . . .' – he mimed taking a photo through the glass – 'picture of self only . . . self in glass.' He tapped the window, the reflection of his own knuckles. '*Tzis* camerah . . . press button . . . camerah look *through* glass . . . Picture of world outsigh!'

'I'll try and get one of those,' promised Morton.

On time, the bus pulled away from Tain, without Nick Kline. Morton was nodding off next to the Japanese tourist, who was still pushing buttons on the magic camera and explaining how close you could get to the flowers. Fay was leafing through her copy of *The Glory of the Highlands*. June Laboyer-Suk just settled back and looked through the window, which was just as well, or they might all have missed the extraordinary sight, just outside Alness, of a huge broken slab of concrete freshly painted orange, and daubed with the indigo message

ARTIST ⇨ GLASGOW

⇩

There was no one underneath the arrow anymore.